THE WAKE

A BRUDER HEIST NOVEL

JEREMY BROWN

WOLFPACK
PUBLISHING
— EST 2013 —

WOLFPACK
PUBLISHING
— EST 2013 —

The Wake

Paperback Edition
Copyright © 2021 Jeremy Brown

Wolfpack Publishing
5130 S. Fort Apache Road 215-380
Las Vegas, NV 89148

wolfpackpublishing.com

Paperback ISBN 978-1-64734-860-1
eBook ISBN 978-1-64734-861-8

THE WAKE

THE WAKE

PART ONE

PART ONE

CHAPTER ONE

When the man came out of the Porta John shotgun first, Bruder yanked it out of his hands and slapped the butt into his throat.

The man sprawled back into the phone booth-sized bathroom, choking and clutching at his neck, and Bruder saw him fall onto the seat before the spring-loaded door clapped shut.

He carried the shotgun in gloved hands to the opposite side of the john and set the gun on the ground, then lifted and pushed the structure until it tipped forward and landed on its door.

Liquid sloshed and a body thumped around.

The john was mounted on a wooden pallet, so it wasn't going to roll, but Bruder put a boot on one of the boards to make sure.

This happened on the edge of a construction site—a new parking garage or something—at nine-thirty on a chilly, wet Sunday night in March outside of Salt Lake City.

Nobody was around to hear the man inside when he choked some more, and sputtered, then managed to croak out, "Bruder, what the hell?"

Bruder picked the shotgun up again and looked at it, a black Mossberg 500 FLEX. He pressed the action release lever and pulled the fore-end an inch to the rear, partially opening the action.

The chamber was empty.

Bruder slid the pump forward and stuck his thumb into the magazine tube and could feel the first cartridge in there, waiting on deck.

He wasn't surprised.

Keppel was the sort who thought the sound of a shotgun pump was enough to scare people away.

He said, "Keppel, is that you in there?"

After some more sloshing and thumping around, Keppel pressed his mouth to the vents along what used to be the top of the john and said, "Ah, fuck! Let me out of here!"

"Why did you bring a shotgun to a meet?"

"A what? This is about the damn *shotgun*?"

"I have it right here, in case you have anything else in there and think it's a good idea to start shooting at me through the wall."

Keppel slipped and fell away from the vent.

He gagged, then said, "No, man, come on. I wouldn't."

His voice sounded like it came from down in a well.

"Then why bring the scattergun?"

"Protection, man. Self-defense."

"From me?"

"From whoever! Now let me out! There's—what the hell is that?"

White light showed through the vents, Keppel using his phone's flashlight to see what was floating around him.

"Oh, hell no! Bruder, get me out of here!"

"Why do you need protection at a meet? I thought this was just a friendly chat."

"It is! It is. It's just...when I tell you about the job, and the people it's for, you'll understand."

Bruder sat on the corner of the pallet.

"I'm listening."

***

From inside the john Keppel said, "I'm recruiting guys for a job that's already bankrolled. They have the money, they just need a crew to pull the job."

"What's the job?"

"I don't know."

Bruder frowned at the skeletal iron looming above the dirt lot and job trailer, which had the only light source around, a sodium lamp attached above the trailer door.

Keppel said, "Can I come out now?"

"No. You're putting a string together for a job you know nothing about?"

"Well, I know some things. I know it's in Florida. I think."

Bruder's frown deepened.

"What else?"

"I know when you're supposed to meet the bankroller."

"And who's that?"

"...I don't know."

"Keppel."

"Listen man, it's a legit job! I know it sounds sketchy, but the people I'm working for are super careful. They don't want anyone to know they're involved in this...whatever it is. They want a professional crew to pull the job, and they're willing to pay for that kind of expertise."

"How much?" Bruder said.

Keppel was silent.

"You don't know."

"It'll be a lot, I know that. They're even willing to pay for the initial meet, to make sure you're a good fit."

Now the frown turned into a scowl.

"Hold on. You're pulling me into a job interview?"

"No, not really. Well, sort of. The bankrollers, I haven't met them, but I get the idea they're corporate. You know, used to having meetings and shit like that. They want to make sure they get the right people for this."

"And when they laid this all out for you, you thought of me."

"You're the first person I thought of, man. They want a real pro."

"It sounds like they want someone to jump through their hoops."

"No, no, they'll be hands-off, I know it."

"Oh, so that part, you know."

"Bruder, I swear to you, this is a sweet deal. These bankrollers, they're some kind of big shots. I smell old money and restlessness. They probably want to pay you a couple hundred grand to steal a racehorse or some shit."

"A racehorse?"

"Just an example. Not really. I think."

Bruder thought about it while Keppel sloshed around in the john.

"None of this explains why you felt the need to bring a shotgun."

Keppel was quiet for a while, then said, "Ah, shit. So, you're the first person I thought of but not the first person they interviewed. Talked to, I mean. About the job."

"How many others?"

"Oh...fifteen or so."

Now Bruder looked around the job site, checking the shadows.

"Fifteen other guys know about this job?"

Keppel picked up on the tension and the reason for it.

"Well, the bankrollers got one look at them and passed, and I was the go-between. So, nobody else has any details about the job. Including me, right?"

He barked a laugh from inside the john.

Bruder said, "But they *think* you might have some details.

And if they get their hands on you, they can cut in on it."

"Pretty much, yeah."

"Why did the bankrollers pass on the others?"

"I don't know, man. They don't bother to tell me stuff like that."

"Here's one you ought to know: I'm the first guy you thought of, so why did fifteen other guys get in on this before me?"

"Because I couldn't find you! I reached out through the usual channels and got nothing."

Which was true.

After a decent score in New York the previous summer, and a three-million-dollar cut from a November job in Iowa, he'd been off the radar and not looking for any more work.

Lola had let him know about Keppel's calls but Bruder ignored them.

When Kershaw called and said Keppel was looking for him, Bruder decided to meet up just to keep the guy from kicking over more rocks.

He didn't need the money, no matter how much the bankrollers were paying.

But it wouldn't hurt to listen.

He stood up and used the sole of his boot to push the pallet and john over, rolling it ninety degrees so the door fell open and discharged Keppel and a pool of dark blue sewage.

Keppel crawled out of the mess, choking and gagging some more, while Bruder slid the cartridges out of the shotgun's magazine tube and dropped them in the mud.

"So where do I meet these bankrollers?"

CHAPTER TWO

One week later Bruder was in a South Beach hotel overlooking the sand and ocean.

The hotel was horseshoe-shaped and he was on the tenth floor of the southern wing, standing on a balcony perched above the pools and bars in the middle of the U.

He didn't like the room.

The view was fine, and the bed looked like it worked, but he didn't like having a single point of egress.

He'd go over the railing to the balcony below or jump to those on the sides if he had to, but he'd rather not.

He'd still have to get off the tenth floor, then out of the hotel, and even then he'd still be on an island with limited routes off unless he stole something on the water.

And the water had its own problems, like nothing to hide behind.

Bruder had never liked feeling trapped, and after the job in Iowa he vowed to never let it happen again.

Yet, here he was.

He watched the people below for a while, most of them trying hard to be watched while looking like they couldn't care less about anything.

There were some young kids acting like they were on spring break, but the hotel was too high-end for the kind of things they really wanted to get up to.

Bruder wore a blue linen shirt with the sleeves rolled up and swimming trunks with sandals.

Black sunglasses covered his eyes.

If the bankrollers, whoever they were, made him wait much longer in this box they'd have to come find him at the pool or beach.

He went back into the room and was looking into the mini-fridge for something interesting when knuckles rapped on the hallway door.

Bruder picked up the Beretta Pico in .380 ACP, a tiny thing he could hide in the palm of his hand if he curled his fingers.

For now, though, he kept his finger near the trigger and called out, "Yeah?"

"Time for your meeting."

Bruder walked to the door.

He didn't bother with the peep hole—if whoever was on the other side wanted to cause trouble, the door wasn't going to stop them.

He kept the gun in his right hand and used his left to unlock and crack the door, leaving the gun hidden near the knob.

The two men in the hallway wore linen suits with dark ties.

They were both large but lean, and their skin and eyes had the look of men who'd spent a lot of time peering through scopes from hilltops.

Their hands were empty at their sides.

Bruder stepped to the right as he opened the door and slid the Beretta into his pocket.

"Come on in."

The one on the left said, "The meeting isn't with us. Come on."

"Where?"

"Just follow us. And leave the peashooter here."

Bruder looked down at his trunks.

The gun was invisible unless you were the one who'd put it there.

"I think I'll keep it."

"You can leave it here," the man said, "or bring it, and at some point we'll take it away from you. Then we'll have a gun with your prints on it."

Bruder looked at him, then the one on the right, who gave off a coiled energy and seemed ready to fight or take a nap—it made no difference to him.

There wasn't any point to posturing further, and Bruder knew if it came to a tussle someone was going off the balcony, so he dropped the Pico into his open suitcase on the kitchen counter and covered it with a shirt.

Two other pistols were in the room, both larger than the Pico, so he didn't consider them.

When he got back to the door the one on the left said, "You're wearing that?"

"I'm in Miami," Bruder said. "Let's get on with it."

***

They escorted him to the elevators, then up to the top floor, then around a corner until they were in the middle of the U-shaped hotel.

The hallway only had three sets of double doors on the beach side, and when Bruder went through the center pair he saw why.

The penthouse suite was enormous, more like an open-concept apartment than a room, with floor-to-ceiling glass doors showing the beach and water beyond the hotel's pools and landscaping.

The glass doors were on a rail system and they'd been pushed all the way open to turn the interior and expansive balcony into one space.

A compact kitchenette and bar were to the left. A spread of fresh fruit and charcuterie covered the countertops, along with ice buckets filled with assorted beers and soft drinks. None of it had been touched yet.

To Bruder's right was a set of leather furniture on a massive rug, all of it arranged into a square meeting space with a low table in the center.

He walked past the food spread and scanned the closed doors on both side walls—leading to bedrooms and bathrooms, he assumed—then continued past more rugs and furniture to the balcony.

Small palm trees and bright flowers blocked the sides, creating a private deck with padded chairs and couches around a dormant fire pit.

Some of the furniture was under a pergola covered in more flowers and vines, which created a spot of shade without losing the tropical feel.

A large sunken Jacuzzi grumbled off to the left.

Maybe it was all meant to impress him, but so far he just saw a lot of wasted money—money that could have gone into his pocket if he took the job, whatever the hell it turned out to be.

He looked at the two suits, still standing inside.

"Well?"

"Wait there."

The one who did all the talking went through a door on the left.

Bruder couldn't see what or who was on the other side.

He hadn't had lunch yet, so he went back to the spread and helped himself.

The remaining suit didn't say anything.

"Help yourself," Bruder said. "I won't eat all of this."

"Maybe later," the guy said.

Bruder shrugged and cracked a bottle of sparkling water.

"How long is this going to take?"

Then the side door opened and the first guy came through, followed by another man.

At that point, Bruder realized this wasn't a job interview.

It was a manhunt.

***

The last time Bruder saw him, McIntyre was in golf clothes, bound and gagged in a grassy ditch along a Pennsylvania carpool lot.

Bruder had left him there after the job in New York.

Now McIntyre smiled, wearing a different set of golf clothes and showing straight, capped teeth.

His teeth and hair seemed even whiter because of the tan skin.

He said, "Bruder," like the name was a trophy he wanted to relish, even show off.

Bruder just stood there and waited for whatever came next.

McIntyre was somewhere high up in the New York branch of an organization called the Labyrinth, a group of people with influence across corporations, industries, and governments.

They were criminals, with criminal interests, but once you got high enough on the food chain that word changed to things like CEO, Founder, Senator...

Maybe somebody knew how wide and deep the Labyrinth went but Bruder wasn't one of those people.

McIntyre said, "Are you enjoying the food?"

"Not anymore."

They looked at each other for a while, then McIntyre said, "Let's sit down."

To the man in the suit next to him, he said, "Cancel the rest of the interviews. This is him."

***

No one had pulled a gun yet, and McIntyre seemed fine without having any additional bodies standing between him and Bruder's hands.

So this was either a very casual execution, or something else.

Bruder sat in one of the chairs with his back to the balcony.

He knew nobody was out there and wanted to keep the three men in the room in front of him.

McIntyre sat across from him in the middle of a sofa, and before he could get done adjusting his golf khakis, the quiet muscle put a tall glass filled with golden liquid and ice in his hand.

"Would you like something besides the water?" McIntyre asked.

Bruder shook his head.

McIntyre looked at his new drink like it confounded him.

"In New York, I never drink iced tea. But as soon as I get on the jet to come down here, it's all I want. Why do you think that is? Some Pavlovian response, I suppose."

Bruder waited while the man had a conversation with himself.

His left hand was noticeably paler than the rest of him, showing how much time he spent with a golf glove on.

Maybe it was a status symbol to people like him.

Eventually McIntyre looked up with a glimmer in his ice-chip eyes.

"So. You must be wondering why you're here."

"Not really. Keppel gave me up."

"Ah, Mr. Keppel. You needn't hold any grudges against him. He had no idea what was going on, or even who it was for. A useful idiot, if you will."

"I'm here because of him," Bruder said.

McIntyre flashed a brief smile.

"I see. Hold the grudge if you like, Mr. Bruder. Bruder is your last name, correct? Not your first?"

"Sure."

"Grudges are for amateurs, Mr. Bruder. People with low self-esteem. Because if you make me look stupid, and I secretly agree that I am, indeed, stupid, I have to work to prove you wrong. For my own sake. My own illusion of worth. But my worth is not an illusion, to me or others."

"Okay."

"Keppel was one of a dozen or more people I reached out to through cutouts and go-betweens. One of them was going to contact you eventually, and it happened to be Keppel. So kill him if you like, but it would be a waste of your time."

Bruder said, "You have more than a dozen people putting feelers out for me? That sounds like a grudge."

"I can understand why you might make that assumption. Our last meeting was…unpleasant for Bertram and myself."

"Who's Bertram?"

"My former driver and personal bodyguard."

Bruder nodded.

He and Kershaw had left Bertram bound and gagged in the ditch right next to McIntyre.

Bruder said, "You're not getting the money back."

McIntyre blinked.

"You think this is about the money you stole?"

"What else could it be?"

McIntyre's eyes widened at the floor, like he realized this was going to take some patient hand-holding.

"This meeting is not about that. I hold no ill will."

"So you have a dozen headhunters out there, sending guys who *might* be me to meetings like this, for what?"

McIntyre sipped his tea.

"First, let me assure you, the effort wasn't that strenuous. Most of the people like Keppel were able to send photos of the prospects before meetings were set."

"Prospects," Bruder said. "What sort?"

"Someone who can run a job like the one you pulled

in New York. We didn't mention that one specifically, of course."

"And these people—people like me, supposedly—they let Keppel and the others take photos?"

McIntyre shook his head.

"Covertly, of course. We told our headhunters we needed a man who looked a certain way in order to execute the job. We didn't describe the look. We didn't even ask for names, because I didn't know yours. Just send us a photo. Because I do know your face."

"Keppel didn't take my picture."

"Well, no. As I understand it, you locked him in a portable toilet and nearly drowned him in sewage."

"That's an exaggeration," Bruder said.

"To answer your larger question, you are the only person I've actually met with in person. Anyone who got as far as a hotel room like yours here—because of a lack of photos or uncertainty on my part about them being you—never got past the room."

He gestured to the talkative muscle, who brought out an iPad and showed Bruder the screen.

It had various shots of him in his hotel room, close-ups and different angles from cameras hidden in the ceiling, above the refrigerator, above the toilet.

Bruder said, "That's how you knew about the pocket gun."

The muscle shrugged, his magic trick exposed.

"When I saw those," McIntyre said, "I put your face together with the name Keppel gave us for the meeting. Bruder."

"But not because of a grudge," Bruder said.

"I assure you, no. Let's see if this helps you break the narrative you have playing in your head. While I was riding around in the trunk with Bertram, you were hijacking the meeting outside Yankee Stadium and stealing my money.

For the second time."

Bruder stayed quiet.

When it came to things he'd done, his policy was to say nothing and admit less.

Besides, McIntyre was doing enough talking for both of them.

"The Yankees," McIntyre said, "are a wonderful organization. Elite, compared to the other allegedly professional teams in the league. Do you follow baseball, Mr. Bruder?"

"No."

"Well, this should still help. When the Yankees come up against a player who has their number—say he's a pitcher who regularly stymies their lineup, or a hitter who ends their playoff hopes with a walk-off home run—what do the Yankees do? Hold a grudge and vow to get revenge the following season?"

He raised his eyebrows at Bruder, waiting for an answer that wasn't coming.

Finally McIntyre said, "No. They go out and buy that player. They hitch him to their wagon."

Bruder said, "You're interviewing me for the Lab?"

McIntyre couldn't help smiling.

"No, I'm afraid not. The Labyrinth would certainly have a use for you, probably short-term, but no. You lack a certain refinement we require. Which is why you're perfect for this."

"And what the hell is *this*?"

"This," McIntyre said, "is something you're going to do for *me*."

***

Bruder sat and waited.

He was still wary of the room shifting, going from a civil conversation to having to fight like the third wolf on the ramp to Noah's Ark, should McIntyre change his mind.

As a result, part of his brain listened while the rest of it judged angles and distances and furniture and which hands the muscle would use to reach for their guns.

McIntyre said, "You're going to steal a yacht for me."

Because he was looking at the calluses on one of the bodyguard's hands, a strap of thick, rough skin along the webbing between thumb and forefinger indicating pistol range time bordering on fanatic, Bruder wasn't sure he'd heard it right.

"Did you say a yacht?"

"That's right."

"How about I just lend you some money instead?"

McIntyre found that amusing.

"It's not for me. And affordability isn't the issue. If money was the obstacle, you wouldn't be necessary."

"So tell me why I am. But be careful. I don't want to know anything that keeps me from walking out of here."

"Expand on that," McIntyre said.

"Don't tell me where and when. If I know those details and turn the job down, you might get it in your head I'm a liability."

McIntyre nodded, understanding, but with an expression that said Bruder was the one who didn't get it.

It almost looked like pity.

He said, "Then it seems I need to adjust my presentation a bit, move the facts to the front and save the details for later. Fact: You will be taking this job."

"Start over," Bruder said.

McIntyre held his hand out and the muscle with the iPad put the device in the open palm.

McIntyre tapped the screen, which Bruder couldn't see, and said, "You're correct. You do have the option of refusal. And now that I know how to get in touch with you, I can reach out when the next opportunity comes along."

"I won't be taking any more calls from Keppel."

McIntyre looked up.

"Keppel? Oh, I meant Lola."

He turned the device so Bruder could see the screen.

It showed a photo of Lola, taken across the street from her yoga studio in Austin.

She was walking toward the door with some kind of drink in her hand and a large bag hanging from her shoulder. She didn't know the camera was there.

Lola was Bruder's ex...whatever they had been...and helped him out as a point of contact for people who needed to get in touch. They called her and left the message, she passed the information along, and if Bruder wanted to call them back he did.

Occasionally, when a job needed someone who could climb the side of a building and slip through security systems like a snake through grass, she also did that.

"This just came through," McIntyre said. "We already knew how Keppel got in touch with the man known as Bruder. As soon as I saw your face, I issued an order to our Austin branch. And now I have this."

He turned the screen back and gazed at it.

"You said this isn't a Lab job," Bruder said, working to keep his temper in check.

McIntyre brushed a hand aside.

"This is routine surveillance work. The Austin branch doesn't need to know why. Or why I might need to speak with her in person."

"Anyone you send after her won't be coming back."

"Then I'll send someone expendable. Or these two, who should know how to deal with a yoga instructor."

"She's useless to you," Bruder said. "She doesn't know how to find me. I call in to check messages. She doesn't know or care where I'm calling from."

"I see," McIntyre said. "Then, what I should do—if you refuse the job, that is—is take you from here and put you in a cinderblock room while my associates have a chat with her. Because I believe she knows who you work with on a regular basis. For example, in New York. And how to get a hold of them. Then my associates will pay them a visit. And so on, and so on, while you sit in your cinderblock room knowing you are the sole reason people who trusted you are experiencing agonizing deaths."

Bruder chewed the inside of his cheek.

McIntyre said, "And we'll be sure to let them know why. Them, and everyone else in the cesspool you call a network. At that point, you might be too weak from hunger and thirst to be much of a threat to me. So maybe I'll put you on the street and let whoever is left of your friends deal with you. Or maybe I'll take you out on my boat and keelhaul you. When's the last time that happened to someone?"

He glanced behind him at the muscle, who offered thin smiles in return.

He looked at Bruder again.

"So. Are you ready to hear about the job?"

Bruder tasted blood in his mouth.

"Grudges are for amateurs, huh?"

"Absolutely," McIntyre said. "Extortion, however, is for professionals."

***

"So I need to steal a boat," Bruder said.

"A yacht," McIntyre corrected. "It's currently in an impound marina near St. Petersburg."

"Florida or Russia?"

McIntyre smiled.

"Florida."

"What's this impound lot like? Heavy security?"

"That's for you to determine, Mr. Bruder. And this has to happen in the next two weeks. No, less than that. Eleven days."

"Why?"

"Because eleven days from now, the yacht is being relocated to an impound facility in New Jersey, where it will be sold at an exclusive auction."

Bruder's mind started to pick at the scenarios.

"What about hijacking it along the way?"

"No. The crew piloting the vessel to New Jersey will be high-end, hired by the government. They might even have an armed escort, due to the yacht's...history."

Bruder said, "And the Jersey lot will be better equipped than the St. Pete one."

"Correct. This is your best opportunity. And if you miss it, it will be up to you to figure out how to get the yacht, regardless of where it is."

"Eleven days," Bruder said.

McIntyre nodded.

"Once you have it, you need to take it from the marina down past Key West to a group of small islands called the Dry Tortugas. Are you familiar?"

"No."

"They're about seventy miles west of Key West, almost due north of Havana. There's an old military fort there that was converted to a prison during the Civil War. Did you know, the doctor who set John Wilkes Booth's broken leg after he assassinated Lincoln served time there?"

"I just found out about the islands," Bruder said. "And this is probably a good time to tell you I don't know a damn thing about boats."

"Do you know how to steal them?"

"It's probably like stealing anything else. But once I have it, then what? You don't want me driving the damn thing."

"We don't call it *driving*," McIntyre said, then caught himself and seemed to decide any maritime lessons were wasted on Bruder. "I will supply you with a crew to pilot the vessel."

"No."

"No?"

"I pick the crew."

"Oh, I see. Will I get to meet the other gentlemen from our New York incident?"

"No," Bruder said.

He had no intention of bringing Kershaw or anyone else he knew in on this fiasco. He'd have to find and vet a new string, people who knew boats.

"I thought not," McIntyre said. "But it's a moot point. I will supply the crew, and the bankroll, and you will plan and execute the job. When you deliver the yacht to the men waiting for you at the Dry Tortugas, you'll receive payment."

"How much?"

McIntyre pretended to think about it.

"Ten thousand dollars."

"Ten grand wouldn't even get you this meeting."

"And yet, here we are."

His lips curled into a smile, knowing he'd just slapped Bruder across the face with the meager sum. Hell, the room they were sitting in probably cost more per night.

Bruder remained calm.

"Why the Dry Tortugas? Why not just have that crew with me in St. Petersburg? I steal the boat, they take it away."

McIntyre looked past him, out the balcony doors toward the sky and feathered clouds over the ocean.

"Those islands are as close as these gentlemen would like to get to the continental United States. And as far out as I'm willing to send you and the rest of the crew."

Bruder said, "Whose boat is this?"

"You needn't concern yourself with that."

"Why are you stealing it for them?"

"Again..."

Bruder sat back in his chair and studied McIntyre for a few moments, then said, "You need me to do this job because the Labyrinth doesn't want to touch it. Maybe you already asked, and whoever is above you said no. Which means whoever this boat belongs to is radioactive. Who is it?"

"Does it matter?"

Bruder shrugged.

"Not really."

"My associates are being short-sighted on this," McIntyre said. "They're only looking at the here and now, and how helping this person will negatively impact other endeavors. But I see the big picture, and the eventual dividends from this are...substantial."

"Good for you. Why this boat? Why not just buy him—or her—another one?"

McIntyre shook his head.

"It doesn't matter. This person wants their yacht back, and you will deliver it. Maybe it's sentimental value. A so-called moral victory? Who knows?"

"And I get ten grand. What else?"

He wanted McIntyre to say it without him having to ask for it, specifically.

"Peace of mind."

"I already have that."

"I mean this," McIntyre said, waving a hand at the iPad. "Your information, your contacts, your known associates. I delete all of it and forget about you."

"I'm supposed to take your word on that?"

McIntyre adjusted the fabric stretched over one of his knees.

"Take my word on this, Mr. Bruder. If I wanted to punish you, it would happen. You have no say in that. Any moment I spend with you, thinking about you, is a waste of my time. It costs me money and attention better spent elsewhere. So forgetting about you will be more of a relief for me than for you. Get this job done so I can forget you exist. How does that sound?"

Bruder said, "Let's get it over with."

CHAPTER THREE

At one-thirty in the morning on a Tuesday, with ten days left to steal the boat, Bruder was parked in a rented sedan outside of a Florida town called Gandy looking at sandy road shoulders and battered asphalt and a cluster of mismatched warehouses surrounded by cyclone fences.

Most of the streetlights worked but they were far apart and left plenty of dark pools in between.

Bruder was in the middle of one of those pools about a quarter mile down the road from the target, watching and listening with the windows down.

The street was empty and quiet, nothing residential within a few blocks.

He had the layout of the area memorized from satellite maps, but it all still looked slightly different than he'd expected.

Things were bigger or smaller, taller or shorter, closer together or farther apart.

On the other side of all the warehouses was a small, protected splotch of water that connected to Old Tampa Bay, which led south to Tampa Bay, then the Gulf.

And one of the warehouses was the impound marina where the boat was supposed to be docked.

Yacht, Bruder corrected himself, then made a disgusted face.

It was called *Destiny Fulfilled*, and Bruder had the identification number scrawled on a scrap of paper he could toss away or chew up if necessary, but he doubted he'd need either piece of information to identify the vessel.

The damn thing was ninety feet long, twenty feet across at its widest point, and had three levels to it.

The problem of stealing something that big and making a getaway had been in the center of Bruder's mind since he walked out of McIntyre's suite the day before.

He found satisfaction in the dissection of it, finding the angles and cracks and prying on them to see if they got him closer to what he needed, but he had to ignore the part about doing it for McIntyre and a pitiful ten grand.

Otherwise it all turned sour.

He had to think of it as just another job.

And now it was time to scout the impound marina and see if it was even possible.

If it wasn't, or if getting caught or killed was the most likely outcome, he'd put the word out to Lola and Kershaw and the others to disappear, then vanish himself.

After he killed McIntyre.

Bruder put the windows up and got out of the car.

He smelled fish and salt and a brief tang of fuel before the breeze changed.

He wore dark, quiet running clothes and shoes that didn't thump when he walked.

The headband could be pulled down to cover his face if necessary.

He started walking, looking for a crack to pry.

***

The impound lot didn't offer any help but the business next door, which looked like a boat sail and upholstery fabricator from what Bruder could tell, wasn't as serious about their perimeter security.

He went through a gap in a chained gate, scraping his chest and shoulder blades to squeeze through, and crouched among some waist-high fiberglass bins set on pallets.

He moved quietly for a man his size. No one would call it graceful, but there was an ease to the movements with a clear reserve of strength beyond what was required to pull and push and kneel and climb.

The bins next to him were full of rusty grommets and shredded bindings and things he couldn't identify but looked like they belonged on a boat.

He listened for anything new—alarms, footsteps, dogs— but didn't hear any shift in the nighttime patterns.

The fabrication building was tall and narrow, made of faded blue metal siding with two overhead doors taking up most of the facade. The sign over a personnel door at the nearest corner was sun-blasted, just chips of black and red paint on a white background.

A sailboat on a trailer sat outside one of the overhead doors with its mast up and no sail attached.

Bruder scanned the roofline and corners of the building and saw light fixtures but no cameras or motion sensors—if they were there, they were tiny. But from the look of the rest of the place, nobody was going to spend money on something like that.

Beyond the sailboat, the impound lot had some parked cars inside the cyclone fence but they all looked like permanent fixtures—possible seizures waiting for auction or destruction—except for one.

The standout was dark and clean with a light bar on the roof.

It wasn't a police car. Bruder knew what the local cruisers

looked like and this wasn't one of them.

Night watchman?

Private security?

He didn't like any of the options.

Above the cars in the impound parking lot a flagpole with banners twitching in the breeze had a cluster of cameras at the top, pointed in all directions and angled toward the ground.

Bruder risked moving to the sailboat with a wary eye on the fabricator's lights, waiting for them to kick on.

They never did.

He got to the boat and leaned around the stern to get a look at the front of the impound warehouse.

He spotted more cameras mounted above the door and on the corners of the building.

He couldn't tell if they were already running or motion-activated, something that would send an alarm to whoever the clean car belonged to.

Maybe that person was inside the warehouse staring at monitors, waiting for somebody in dark clothes to creep around.

But he doubted it.

These days, most cameras were used to trip an alarm for someone off-site or as forensic evidence after something already happened.

But Bruder had no interest in getting trapped somewhere between his car and the bay, picking his way through mangroves and laying low until he could get clear, so he backed away from the boat and went around the far corner of the fabrication warehouse to get a look at the water from there.

He didn't like the cameras or the car with the light bar on top.

Neither one was a deal breaker, but if he saw one more red flag—and if this was his job—he'd walk away.

Not worth the risk and damn sure not worth ten grand.

But McIntyre, the bastard...his leverage carried too much weight.

It threw everything off balance.

Bruder got to the back side of the warehouse and found a sea wall almost right up against the fence running back there.

The wall dropped straight down to a boardwalk, which spread into a half dozen docks with sailboats moored at every available slip.

Sailors getting ready for the summer, Bruder assumed.

Two of the boats had lights on inside and soft music was coming from somewhere in the marina, barely audible within the breeze and sounds of water and night bugs.

So some of the sailors brought their boats to the fabricator and stayed aboard while the work got done.

Next door, the impound lot had a concrete platform below the sea wall instead of a wooden dock.

At the corner nearest Bruder the platform turned ninety degrees and narrowed into a barrier sticking above the waterline.

It extended fifty yards or so into the water with cyclone fence running along its top. The barrier was wide enough to make a walkway on the inside of the fence and short concrete docks stretched away at regular intervals.

Out in the bay, the concrete and fence turned the corner and paralleled the shore for what looked like another fifty yards, half a football field, then cut back in and connected to the seawall on the far side.

He could see the same setup on that side—shorter concrete docks coming away from the wall toward the middle.

Tall poles with sodium light racks stood at each corner, like something from a football stadium or prison yard, but only one bulb in each rack was illuminated, some kind of nightlight setting.

Even with just those bulbs lit, the marina was on full display and the four-corner barrage left no shadows.

Halfway along the outer wall was a gate.

Or a port, since it was for boats.

Whatever.

It was a gap in the concrete barrier with fence panels set on a rail system so they could slide open and shut to let boats in and out.

How that happened, he didn't know yet.

He was staring at the whole thing when something happened with the water and he caught a flash of light coming through the concrete barrier nearest to him.

He watched, and as the water rose and fell he spotted round holes in the side of the barrier, maybe twelve inches across, running all the way through the block.

Connecting the water outside to the water inside, he supposed, for flow and to let the sea creatures in and out.

His eyes tracked up to the concrete platform along the sea wall, up a short set of open stairs to the back side of the impound warehouse, which had a lot of windows overlooking the water.

The windows looked dark but his angle was bad—looking almost straight across the face of them—so he didn't count on that being true.

There were maybe ten vessels moored in the entire lot, most of them shabby, likely abandoned and sent here until they could be claimed or sold at auction or junked.

The whole thing seemed like a lot of work and expense to protect a bunch of boats no one wanted, but among the peasants stood a king.

The yacht was impossible to miss, looming over the other boats like a shark swimming with guppies.

Maybe the marina was like the Alcatraz of watercraft impound lots—mostly full of dirtbags and empty shells, but every now and then they needed a place to put a Capone, so they built this place.

The yacht had its own dock because there wasn't room for anything else along the entire side.

It glowed bright white under the sodium lights and had black windows and, for some reason, a thin line of smoke drifting from the top deck.

Bruder looked at the boat, knowing it wasn't his problem to figure out how to steer it into the channel and out to sea, but still trying to picture it.

Then he came back to what *was* his problem: Getting it free of the impound lot without anyone knowing it was gone until it was too late to do anything about it.

He'd have to get inside the building.

Maybe not tonight, but before the job.

He needed a better idea of how they did things, where the weak points were.

He needed—

He stopped thinking.

He didn't blink or breathe.

On the top level of the yacht, from beneath the line of smoke, a man stood up and stretched.

Bruder saw the flare of a cigar in his hand, one more puff, then the man turned toward Bruder and tossed it overboard, into the water.

Bruder made note of the M4 Carbine strapped across his chest.

He watched for a few more minutes until the man sat back down and disappeared below the white wall surrounding the top level.

Then Bruder turned and went back the way he'd come, all the way back to the car and away from there.

He'd stopped thinking about the job and was now figuring out how he was going to kill McIntyre.

***

Bruder stopped at a 24-hour gas station outside of Bradenton and went inside and paid cash for coffee, sandwiches, two pre-paid cell phones, and thirty dollars' worth of gas.

He was wearing a golf shirt and shorts now, just another guy in Florida.

He started driving again and called the number he had for Kershaw, let it ring a few times, then hung up.

Four minutes later the cell buzzed with a call from a number he didn't recognize.

"Yeah?"

"What's up?" Kershaw said.

"You near a safe computer?"

"Depends on what you need me to do. Safe enough for light research, no good for launching North Korean missiles."

"Just some questions," Bruder said.

"Fire away."

"I need you to look up a boat."

"A boat?"

"That's right."

Bruder gave him the name, *Destiny Fulfilled*, and the identification number from the slip of paper.

Kershaw was quiet while he worked, then said, "Okay. Uh, are you buying this boat?"

"No."

"This is for work?"

"Right."

"Well...it seems to belong to a man named Hazza Rai. He's from the United Arab Emirates, part of a royal family. He's a Sheikh, apparently."

"What's it say about the boat?"

"I think you mean yacht."

Bruder didn't respond.

Kershaw said, "Hold on, I'm reading. Royal family... cricket...goddam, the lead-in on this is longer than an online recipe. Okay, here we go. Rai's US-based assets, including the yacht, were seized and frozen last year due to his involvement with people and groups on a government watch list."

"He's a terrorist?"

"Ehh, maybe? If he isn't, he hangs out with them. So Uncle Sam took his toys away."

"Including the boat."

"Yacht. And yes. Can you say what this is about?"

Bruder wouldn't put any specifics through the electronics. He asked Kershaw, "Are you on the east coast?"

"No."

Bruder thought for a moment, then said, "You remember the golfer we ditched in Pennsylvania?"

Kershaw barked a laugh.

"Of course. Wait, did he come back on you?"

"Yeah. Tracked me down."

"How in the hell did he do that?"

"You wouldn't believe it. But I'm doing a thing for him to get clear."

"He wants the money back?"

"No," Bruder said. "He doesn't care about that part at all."

"Well, that can't be true, but okay. So where do you want me?"

"Out of it. He doesn't know your name, but he'll put in the work to find you if I don't do this."

"Ah, shit," Kershaw said. "Does he have anybody else?"

"He knows about Austin. That's it. He'll go through there to get to you and the rest."

"This thing you have to do—the yacht?"

"That's right."

"This is a government-seized asset, my friend."

"I know that, now. And it has at least one armed guard on it."

"With a badge?"

"I didn't get that close."

"Huh," Kershaw said. "You know, all this info is out in the open, I didn't have to do anything special to get it. You didn't look this stuff up before looking at the boat?"

"I didn't care about any of it until I saw the gun. The job is to get the boat, who cares about the backstory?"

"You do, now."

"Yeah."

Kershaw said, "What about just removing the golfer from the situation?"

"I'm considering it."

"I can help with that. What about the rest of his organization?"

He was asking about the Labyrinth.

Bruder said, "He's freelancing this. They aren't involved, which makes sense, now that I know who the boat belongs to."

"Which you didn't bother to research."

Bruder let him have his fun.

He said, "But if the golfer drops off the map, they'll get interested. If I go that route I'll give you time to prepare, if I can."

"Appreciated. So you're doing this job on your own?"

"The golfer's putting together the rest."

After a pause Kershaw said, "You know this is a setup, right?"

"Yeah."

"Keep your head on a swivel, pal."

"I'll be in touch."

He drove on and waited until he saw water along the side of the road and threw the phone into it.

***

Bruder used the second phone to call the number he had for McIntyre.

It was close to three in the morning but the call was answered right away and a man said, "Yes?"

Bruder recognized the voice, the talkative muscle whose name was Penza.

"I need to talk to McIntyre," Bruder said.

"He's resting."

"In person. I'm on my way. I'll be there around seven-thirty."

"See you then."

Penza ended the call.

Bruder knew he wouldn't get a weapon through the door, so if getting rid of McIntyre was the way to go, he'd have to use his hands until he took something away from Penza or the other one, Reed.

He drove south on 75, heading toward the turn east that would take him across Florida.

He had about four hours to figure out how to kill the three men waiting for him in McIntyre's suite, and driving through the Everglades was perfect for that sort of thing.

CHAPTER FOUR

Penza, the talkative one, let him in and checked him for anything dangerous.

Reed stood on the other side of the counter, watching, like he was prepared to draw and take cover should Bruder get frisky.

The counter held a spread of fresh fruits, juices, sweet rolls, and coffee options.

Bruder nodded at Reed and took a pineapple juice and carried it to the balcony, already open and letting in the breeze coming off the Atlantic.

He was tired of sitting in the car, so he stood back from the railing and waited.

After a few minutes McIntyre came out, freshly scrubbed with his hair still wet. He had an espresso on one small plate and fresh fruit on another.

"So you saw her," he said.

It took Bruder a moment to realize he was talking about the boat; these people referred to their possessions as female.

"I did. You didn't mention the armed security."

"Well, it's an impound marina."

"No, not the marina. Just the one boat. A man on the top level—"

"The flybridge," McIntyre said.

"...With a long gun. He was guarding the boat, not the impound."

McIntyre nodded and put his plates on a round glass table, then sat in one of the padded chairs next to it, crossed his legs and looked up at Bruder.

"Why should I care about this?"

"This changes the job."

"No, it doesn't. When I tell my pool guy to clean the pool, he doesn't come back and tell me there's a hornet's nest in the pool house. He takes care of it and cleans the damn pool."

"Are those hornets from the government?"

McIntyre frowned.

"What does that mean?"

"The boat is a seized asset."

"Oh, you've done some research."

Bruder said, "Who's guarding it? FBI? Homeland Security? Because that, like I said, changes the job."

McIntyre waved that away.

"No. Anyone relegated to that sort of duty is rented by the Feds. A contractor, a mall cop. Federal employees won't be involved until the transport to New Jersey. Even then, they might be contractors, but higher tier."

"So he's just a mall cop. With an M4 Carbine."

"Probably not even loaded. A show of force to spook the gawkers and petty criminals. Certainly not enough to dissuade someone of your caliber."

"Flattery doesn't work on me."

McIntyre sipped his espresso. Above the cup, his eyes showed amusement.

"Let me tell you what won't work on me, Mr. Bruder. If I have you pegged right, you see two available options. One, do the job as asked. Two, kill the man demanding the job. You might think that will solve your problems, but it won't. Assuming you could pull it off..."

He glanced toward the opening into the suite, where Reed and Penza stood listening.

"...which I doubt, but if you could, everything I know about you and your associates goes to my associates in the Lab. Not everyone in the organization shares my feelings on grudges. There are some who, given the opportunity, would make a definitive example of you and the people you work with."

He let that sink in for a bit.

"So you don't really have two options, do you? You're stuck with me, and the job, and the sooner you realize that and accept it, the happier we'll all be."

Bruder finished his pineapple juice and looked out at the water and sky.

The sun was already a hand's-width above the horizon, flashing on waves and warming the sand.

He thought about smashing the glass and using a shard to cut McIntyre's throat, but that would only get him shot by Reed and Penza.

He could grab the old man and use him as a shield until he figured out what to do next, but that would probably end the same as the glass.

Toss McIntyre over the railing and throw furniture until he closed the gap on Reed or Penza...he'd still get shot.

He already knew McIntyre was right.

Like the man said, he just needed to accept it.

He went back inside, put his empty glass in the sink and filled a mug with coffee.

Reed and Penza watched him come out onto the balcony again and pull a chair to McIntyre's table and sit down.

He said, "What do you know about the impound marina?"

McIntyre pointed in the general direction of Penza, who

disappeared into the suite and came back with an open laptop.

He set it in front of Bruder, who saw the browser was on a subpage of a municipal-looking website.

The name of the impound lot was there, with a photo of the marina and fence and a paragraph about the purpose of the facility but nothing else.

A hyperlinked sentence beneath the paragraph identified the third-party company who handled auction services for the impound.

Bruder tapped the link with a knuckle.

It wasn't his laptop so he didn't care about electronic trails, but he did care about fingerprints.

The auction company's site came up with a mess of links to estate sales and business liquidations, office furniture...

He found and tapped the link for watercraft auctions, then the impound marina, and saw the next scheduled auction was at the end of the month, a week past the eleven-day deadline.

Worthless to him.

He leaned back and looked at Penza, who just returned the stare.

"You can take it away," Bruder said.

He didn't like the camera embedded above the screen staring at him.

Penza pressed his lips together but carried the laptop back into the suite.

Bruder said to McIntyre, "The other people you have in mind for this job—they know each other?"

"Yes. They've worked together, mostly with stolen watercraft, which is why I chose them."

"Are they part of the Labyrinth?"

"Heavens, no."

"Do they know my name?"

"Not yet."

"Let's keep it that way. I'll be Mr. Kline to them."

"Fine. I don't think they'll ask for identification, but for my own purposes, do you have documents to support that name?"

"I do."

"Nice to meet you, Mr. Kline."

Bruder said, "How long until you can get this crew together?"

McIntyre showed his straight white teeth.

"Is today too soon for you?"

***

Bruder spent the late morning and early afternoon on the beach, moving in and out of the shade of a cabana tent with white linen walls branded with the hotel's name and logo.

He wore the sunglasses and swim trunks and kept a shirt meant for fishermen nearby, something that would keep the sun off but let the breeze through when he'd had enough heat.

He thought about the job as he watched various kinds of boats and wave runners cruising past, nothing close enough for him to read numbers or names, which was good for what he needed to do with the sheikh's boat.

He'd started thinking of the boat that way—belonging to a sheikh—since the call with Kershaw.

And if he and whoever McIntyre brought in on the job moved the boat down the shore from St. Petersburg to the Dry Tortugas, it wouldn't be odd for them to be a white dot to anyone standing on the beach.

Bruder was sure the sailing expert—McIntyre's label for one of his guys—would have something to say about where the boat could and couldn't go and they'd come to an agreement on it one way or another.

He had a light lunch delivered to the tent and napped on and off, making up for the night of driving, but he was awake and ready when he saw Penza plodding through the sand in his suit and black shoes, peering into other tents and checking the bodies scattered on towels and blankets.

Penza finally spotted him and stomped over, wiping sweat off his forehead.

"Why can't you just keep a damn phone on you?"

Bruder looked at him from behind his sunglasses but didn't turn his head.

"I don't need to call anybody."

"You're a pain in the ass, you know it?"

"You came out here to tell me that?"

Penza didn't think it was funny.

"Mr. McIntyre and the others are in the suite. Waiting for you."

"I'll be there in a while."

"No, let's go. Now."

"I need to rinse off."

"Nobody gives a shit if you smell or have sand in your ass crack. Come on."

Bruder stood up and put his shirt on.

"You know these guys McIntyre picked?"

"No."

"How do they look?"

"Impatient," Penza said, looking at his watch.

Bruder shook his head.

"That's a bad sign. Impatience is unprofessional."

He took his time shaking the sand out of his sandals, then carried them toward the hotel with Penza sweating right behind him.

***

McIntyre sat with three other men on the balcony, under the pergola.

Nobody stood up when Bruder came out from the suite, but McIntyre swept an arm toward him and said, "The man of the hour. Mr. Kline."

Bruder stopped at a rolling cart and poured himself an iced tea.

He took the last empty chair at the round table, across from McIntyre.

"Fellas."

He looked each man in the eye to see if he knew them.

He didn't.

McIntyre said, "Mr. Kline, we were just talking about the weather for the next week or so, which, at best, can be an educated guess this time of year on the Gulf side. But that's for you men to discuss. I'll make the introductions and step away so you can get to work. As you all know, this is Mr. Kline; he's the man in charge. He'll make the plan and the necessary preparations to execute said plan."

McIntyre turned to his left.

The man there was slouched in his chair, watching everything with amusement. He had wide shoulders and dirty blonde hair pulled back in a pony tail, framing a high, tan forehead and large jaw that jutted forward like he was chewing a piece of gristle.

"This is Mr. Turley. He'll be your captain—anything to do with how to move or treat the vessel, listen to him."

Turley wiggled his eyebrows and raised his glass toward Bruder, then dumped tea and ice into his mouth and crunched the cubes.

McIntyre held a hand out to the man on Turley's left, directly to Bruder's right.

He was smaller with darker skin and black stubble for hair.

"This is Mr. Valenti. What would you call him, Mr. Turley? Your second-in-command?"

Turley grinned.

"My left-tenant. My gopher bitch."

"Fuck you," Valenti said, smiling.

He had a heavy-lidded calmness to him but Bruder saw a watchfulness, an awareness, beneath the nonchalant face.

McIntyre cleared his throat, displeased with the vulgarity.

"As I understand it, Mr. Valenti will be handling any mechanical responsibilities on the yacht, and can also pilot the craft if needed. Is that accurate?"

"Yes, thank you," Valenti said. "Much better than gopher bitch."

"Is it?" Turley said, pleased with himself.

McIntyre turned to his right.

The man there, on Bruder's left, was tan and bald with small ears that moved every time he chewed the gum in his mouth. The muscles along his jaw and across his scalp rippled and Bruder looked at the rounded deltoids, peaked biceps, and thick forearms tapering down to skinny wrists and pegged him as a juicer.

"This is Mr. Domm, who will provide security and apply force and intimidation, as needed, which is unlikely. Mr. Domm, would you say that's accurate?"

"I would," Domm said, looking at Bruder the whole time.

"But he's also my bitch," Turley said and the three men laughed.

McIntyre stood up.

"I'll leave you to it, then. I don't want to know any details, other than how much financing you need to get the job done."

Turley grinned up at him.

"Plausible deniability, huh?"

McIntyre offered a thin smile in return.

"No, Mr. Turley. I just don't care."

He walked inside and Reed closed the doors.

***

Turley set his empty glass on the table and looked at Bruder, along with the other two.

Turley, apparently, spoke for all of them.

"Well?"

Bruder said, "What's the biggest boat you ever stole?"

Turley blinked, caught off guard.

"I took a fifty-foot Beneteau for a joy ride once."

"And that's a boat?"

"Uh, yeah. A sailing yacht."

"The one we're taking doesn't have a sail."

"I know, man. McIntyre told us about the boat. We're good to go on that."

He spread a large hand toward Bruder, like he needed to settle down.

"You're the one who's supposed to get us onto the yacht and out of the lot. Just get us aboard the damn thing and we'll do our jobs."

Bruder looked at the others, who gazed back with flat faces.

He said, "What happens if someone chases us? Can you outrun them?"

"My man, have you heard the term 'boat raced' before?"

"The question stands."

Turley took a moment to share his infinite patience with Valenti and Domm.

"Well, it depends on what they're in, but if we get a good enough head start, yeah, I can outrun any pursuit."

The hand came out again, telling Bruder to hold up.

"But if we're talking some kind of Coast Guard interceptor, or a helicopter, then no. Same goes for a radio."

"Can't outrun a radio," Valenti said, like he was imparting great wisdom.

"You guys have a police scanner?"

"Two," Valenti said. "Plus some radios we can use instead of the boat's. Keep us off the open channels."

"Good. How many radios?"

"Three," Turley answered.

"Get one more. You have earpieces for them?"

Turley breathed out through his nose.

"I guess we'll get those too, huh?"

"Today," Bruder said.

Turley looked around the table, either calming himself down or pumping himself up.

He finally said, "But we shouldn't need them, right? I mean, isn't that why McIntyre brought you in on this? So you can come up with a plan to break the yacht out without anyone knowing about it? I thought the whole point of having a *master planner* is to make it so we don't have to outrun anybody."

He used finger quotes on "master planner", making the other two smirk.

"I need to know what I'm working with," Bruder said. "You say you can steer the boat and make it go fast if needed. Regardless of where we are?"

Turley frowned.

"What's that mean?"

Bruder pulled out one of the maps he'd collected from various gas stations and fishing charters around St. Pete.

He spread it on the table and stabbed a finger where the impound marina was.

"We need to get from here to the gulf."

He traced a finger along the twisting route they'd have to take to get out of the cove and bays to open water.

"You can do that at high speed?"

"Well..." Turley said. "I need to look at some depth charts, but yeah, no biggie."

Bruder set his forearms on the table.

"I need a serious answer. If you can't do it, it won't change my opinion of you. I just need to know."

"I said yes."

They stared at each other until Valenti said, "Do we have time to make the same run in another boat? Like a test?"

"Yes," Bruder said. "Do you have one?"

"Of course," Turley said.

"One that isn't stolen?"

"Same answer."

"Where is it?"

"Around here."

Bruder shook his head.

"How soon can you get it to St. Pete?"

Turley looked at Valenti and Domm.

"What's today, Wednesday? We take it up the coast and into Lake Okeechobee, then the Waterway to Ft. Myers and up the Gulf…I mean, we could do it in less than twenty hours if we had to."

Bruder pointed at the map again, along the southeastern coastline of Tampa Bay.

"Sun City. I'll get you rooms at the Bay Breeze Inn, you need the address?"

Domm said, "Bay Breeze Inn? That sounds like a shit hole."

"It is," Bruder said. He'd looked it up using a computer in the hotel's business suite.

Turley said, "No, no, McIntyre is footing the bill on this."

"So?"

"So he makes one call, we got a penthouse in Tampa."

Bruder said, "You heard him, he doesn't want any details. And starting now, he doesn't get any information about where we are or what we're doing until we show up with the boat. Even if he changes his mind and demands to know."

"Why not?" Valenti asked.

"Because that's how I operate. Bay Breeze Inn—you can find a place to put your boat near there?"

Turley seemed a bit stunned by the destruction of his expectations.

"I guess we'll have to. But why Sun City? And why are you driving instead of cruising with us?"

"We don't stay anywhere near the job," Bruder said. "This place is as close as I'm willing to go. And St. Pete may as well be an island for the number of ways out. We want more exit options than that if it comes down to it."

Domm said, "And you'd rather drive because…"

"Because a boat *is* an island."

He stood up and headed for the door.

"I'll see you at the motel tomorrow. Bring the gear we talked about."

He didn't wait around to see if they were happy about it.

***

McIntyre was in the small kitchen talking on a cell phone.

Bruder closed the balcony door and made sure the other three were staying at the table, at least for now, then crossed the suite and stood on the other side of the counter and looked at McIntyre.

Reed and Penza sat in the conversation area behind him, reading sheets from a newspaper, though he could feel them watching.

After a few seconds McIntyre ended the call and offered Bruder a patient smile.

"Yes, Mr. Kline?"

"These guys are the best you can do?"

"You aren't impressed?"

"They seem like small-time hoods who just got a promotion."

McIntyre nodded.

"I can see why you'd think that. Mr. Turley has a certain amount of hubris, and he lacks the sort of consistent motivation I'd like to see, but I can assure you: when the time comes to perform, he will do so."

"How do you know?"

"I won't talk about that. But ask yourself, why would I provide you with a crew who can't perform the task I need done? Just to watch you fail? I don't need any additional reasons for killing you, Mr. *Kline*. So what's the problem? You can't get along with those men out there?"

"Getting along doesn't matter. I don't trust them."

"That's your problem. Now, what do you need from me to get this thing done?"

Bruder examined the situation to see if any new angles had appeared in the last fifteen minutes, options other than exactly what McIntyre wanted.

He found nothing.

He said, "How do I get in touch with the people we're meeting at the Dry Tortugas?"

"You don't. I do."

Bruder had expected as much and still didn't like it.

"So I call you and you call them. What then, you call me back to say everything is sweet?"

"You can assume things are in motion as soon as you call me. No need for confirmation."

Bruder grunted.

"How long from the call until they can be at the meet?"

"Within a few hours."

Which, if Bruder recalled the maps correctly and they were traveling by boat, put them in Cuba.

If they were using a helicopter or parachuting in or some such nonsense, they could be just about anywhere in the Gulf.

"Okay, so I call you when I know the delivery window. The same number?"

"Why would it be any different?" McIntyre said.

And that was the Labyrinth, Bruder thought.

It didn't matter who knew your number or where you were staying because nobody was going to use those things against you or take them away.

Except Bruder had done that, back in New York, and the gleam in McIntyre's eye seemed to be daring him to bring it up.

He let it go and said, "How much cash do you have here?"

"How much do you need?"

"Twenty."

He expected McIntyre to demand an itemized list but he just looked past Bruder's shoulder and nodded at Penza, who went through one of the doors and came back a minute later with twenty thousand dollars in banded stacks of twenties and fifties.

He put the cash on the counter and sat back down.

Bruder looked at it like it was a crumpled fifty on a motel nightstand.

"You can show yourself out," McIntyre said.

CHAPTER FIVE

The next day at two in the afternoon Turley knocked on Bruder's second-floor door at the Bay Breeze Inn, which overlooked a semi-busy two-lane road and, beyond that, a marshy stretch of grass leading to water.

When Bruder opened the door, Turley said, "This place is even more of a dump than we thought. I think I'll stay on the boat. You want to see her?"

Bruder stepped out and closed the door on the slightly cooler room. The air conditioning unit stuck in the wall had been rattling and churning all day without much progress.

He carried a plastic tube designed for transporting a disassembled fishing pole.

Inside were the maps and charts he'd been working on.

His linen shirt immediately started sticking to his back and his feet got a little slippery inside the sandals as they walked along the open hallway and down the concrete stairs.

His shorts, a little baggy with pockets meant for phones and wallets but holding only a clip knife at the moment, were cinched by a wide, stiff belt at the top to secure a cross-draw holster under his left ribs. The holster held a

Glock 19—the Beretta Pico stayed in the room after Bruder had a short, private debate over whether it was too small for a guy the size of Domm.

They crossed the road and Bruder was glad it was March instead of August; he'd need an IV of electrolytes just to walk around.

He said, "You get the radio gear?"

"Yeah, we got it. Relax. And it turns out these grand accommodations you picked have an agreement with one of the dinky marinas over here. Fifty percent off the usual fees if you're staying at the Bay Breeze."

"Good," Bruder said.

He didn't want to have to go back to McIntyre for more money.

He also didn't like being told to relax, but he let it go.

The far side of the road was lined with small shops—fishing gear and tourist garb and Cuban food—and he followed Turley into an alley between two of the shacks. The alley had an open wooden gate with a sign: Marina Customers Only

When they got past the shacks and assorted trash bins and junk, stuff the tourists weren't supposed to see, the alley turned into a wide dock with tall grass on both sides. Bruder looked into the grass and saw water glittering at the base.

The dock stretched out a few hundred feet until it cleared the grass, then spread left and right into a T shape. There were a dozen or so boats tied up, different sizes and shapes and ages, but mostly white.

They walked past a security booth with open windows and Turley waved at the oblivious teenager inside, staring at his phone.

Turley went left at the top of the T and didn't slow down, so Bruder looked toward the end of the dock and saw Valenti waiting there with two beers in his hands next to a boat larger than most in the marina.

"We're actually on a canal here," Turley said over his

shoulder.

Bruder grunted to indicate he'd heard.

"That's good," Turley said and looked back with a grin.

The tone and smile could have been taken as condescending if Bruder cared.

They got to Valenti, who offered the beers.

Bruder accepted one and looked at the boat.

"This is her," Turley said.

"It can get to the Dry Tortugas and back?"

Turley glanced at Valenti: *Can you believe this guy?*

Then he said, "My man, this a Boston Whaler 345 Conquest Pilothouse. Thirty-nine feet long, twelve hundred horsepower."

"Good for you. Can it make the trip?"

"Uh, yeah."

"And it's legal?"

"Legal enough for what we're doing."

Turley wanted a reaction to that but Bruder kept looking at the boat.

It had a pilothouse enclosed on the front and sides with large windows that took up about half the length and an open deck area on the back half. Two swiveling chairs were fixed to the deck beneath a retractable sunshade.

The short walls around the deck were lined with coolers and bags and bins of gear that looked fishing and snorkeling related.

Turley said, "At top speed, she can go about forty five knots. That's fifty miles per hour. Fuel capacity, we got enough to go two hundred and fifty miles at full throttle. Maybe more, with the work we've done on her, but I wouldn't count on it."

Bruder said, "We'll need to bring extra, just in case."

Turley went to one of the bins and showed him two bundles of folded-up material.

To Bruder, they looked like deflated life rafts.

Turley said, "Fuel bladders. Each one is two hundred gallons. We can only fit one on here when they're full, but we can put the other on the yacht. We transfer the fuel from this bladder to the yacht's tank, or the other bladder, then send this boat back in to fill up again, if we have to."

"Good," Bruder said.

Turley crossed his arms.

"Now, it would probably help if you told us what the damn plan is."

Bruder said, "Where's the other one? Domm?"

Valenti turned toward the boat.

"Domm!"

Through the starboard window Bruder saw the bald head poke out of a narrow opening in the center of the pilothouse, next to the captain's chair.

"Hah?"

"Come out here, the man with the plan is about to drop some wisdom."

"Well, shit, I can't miss that."

He emerged from the pilothouse and dropped into the nearest swivel chair, then spun it until he faced the dock.

"Lay it on us, boss."

Bruder looked around.

No one else was on the dock, but a few of the boats were close enough for eavesdropping if anyone was inside with a window open.

He didn't want to do it but said, "Let's go for a boat ride. I want you all to see something."

***

Turley took the boat away from the marina and headed for the point where the cove turned into Tampa Bay.

Bruder was in the port side swivel chair, facing forward.

Domm was next to him with his feet up on the starboard railing. He was tilted back with his eyes closed behind sunglasses and may have fallen asleep.

There was an empty chair in front of Bruder, inside the pilothouse and built into the body of the craft, facing the bow. It shared a small table with a matching seat that faced the stern, the whole thing like a compact setup for playing chess.

Valenti sat in the rear-facing seat, watching Bruder.

The breeze made by the boat's motion was enough to get through Bruder's shirt and felt good, drying the sweat.

Still, he didn't like moving away from shore.

He could swim fine and didn't mind the water—it was the exposure, out here cutting across the cove with nothing but clear sight lines in all directions, right out in the open for anybody who wanted to watch them.

And if he had to get off the boat for one reason or another, his head would be a beacon out there, just bobbing around.

Turley swiveled the captain's chair enough to look back at Bruder.

"I assume we're checking out the impound marina, yeah?"

Bruder opened the tube and pulled out the rolled-up sheets inside, then worked to keep his balance when he stood and carried them forward.

He dropped into the seat across from Valenti and flattened the maps and charts on the small table.

Turley rooted around in a storage compartment next to his chair and came out with a leather sap and a hockey puck with the Tampa Bay Lightning logo on it.

Bruder frowned at the sap and watched that hand, but Turley just dropped both items on opposite corners to keep the papers from rolling back up and went back to the captain's chair.

Bruder pointed at the map.

"Yes, the impound lot. Here. Now, I don't know how this all works with boating—will we stand out, cruising by the place?"

Turley dismissed the concern with a wave.

"Nah. We're just a group of assholes looking for a place to drop a line. Domm, you want to get some poles going?"

"Aye," Domm said and stretched and groaned and made a big deal about opening one of the bins and pulling out some fishing poles.

Turley looked at the map again.

Tampa Bay is shaped like a curving uppercase graffiti Y, and he stabbed it with his finger near the right ascender.

"We'll stay along the coast on the way up, but we can't get too close to the preserves here. Then we'll sweep west here, along the coast, and curl up into Old Tampa Bay."

His finger traced the route up into the left ascender of the Y.

Bruder pointed at a line running through the water.

"This is the shipping channel?"

"Yeah, those boats have the right-of-way. Freighters and tugs."

"They won't bother us though."

"Nah. They don't give a shit about little water bugs like us unless we get in their way."

"Even once we have the yacht?"

"Still a water bug compared to them, buddy."

Valenti tapped the isthmus of land in the middle of the Y.

"Might see some jets taking off and landing. That's Mac-Dill Air Force Base."

"About that," Bruder said. "Is it going to be a problem?"

The two men shared a look of alarm.

Turley said, "Why would we need to worry about the Air Force?"

"I'm asking you. Do they like to run helicopter patrols over the bay, do they control access or have any sort of curfew in the surrounding waters?"

Valenti stuck his lower lip out and shook his head.

"Nah, man. As long as we don't try to steal a plane or

something, we're good. We aren't stealing a plane, right? Just the yacht?"

"Just the yacht," Bruder confirmed, looking at the map.

He pointed at St. Petersburg, about halfway down the stem of the Y along the western coast of Tampa Bay.

"We'll be going past here on the way out, with the yacht, and there's a Coast Guard station. We'll talk about that after we get a look at the impound marina."

"Why wait?" Turley said.

"Because there's no point in getting into it if you look at the impound and tell me it can't be done."

"Fair enough," Turley said.

Domm finished messing around with the fishing gear and stood at the rear of the pilothouse, reaching up to grab the edge of the roof and have an excuse to show everyone his biceps.

"What are we talking about up here? We get it all figured out?"

"We're gonna look at the lot first," Valenti said.

Domm looked down at Bruder.

"Lemme ask you this: Say we go scout this yacht and the impound marina, and the gate's open with nobody around. What do you think about just idling in, you and Turley jump aboard and follow us out to sea?"

"No," Bruder said.

Domm grinned, like he'd expected the answer and considered it weak.

"Why not?"

"Because the people we're delivering it to might not get to the Dry Tortugas fast enough. What then—we just cruise around in a stolen yacht until they show up?"

Domm shrugged.

"Eh, maybe they don't get the yacht back at all."

Bruder looked from Domm to Turley.

"Is he always like this?"

"Like what?"

"Full of shit."

"Hey," Domm said, taking one hand off the roof. He pulled his sunglasses down so Bruder could see his small eyes.

Turley said, "Yeah, he's just screwing around. He's not serious. Are you Domm?"

Domm was too busy glaring down at Bruder to answer.

Turley said, "Domm."

"What."

"Look at me."

Domm peeled his eyes off Bruder.

"Knock it off," Turley said.

After a moment Domm shrugged and pushed his sunglasses back up, then put the free hand on the roof again.

"All's I'm saying is, if the damn thing is right there for the taking, we ought to keep our options open."

"You want to do that kind of work," Bruder said, "go rob liquor stores. You want in on this job, stick to the plan."

"Your plan."

"Right."

"The one we haven't heard yet."

Bruder didn't bother answering.

Domm said, "And now you're in charge of the string too? Not just the plan?"

Bruder just waited for him to run out of gas.

"Funny," Domm said. "I thought Mr. McIntyre made that call. Not you."

Bruder said, "People fall off boats every day."

Now both hands came off the roof but before they could reach down Bruder hit him with a straight left just above the bladder.

Air rushed out of Domm's open mouth and Bruder clipped his chin with a right cross, making his jaw clack around as he fell backward.

Bruder was up and grabbed a handful of his shirt and

guided him into the swivel chair, where Domm slumped and tried to make his eyes stop rolling behind his crooked sunglasses.

Bruder turned and found Valenti and Turley both watching, neither one having moved, like they were used to this kind of thing when Domm was around.

"Well," Turley said, "I'm glad we got that sorted out."

He opened another beer for himself.

"Now come on. Let's enjoy this beautiful day while David Copperfield here tells us how we're going to steal a ninety-foot yacht without anybody noticing."

***

Bruder went back to his swivel chair on the deck and watched the water and shore for anything new to concern him.

Turley steered the boat like he knew what he was doing or at least knew how to fake it.

He made what seemed like random adjustments, then they'd cruise past a shallow spot off the starboard side or a cluster of buoys Bruder hadn't seen until they were already in the wake.

The cove gradually widened, then spilled out into Tampa Bay, which looked like an ocean with no visible far shore.

Much closer were the cargo ships and accessory boats — tugs and Coast Guard and zippy little crafts that seemed to have an urgent purpose.

Outside the channel, a lot of boats like Turley's were moving or anchored, most of the latter with people fishing off the back.

Turley waved to anyone within a few hundred yards and got return waves from everyone who saw him.

At first Bruder thought he was well-known, then realized it was just a boat thing.

You wave at everyone and they wave back.

A few minutes into Tampa Bay, Domm got himself together enough to push up in the chair and look around.

He touched his chin and peered at Bruder over his sunglasses.

"Did you hit me?"

"Yeah."

"What for?"

Bruder turned to him.

"You don't remember?"

"I remember you hitting me."

"The rest doesn't matter. Just remember that part."

Domm called into the pilothouse, "Hey, why'd he hit me?"

"You were being an asshole," Valenti said.

Domm tested his jaw, which seemed to work fine.

"I'm always an asshole."

"Yeah, but he doesn't know that."

Domm told Bruder, "So now you know. That's just the way I am."

Bruder said, "And now *you* know. I'll smack you around for being you."

Domm stared for a moment, then broke into a wide grin, wincing at the end.

"Goddam, such a hard ass! You guys, I think I'm gonna like this guy!"

Bruder didn't tell him about the blood in his teeth.

***

Turley found a good spot to cut across the shipping channel, then they were at the top of the Y and curling northwest into Old Tampa Bay.

Bruder saw a low bridge spanning the water ahead and it matched what he saw on the main map: Gandy Bridge, which put the impound marina in one of the coves south of the bridge and along the western coastline.

Turley and Valenti mumbled and pointed and shrugged over the pile of maps and charts, some of which had come out of a bin on the boat.

They consulted the depth finder mounted on the console, then Turley pointed the boat toward a spot on the shore he deemed correct.

Valenti sat sideways in the chair in front of Bruder and said, "We got it."

Bruder looked at the shore, which had stretches of green mangrove interrupted by rows of houses seemingly floating on the water.

As they got closer one of the wider spaces between neighborhoods turned into a canal, and Turley kept to the middle and pulled the throttle back.

The canal wound around a few curves with more mangrove and houses, the homes larger and more spread out here, nearly estates, until they swept around a final curve and Bruder saw the impound marina ahead along the starboard shore.

Everything looked different from this angle, and in full sun, but it was unmistakable.

He identified the sail and upholstery fabricator, which was closer to Turley's boat, and the corner he'd crouched at to observe the impound.

The fabricator docks were busy with dark, wiry men lugging ropes and bunches of canvas around, some of them up in the rigging of a few of the boats, either removing old gear or installing new.

Other people—these not so dark or wiry—stood on the docks and watched and chatted and laughed.

The boat owners, maybe the same ones playing soft music when Bruder was there.

Other boats were anchored in the cove, fishing or just floating there while people sat and drank and jumped overboard to swim.

Turley waved at all of them but his eyes were on the impound marina.

"So that's her."

The sheikh's yacht looked like a spaceship crash-landed in a junkyard.

It glowed in the afternoon sun and made everything around it look filmed with grime and dust.

The gate was shut and Bruder could see one person on the concrete docks, a man wearing khaki shorts, a dark blue golf shirt, and a wide-brimmed sun hat. He stood next to one of the scrubby boats with a clipboard or tablet, writing or tapping, then walked along the concrete dock toward the impound warehouse.

The wall facing the marina was mostly black glass and aluminum, the interior invisible from the water.

The man went up the metal stairs from the dock to the top of the sea wall, then through a door made of more black glass and aluminum and disappeared inside.

Bruder told Turley, "Find a spot to fish. Away from everybody else here."

"They took all the good spots," Turley said. "I guess it doesn't matter though. We're here for the Big Kahuna!"

He looked at Valenti for approval and got a smile for his trouble.

They dropped anchor beyond and across from the impound marina, near some mangrove trees overhanging the water. Bruder could smell a dead fish somewhere close and saw small live ones darting around the tree roots and hull of the boat.

Domm passed the fishing poles around.

Bruder took his and held it but didn't do anything else with it.

The others cast lines in various directions and wiggled and tugged the poles around, playing with the reels at different speeds.

After a while Turley said, "So we need to take that beauty from here, down the bay, and into the Gulf."

"Then to the Dry Tortugas," Valenti added.

Bruder said, "Any problems?"

Turley had his back to the yacht, watching his fishing line. "With the trip itself, no. The timing, maybe."

He wanted Bruder to prompt him for more information but it was irritating so Bruder just waited.

Eventually Turley said, "So we shoot south and go under 275, the Skyway Bridge. From there the best option is the Southwest Channel, a straight line running between Egmont and Passage Keys."

He seemed to be talking mostly to Valenti and Domm, or himself, while he ran the route in his head.

"Second option would be to cut further south and hit the Passage Key Inlet, on the south side of Passage Key."

He reeled the line in and tossed it out again.

"Might be some other options but I don't like them at speed, at night—I assume we'll do this at night?"

Bruder nodded.

Turley said, "Yeah, so I don't like those routes in the dark with a vessel I'm on for the first time."

Bruder waited a little longer, then said, "So what's this have to do with timing?"

"Huh? Oh, right."

He brought the line in again and set the rod down so he could consult a few maps and charts in the pilothouse.

When he came back out he looked around for any boats creeping too close, then showed Bruder the route on a map titled *Boater's and Angler's Guide*.

"See, from here to here, it's maybe twenty three nautical miles."

"Okay," Bruder said.

"The sheikh's yacht, if I have her pegged, cruises at about twenty-two knots."

He looked at Valenti.

"You think?"

Valenti pushed his lips out and nodded.

"Top speed around twenty-seven, but we don't want to hit that unless we have to."

Turley came back to Bruder.

"We'll look it up, but it's close to that. So from where we are now until we clear the bay and get to the Gulf, figure on one hour."

Bruder looked at the map again and saw it.

He stabbed the small islands Turley had mentioned, labeled Egmont Key and Passage Key, the last two pieces of land between Tampa Bay and the Gulf of Mexico.

To the north of Egmont was the shipping channel, then a chunk of land called Mullet Key, then a mess of wetlands before St. Pete.

To the south of Passage Key, Anna Maria Island jutted up like a thumb, then there was Bradenton.

Bruder said, "The passage through here is a bottleneck."

"That's what I've been saying."

It wasn't, but Bruder let it go.

"One hour to get from here to the Gulf."

"Yeah, man. Like I said. Do you see the timing problem now?"

Bruder sat back in the swivel chair and looked at the yacht, the impound marina, the whole setup.

He said, "If anyone calls the cops inside that one hour, and they block off those waterways, we're done."

Turley pointed a finger gun at him and dropped the thumb. "Nailed it."

Bruder said, "Fine. I'll work on that. For now, this is how it'll go tomorrow..."

CHAPTER SIX

The next morning Bruder pulled the rental car into the impound marina's lot, which had a half dozen employee cars now, and parked next to the black sedan with the light bar on its roof.

The gray lettering on the passenger door said *Sentinel*. The letters were on top of what looked like a circular radar screen or the reticle of a sniper scope.

Bruder stood and tried to get a quick look inside the other vehicle from behind his sunglasses but the windows were tinted beyond black.

Someone could be sitting inside staring back at him and he wouldn't know it.

So he kept moving, beneath the flagpole with the cameras and through the door, a thick metal slab with a mesh window in the upper half.

The inside was dark and cool, almost cold compared to the blanket of humidity dropping over the parking lot.

Bruder took his sunglasses off so he could see.

The place reminded him of an auto parts store or a high-end scrapyard.

A row of chrome and plastic chairs ran along the front wall to his left.

In the center of the chairs, a low table held fishing and boating magazines.

On the right was a closed metal door with a doorbell button next to it and a sign: Press for Entry.

A long laminate counter ran in front of him with an opening above it and three construction-grade computer monitors facing away.

Through the opening was a separator wall to block whatever was beyond.

Bruder leaned over the counter and could see doorless access around both ends of the wall.

Cameras looked at him from the upper corners and straight ahead.

Nothing to do about those, so he tried to ignore them.

He waited for almost a minute, then pressed the doorbell button with a knuckle.

Nothing happened for another minute, then a tan woman with short blonde hair walked around the separator wall and stood behind the counter.

She had an ID badge on a lanyard around her neck and wore the same style of dark blue polo and khaki shorts as the man working on the concrete docks the previous day—some sort of uniform, then.

The badge said her name was Julie.

She said, "Hey there, good morning. Sorry about the wait."

She had a thin, pale scar stretching up near the corner of her mouth like she'd taken a bad spill off a bike or had a car accident that split her lip a long time ago.

It looked good on her.

"No problem," Bruder said, working to sound at ease but slightly embarrassed.

She said, "How can I help you?"

He winced and paused, like he wasn't sure how to start.

"Well, I'm wondering if you might have my buddy's boat here."

Her eyebrows went up.

"Oh? Has your buddy been up to no good?"

"No, no, nothing like that. He just, uh, had a little too much to drink a few nights ago and passed out, and when he woke up and went to find his boat, it was gone."

"So, stolen," Julie said. "Did you call the police?"

Bruder winced again.

"Not yet, he wanted to check here first. If there's any way to avoid a police report, you know...insurance, all of that. I don't really understand his concerns, but apparently it's a big deal."

She seemed unimpressed by Bruder and his buddy so far.

"Sounds like he's had this kind of trouble before."

"This kind, every kind. He's a jackass."

Bruder put his elbows on the counter and leaned forward a little, confiding.

"Here's the thing. He doesn't really remember tying the boat off."

"That's a problem."

"Yeah. He might have, and somebody might have stolen it. But...there's a chance he just let it float away. Which is why we're checking places like this."

She turned to the middle computer monitor.

"What's the vessel's ID number?"

He took out a slip of paper and read the hull identification number they'd pulled from one of the boats at the Sun City marina.

Julie started working the mouse and keyboard below the counter.

"What's your buddy's last name?"

"Salas."

Valenti had gotten the name of the owner the night before, just making idle boat chatter.

She clicked around some more, then shook her head.

"We don't have it, sorry."

Bruder thumped the counter lightly with a fist.

"Dang it. Wait, do you have anything with a missing number? Or scuffed up?"

"Scuffed up?"

"He doesn't take care of the boat. Which you probably gathered, what with him possibly forgetting to tie it off and all. But I don't remember seeing this number on the hull. I mean, I never really looked for it, but when he rattled it off it struck me that I don't think it's actually on the hull."

"HINs are required by law," Julie said.

Bruder shrugged, helpless about how disgusting his friend was.

He also knew, from the fake fishing trip yesterday, there were at least three boats in the impound with no hull identification numbers.

***

Julie said, "What kind of vessel is it?"

Bruder flipped the scrap of paper over.

"It's a twenty-six foot Osprey Fisherman. From 1998."

Julie looked up from the screen.

"1998? And he doesn't take good care of it?"

"Nope."

"It probably sank."

She was being smart and Bruder laughed, a short bark.

"You might be right. Do you have anything like that out there?"

He already knew she did.

Julie went back to the screen, then said, "Well, huh. As soon as you said Osprey a little bell went off in my head, because we do have one, and we *think* it's a '98. But it's a floating dumpster."

Bruder nodded.

"That sounds about right. Can I take a look at it?"

She looked at him for a moment with an arched brow.

"Okay, assuming this is your friend's boat, I can't let you fill anything out and take it. It has to be the owner."

"Sure, of course," Bruder said. "All I need to do is find it. It's up to him to do the rest."

"And where is he now?"

"Up in Clearwater, calling around to all these marinas he knows, and other drunks, and checking the impound lots around there. That's what he says, anyway. He's probably at a bar."

Julie nodded, considering the situation.

"You're either a really good friend or he's a really bad friend. Or both."

Bruder shrugged again: *What can you do?*

She tilted her head toward the door.

"Step over there; I'll buzz you in."

***

Bruder went through the door, a thick metal slab, and turned left toward the back of the building.

He walked down a short hallway and when he got past the rectangle enclosing the lobby and the floating separator wall, he saw the interior was one big open space.

It had a high ceiling showing metal joists and exposed conduit and ductwork.

Large light fixtures descended from the joists but they were off because the windows facing the marina allowed plenty of light—almost too much—even with the curtain wall of tinted windows.

The middle of the room held a bullpen of large cubicles in three X patterns, twelve desks total, with fabric half-walls forming the X dividers.

Most of the desks had a person in a dark blue golf shirt, looking at screens or talking on phones.

Bruder spotted the man he'd seen on the concrete dock yesterday; the wide-brimmed hat was on his desk next to the tablet.

He didn't see any kind of master control center or security booth, but based on the number of monitors at each workstation he erred on the side of paranoia and assumed they could all access the security camera feeds and gate controls.

Julie led him along the right wall, down a wide swath of low-pile carpet, toward the windows.

Bruder said, "All of this for some crappy boats?"

"You'd be surprised," she said over her shoulder. "This is a hub though—we coordinate what happens with the seizures and derelicts from here down to Fort Myers."

"And that's a lot?"

"Like I said, you'd be surprised. We spend half the time arguing with other hubs and offices about whose responsibility a vessel is. Did it get abandoned here but float into Naples' turf? That's why you see some boats just sitting out there in the water. Nobody wants to claim them."

"Why not?"

She said, "It can cost thousands of dollars to recover a vessel. And that's usually a sunk cost—no pun intended—because nobody is going to pay that much to get their piece of crap boat back, which they abandoned in the first place."

"Huh. I guess I never thought about that."

"Yeah. It's not like tossing a napkin on the ground for someone else to pick up."

She turned left and headed for the aluminum and glass door set near the center of the back wall.

Bruder worked to memorize the office layout, where the corners were, the cameras mounted up in the corners.

If he had to come inside again, it would be at night.

***

They stepped out of the air conditioning into the growing heat and mugginess of the day.

Bruder put his sunglasses back on and looked around and froze when he saw the yacht.

"Whoa."

Julie was already smiling, waiting for it.

"That's not your friend's boat."

He barked another laugh.

"No, not a chance. That thing is impounded?"

"It is."

She went down the steps and Bruder followed, saying, "Up for auction?"

She shook her head.

"Not here. They're taking it up to Jersey, some exclusive nautical club auction. We tried to convince the head office to keep it as a seized asset, like the DEA does sometimes, but they said no way. Not up to them."

"Keep it..." Bruder said. "For what?"

She shrugged.

"I dunno. Company parties. Lunch breaks."

He turned to see if she was kidding.

She said, "The cost to run that thing for a week would take up our annual budget."

"I can imagine. Whose is it? Or was it, I guess."

"I've said all I can say. And no, we can't give tours. Now come on—if your buddy's boat is here, it's one of these."

She started walking to the right.

Bruder lingered a moment, studying the yacht like a gawking tourist but really watching for movement.

He didn't see anyone with a rifle on the upper deck—the flybridge, McIntyre called it—or moving on the lower decks.

Maybe they were inside the cabin, behind the tinted glass, or below.

Before he turned away he looked down at the railing, meant to keep people from falling off the concrete into the marina.

An aluminum box was mounted there, about the size of a personal cooler.

It had a scuffed Plexiglass lid angled down at the front to let water run off.

Through the Plexiglass, he saw knobs and indicator lights and a large raised red circle, like an emergency stop button.

A laminated piece of paper was duct taped to the front of the aluminum housing. The tape and laminate were beaten up by the weather, strands of the tape twitching in the breeze.

The paper said:

INCOMING VESSEL: DO NOT CLOSE GATE
UNTIL VESSEL IS DOCKED
OUTGOING VESSEL: DO NOT CLOSE GATE UNTIL
VESSEL CLEARS FIRST BEND

So someone, at some point, had closed the gate on a vessel.

Maybe more than once, if a sign was necessary.

He followed Julie, who waited at the corner of the concrete dock, which doubled as the barrier wall once they walked out over the water with the cyclone fence on the right.

Bruder looked at the mesh and poles.

There weren't any rust spots or gaps or chipped concrete along the base of the fence to be exploited.

The razor wire along the top looked as sharp as it needed to be.

He glanced out into the cove, where a dozen or so boats were idling around or anchored.

One of them was Turley but he couldn't tell which and didn't want to stare long enough to figure it out.

Julie turned left and took them down the first branch extending off the barrier wall.

Two miserable-looking boats squatted there. Most of the paint had chipped and flaked away, exposing gray, cracked wood underneath.

The first boat had a pilothouse with a missing windshield

and a nest of crushed beer cans in one corner.

The second had an extension cord running into the cabin from an outlet mounted on the dock. Bruder could hear a pump motor working from somewhere inside the vessel, and a constant stream of water spewed from a hose hanging over the side.

Julie pointed at the one not taking on water.

"That's an Osprey," Julie said. "The other one isn't, but I'm hoping it's your buddy's just so we can get it out of here."

Bruder shook his head.

"Sorry. Neither one."

"Damn. Come on."

She walked back down the dock and Bruder took the opportunity to look at the holes running through the barrier wall.

Water sloshed in and out, tugging at strands of green, filmy seaweed that had attached itself to the concrete.

A long, narrow fish peeked out from one of the holes then disappeared into the marina water.

Bruder turned left and trailed along to the next branch, which had a pontoon boat and two sailboats, all of them afloat but otherwise unimpressive.

The fourth craft was another Osprey, spotted by Turley the day before.

Julie held a hand out toward it.

"'98 Osprey with no HIN. Please tell me it's his."

Bruder stood next to it and peered into the pilothouse, which had a moldy bedroll on the deck and a tangle of fishing gear. He could smell the tang of old fish blood coming off the equipment.

"You're not going to believe this," he said.

Her eyebrows went up.

"It's his?"

"Nope. What are the chances? Two '98 Ospreys with no hull numbers, both of them beat to hell and clearly owned by jackasses."

She seemed more disappointed than him.

"Like I said before, you'd be surprised. You name any make and model, we've seen it, usually mistreated."

They both looked at the boat for a few seconds, then Bruder said, "Well, damn. Sorry to waste your time."

"Not a waste. If you don't find his boat, these will be up for auction in a few weeks. You can come get into a bidding war with a bunch of salvage guys."

Bruder shook his head.

"He doesn't deserve another boat."

"Yeah, you're right."

He picked up on a tone and realized she may have been probing for any interest on his part to see her again.

The auction would be after the job, and so far he wouldn't mind spending more time with her.

As long as they didn't talk about boats the whole time.

He said, "But just in case, what's the date?"

She looked up at him and he couldn't tell if she was squinting or smiling but it looked like the latter.

"Let's go back inside, I'll give you a flyer."

"Great."

As they walked Julie said, "So what's the next step in Operation Jackass?"

"I have no idea. I'll check in with him and see if he's had any luck. But if he's at a bar..."

He left the rest unsaid and she laughed.

When they got to the stairs something bobbing in the marina caught Bruder's eye.

It looked like a small stick, or piece of feces, then he caught a whiff of cigar smoke and knew what it was.

The same guy he'd spotted that first night was on the yacht, smoking his cigars and carrying his rifle.

Bruder followed Julie up the steps and into the office

He felt eyes on his back the whole way,

***

Bruder took the Sun Skyway Bridge south over Tampa Bay with the morning sun still bouncing off the water.

As he crossed he tried to eye the water below, knowing he and Turley's crew would be down there on the yacht soon.

He cranked his head around and tried to spot the two Keys, Egmont and Passage, but had no luck.

He didn't know how the ocean worked, if he had any right to expect to see them from the bridge.

As the bridge dropped back down toward land he spotted an exit for the South Skyway Fishing Pier and took it, then wound around until he was driving back the way he'd come with the water there on his left and the Skyway bridge above him on the right.

He passed cars and trucks parked along the side with people standing nearby holding rods over the side of the pier, three miles of two-lane highway just for fishing.

Bruder took the road as far as he could go, then parked and got out and looked around.

Water and boats and maybe a smudge of land way out to the southwest, but it could have been a cloud.

It didn't tell him much but he was glad he saw it.

If there was time, he'd have Turley take them out to Egmont and Passage to see how those chokepoints looked.

One hour to get from the impound lot to the Gulf.

Then, according to Turley, they'd be a needle in a haystack.

So far, Bruder agreed.

The water was big and the sheikh's yacht was small, relatively, and it would be hard for someone to find them.

But not impossible.

He got back in the car and curled north to Sun City and the motel.

The entire drive took just under ninety minutes and Turley and the others weren't due back at the dock until later, so he walked two blocks to a diner and had a more substantial breakfast than the gas station donut and coffee he'd picked up on the way to the impound lot.

He chose a booth by the windows and looked out at the water, beyond the street and mess of low buildings on the far side.

After the close-up look at the impound marina, he had a way to get the yacht out.

The plan counted on Turley, Valenti and Domm playing a part, so he had to assume they would come through.

He worked through the details of what he considered Plan A—the gear they'd need, the timing to make sure they'd make the Gulf inside an hour, who would do what.

When that was done he moved on to Plan B, which in just about any other job would be to walk away from it.

That wasn't possible, thanks to McIntyre, so he had to figure out a way to get the job done if Turley and his crew failed to meet the moment.

Whether it happened through ineptitude or malice didn't matter—if they became a problem, he'd have to deal with it.

The server refilled his coffee and he took his time draining the mug, looking out at the water and thinking about how to kill three men on a yacht without sinking the damn thing.

CHAPTER SEVEN

A thump on the motel room door woke Bruder from a light nap.

He glanced at his watch: 2:20 in the afternoon.

He opened the door and Valenti was there, standing with his hands in his back pockets and his head jutting forward, gnashing a piece of gum.

"We got a big problem," he said.

***

Bruder stood on the dock and looked down at Turley in the captain's chair.

"Well?"

"Not here. Hop on."

Bruder checked each man for any sign of hostility.

They were vigilant, on alert, but not because of him.

He stepped onto the boat and sat in the same swivel chair as before.

He considered it his seat until the job was done.

Valenti was in front of him again, and Domm was in the other swivel, so everyone had settled on their spots.

If there was a hierarchy involved, Bruder didn't know or care about it.

Turley took the boat back out into the cove and dropped anchor before they got into the bay, in a protected nook near an island of mangrove trees about the size of a McDonald's.

Bruder asked the whole boat, "What's the problem?"

Turley made a show of looking around at the empty water nearby.

Five hundred yards to the south other boats cruised toward or away from Tampa Bay, nobody paying them any attention.

"First, we watched the yacht and you were right. They did a shift change at nine. Some dude in khaki shorts and a black golf shirt came out of the offices and met another dude, dressed the same, on the dock next to the yacht. They both had black ball caps with some kind of logo on the front. The one on the yacht had that M4 you spotted."

Bruder lifted a hand to stop them.

"How close did you guys get?"

Valenti picked up on the tone.

"We weren't close. Turley glassed them from below, through the porthole."

Bruder nodded and let the hand drop.

Turley said, "They chatted for a minute, then the new guy took the rifle and boarded the yacht. The other dude went into the office and went home, we assume."

"Shift change at nine a.m.," Bruder said.

"Maybe another later in the afternoon," Valenti said, "but I doubt it. Two guys, twelve hour shifts, and the working shift is sitting on a multi-million-dollar yacht. Not a lot of stress to unwind from, you know?"

Turley said, "Bottom line, nobody is coming and going at two in the morning. You saw that when you scouted it the first time, and if they're switching at nine, the night shift is straight through. Has to be."

"And you got a better look at the boat," Bruder said, "and what it can do."

Turley nodded.

"Yacht. And yeah, it's a Maiora 27. It should have a couple engines in there, maybe Caterpillars or MTUs, with a fuel tank that can take about three thousand gallons."

"What's all that mean?" Bruder said.

Turley pulled out a warped spiral-bound pad he kept in a cockpit cubby and consulted his notes, scrawled diagonally across the page even though the paper had horizontal lines.

"At cruising speed, about twenty-two knots, she can go around three hundred and eighty nautical miles."

He looked up from the paper.

"We figure it's gonna be two hundred and ninety, maybe three hundred to get from the impound to the Dry Tortugas."

"That's with no wind working against us," Valenti added.

Bruder said, "So if the tank is full, we won't need any more."

"The tank won't be full," Domm said.

"Why not?"

"Because why would they fill it up? So some assholes can come take it up the coast to Jersey? Nah. Nobody at the lot will pay for a drop of fuel. Let the transfer crew deal with it."

It made sense to Bruder, especially after what Julie had told him about departmental turf wars and budgets.

He said, "So we need to bring enough fuel to at least get it started and out into open water. Just in case."

Turley squinted at his notebook again.

"The way we figure it we're looking at fifteen gallons per hour, per engine. So at minimum, we'll need thirty gallons to keep us going for an hour, which ought to get us clear of the bay."

Valenti said, "But the tanks won't be dry. Domm's right, they won't be full, but they'll have something in them. We just won't know until we're on board."

"Thirty gallons," Bruder said. "You see anything bad about that?"

Turley shook his head and tossed the notebook into the cubby.

"Only that it's all gonna be heavy as hell. Those fuel bladders each weigh about fifteen hundred pounds when they're full."

"Is that the big problem Valenti woke me up about?"

"No," Turley said.

Bruder looked around the boat.

"So why the hell are we talking about it?"

"Because if the fuel details make you want to cancel the job, the problem doesn't exist anymore."

"The job isn't canceled."

"Yeah," Turley said, glancing at Valenti and Domm.

Bruder worked to stay patient.

Turley said, "So, the big problem is, another crew is scouting the yacht."

***

Turley said, "It's a guy named Dunbar."

"And you saw him," Bruder said.

Valenti nodded.

"Him and his crew—two other guys—and some chicks. We think the girls are just camouflage. They were fishing in the impound cove, just like us. Or like we were pretending to do."

"Maybe they were actually fishing."

"Not a chance," Turley said. "They were scouting. They might have been there yesterday and I missed them, too busy looking at the yacht."

"How do you know they're scouting the same thing?"

"What else is there?"

"The fabricator," Bruder said. "All the boats docked there."

Turley waved that away.

"Not much there worth the time and trouble. And people

are staying aboard some of those boats, which is another hassle for us."

Bruder knew it—the fabricator played a part in his Plan A for stealing the yacht.

"But here's the thing," Turley said. "Dunbar and his guys are a straight-up rip crew. No savvy or elegance, like us."

Bruder stayed quiet.

Domm added, "They're like pirates. Fucking hijackers."

"So what are they going to do?" Bruder said. "Wait until the boat is on its way to Jersey and take it down? Or will they move faster?"

"These guys," Valenti said, "they might ram the gate with a tugboat and try to make a getaway on the yacht. Just on the chance they pull it off."

Turley nodded.

"Exactly. No savvy."

Then, alarmed, he turned to Bruder.

"Wait, that isn't our plan, is it?"

"No," Bruder said. "So they're just watching. Maybe planning."

Valenti said, "Dunbar ain't much of a planner. He's a cruiser, a shark, moving around and looking for targets of opportunity. He's got no impulse control. He sees something he thinks is worth taking, he goes for it."

Bruder said, "How do you know this much about him?"

Valenti and Turley shared a look, then Turley said, "We've worked together before."

Water slapped against the side of the boat and an airplane buzzed overhead.

Some kind of bird complained about something from the mangrove trees.

Bruder said, "So he knows just as much about you. Including your faces. What about this boat?"

"He hasn't seen us with this one," Turley said.

"Did he spot you in the cove?"

"Nah," Domm said but nobody considered it a fact.

Bruder looked at Turley, waiting.

"I don't think so," he said. "They were pretty focused on the yacht."

"You had to cruise past them to get back here."

"Uh-uh. They left before we did, by thirty minutes or so. They were long gone when we moved out."

Bruder thought about it.

"If they break the boat out, what happens then? Where does he take it?"

Valenti shrugged.

"Probably south, Cuba. Or over to Mexico. Or farther. Looking for a buyer if he doesn't already have one lined up. We watched him do that once, remember the bar?"

Turley grinned, then caught himself.

"Yeah, some guy pulled up in a forty foot Sea Ray at this dockside bar, tied off and ran into the bathroom. Dunbar watched him, pulled out his phone and called somebody and goes, 'Hey, can you do anything with a forty foot Sea Ray? Okay, see ya.' Hangs up and tells us 'Later,' then jumps on the boat and takes off."

Bruder looked out at the water and chewed the inside of his cheek.

"So he could make his move any time. Assuming he'll make it at all."

Turley nodded.

"Yeah. Probably at night, though. He's not a complete idiot."

Bruder said, "What kind of weapons do you have?"

The question caught them off-guard.

"Uh," Turley said.

He lifted his shirt and showed the butt of a pistol stuck in his shorts.

Valenti patted his right side near the belt line, not wanting to lift his shirt.

Domm pulled out a Glock 17 and waggled it at the deck.
"We also got a harpoon gun in with the snorkeling shit."

Bruder nodded.

"Can you find Dunbar's boat?"

"What for?" Turley said, suddenly wary.

"To see if we can remove him as a concern."

"Hold up," Valenti said. "You want to kill him?"

"No. But if we sink his boat, he'll have other things to
worry about besides the yacht."

The crew took this in, stunned by the rapid turn.

Turley said, "It's pretty hard to sink a boat, man."

Bruder shrugged.

"Then we sink his engine. Or break it. Whatever you do
to a boat to make it not work anymore."

"No, no," Turley said. "Even if we could find him and
his boat, it's way too risky. If we get close enough to do
anything like that, we may as well kill him, because he'll
sure as shit kill us."

Bruder thought about that, then checked his watch.

"Okay. Get me back to the dock. I need to find a hardware
store."

Valenti said, "Hardware? For what?"

"Everything. We're stealing the yacht tonight."

PART TWO

PART TWO

CHAPTER EIGHT

Bruder took the rental car to Bradenton and found a big box home improvement store.

He checked the grill section first and found a short propane tank hose with a built-in regulator but had no luck with the kind of igniter he needed.

He moved through the rest of the store and grabbed a hundred-foot gray garden hose and a ten-foot black soaker hose, a roll of black duct tape, heavy-duty black zip ties, and a handful of PVC connection adaptors.

The adaptors were in an aisle-long rack of bins and boxes with everything looking more or less the same, and he went through some trial and error with the propane and garden hose before he found what he needed.

The store had a locker of propane tanks outside the exit, and at the checkout he told the man in the apron to add one to the bill.

Then he found a marine supply store and grabbed four inflatable fenders made of black marine-grade vinyl, each one about six inches across and two feet long.

The supply store shared a parking lot with a gas station

the size of a small airport, and Bruder went inside and bought gas for the car and some lunch and water and a handful of pre-paid phones with browser capabilities.

He used one of the phones to look up grill supply stores and found several, most of them looking like they focused on outdoor kitchens and high-end installations.

He called around until one of them, down in Sarasota, had what he needed.

It took forty minutes to get there and he bought a remote grill ignition kit and batteries; the kit had batteries in the packaging but he didn't trust them.

He used McIntyre's cash to pay for everything.

***

Bruder parked at the motel in Sun City and lugged the propane tank and hoses and bags across the road to the marina, where Turley and the others were getting the boat and their gear ready.

Domm had a black wet suit spread out on the dock and was blowing air through a snorkel.

Bruder stepped onto the boat and went to his swivel chair.

He pulled the soaker hose out and started working on it with the black bumpers and zip ties and duct tape.

Turley came up from the cabin and stopped halfway out of the hatch to eyeball the propane tank and hoses.

"I got food and water for a couple days down here, a week if we need to make it last."

"Good."

"We should grab dinner off the boat tonight. I don't want to tap any of this stuff before we get started, and it'll give the guys a chance to relax a bit. We'll fill the first bladder then."

"Fine," Bruder said, pulling and tearing the tape.

Turley kept looking at the propane tank.

"Man. This makes me real nervous."

"That's the point," Bruder said.

***

When Bruder finished putting everything together the hundred-foot garden hose was attached to the propane tank via the adaptors, with the black soaker hose at the other end.

The black bumpers were taped to the soaker hose, and the grill ignitor was affixed to one of the bumpers.

He told Turley, "Let's take a short trip."

They motored across the cove into the late afternoon sun and Turley found a spot along the western shore, close to where they'd discussed Dunbar's crew, and dropped anchor.

Bruder eased the soaker hose over the port side, which faced nothing but thick vegetation and some birds. The bumpers kept the hose afloat, looking like some kind of bulbous water serpent.

He reached for the propane tank.

"Easy," Valenti said. "Easy."

He had a fire extinguisher clamped between his feet.

Domm sat in his swivel chair with a beer, watching the show.

Turley was still in the pilothouse. He looked ready to pull the boat away should Bruder's handiwork go sideways.

Bruder opened the propane valve a half turn, then more, until he heard the gas moving.

A moment later he caught a whiff coming up from the soaker hose.

He pushed more of the garden hose into the water, sending the soaker and bumpers about ten feet away from Turley's boat, and pressed the button on the grill igniter's remote.

Staccato clicking carried to them from the floating hose, then the gas caught with a heavy *whump* that sent a wave of hot air into Bruder's face.

"Oh hell," Valenti said. "Oh damn."

He took a step toward Bruder with the fire extinguisher.

The flames from the soaker hose rippled and fluttered anywhere from a few inches to nearly two feet above the water.

Bruder pushed and tugged the garden hose around to see if the fire would go out.

It did not.

It moved and huffed and hissed, a ten-foot snake of flames angered by the disturbance.

Turley was next to Bruder now, watching the flames dance.

"Huh. Well, if I didn't know what it was, I'd be shitting my pants right about now."

Valenti said, "I'm shitting my pants and I *do* know what it is. Can you shut it off?"

Bruder studied the flames for a few more seconds before closing the tank's valve.

The flames rippled and huffed and died.

It didn't look perfect, but in the dark, with everything else going on...it would work.

***

As the sun started to dip into Tampa Bay they took the boat up the coast to a filling station in an Apollo Beach marina.

Turley topped off the boat's fuel while Domm and Valenti spread one of the bladders out on the stern deck. It was about six feet by five and a half and took up almost all of the deck, and when it was full it looked like a waterbed mattress.

Turley paid with cash from Bruder's reserve and idled through the marina until he found an open slip.

He used more of the cash to pay the dock fee and gave the attendant a healthy tip, then the four of them walked inland past condos and modest homes in pastel stucco and boat storage yards—Bruder had never seen so many damn boats in his life—until they got to a restaurant with water frontage on another part of the marina.

They got a table on the deck, overlooking more boats.

The hostess asked what they'd like to drink and Turley told her, "A bucket of Coronas, sweetie."

When she left Turley caught the vibe from Bruder.

"What?"

"Nobody gets drunk."

"It's Corona," Domm said.

Bruder told them, "One each. Then switch to something that will keep you awake and alert."

Domm lifted his menu and squinted at it.

"They got cocaine here?"

Turley and Valenti laughed.

They got the beers and ordered food.

The boat crew told stories to make each other laugh more and Bruder ate and half-listened.

His mind was on the job.

He'd had an idea of the plan for a few days, then dialed it in once he got a better look at the impound marina.

Turley and his guys didn't have to do too much, but what they did need to do was critical.

They claimed to have it under control, no sweat, no worries.

Bruder wasn't worried but he was preoccupied.

Normally, this close to the job, he'd be relaxed and ready, everything rehearsed and locked down.

But this was too spontaneous for his taste.

Every angle of the job was getting pushed by an outside force—McIntyre's looming threats, the arrival of Dunbar and his rip crew, moving the yacht to New Jersey.

It was rushed.

And whenever a job was rushed, it went bad.

Bruder was close to leaving the table to use the bathroom and never coming back.

Just keep walking until he found a ride and a phone so he could call Lola and Kershaw and Gator—the three surviving people who had anything to do with the New York job—and give them the news: The Lab was coming for them.

Then he'd find a place to lay low and decide if he was going to keep running or go hunting.

But even though he was on the brink of walking away, he knew he was also on the edge of getting clear of it all.

Assuming McIntyre kept his word.

All he had to do was pull off the job.

Lola would call it infuriating stubbornness.

Kershaw had labeled it as Bruder's custom blend of arrogance and ignorance.

Gator...he'd probably just lock and load and ask where to point the barrel.

In the end, he stayed at the table.

***

It was dark when Turley took the boat out of the marina.

The ride seemed more sluggish with the weight of the fuel bladder, but when Bruder asked about it Turley told him not to worry.

Bruder wasn't worried but he enjoyed being told not to worry about as much as he liked being told to relax, so he chewed his cheek and watched the water to keep from glaring at Turley.

They followed the coastline north before cutting across the shipping lane and wrapping up into Old Tampa Bay.

The air was cool and Valenti handed out dark hooded sweatshirts and black neck gaiters that smelled new, then doled out the radios.

Bruder first pulled a pair of loose quick-dry pants on over his shorts, then stuck the radio on his belt and snaked the earpiece under his shirt to his left ear.

When he was satisfied he zipped the sweatshirt up and slid the gaiter over his head, easing it around the earpiece so it wouldn't snag.

He left the gaiter bunched around his neck, below his chin and ready to be pulled up.

Turley and Valenti did the same.

Domm didn't bother with his yet.

Bruder swapped his sandals for socks and boots with non-slip soles. He stuffed the sandals into a trash bag he'd taken from the motel room, which also held the burner phones, still in their plastic shells, and other things he might need.

It was the first time he'd been on the bay this late and he saw other boats moving around and bobbing at anchor near the shore, but nothing the size of the sheikh's yacht.

He got up from his chair and stood behind Turley's left shoulder.

"Are we going to draw too much attention on the way out?"

"From these people? Nah. I mean, that beast will turn heads wherever it goes but it won't be anything worth calling the news. I'm gonna keep to the middle as much as possible though, stay away from eyeballs."

"You think Dunbar is out here?"

Turley shrugged.

"I'm looking for him, and I'd recognize the shape of the boat he was on by the running lights, but you can mess with that. Cover some of the lights, add more here and there, and it changes the profile. You know, hiding in plain sight."

"So we won't know until he makes himself seen."

"Bingo, amigo."

There wasn't anything to do about it, so Bruder sat back down and waited.

Turley guided the boat across Old Tampa Bay and killed the throttle when they got close to a tangle of small mangrove islands just south of the entrance to the impound's cove.

He let the boat drift until he was happy, then dropped the anchor.

The mangrove trees were pitch black with a halo of lights above from the city further inland.

Bruder checked his watch: 12:47.

He told the boat, "One hour."

***

When they idled into the cove just before two in the morning, Bruder first checked to make sure the sheikh's yacht was still there.

It was.

The stadium lights at the outside corners of the impound lot were on their minimal security setting, the single bulbs blazing down on the star of the show.

Nothing inside the fence was moving.

Bruder scanned the boats at the fabricator's docks.

The slips there were about half full and he saw some cabin lights on but no one walking around.

This was all fine.

Turley took the boat in a wide loop to the left so he could come straight into the fabricator's dock closest to the impound lot's concrete barrier.

There were two open slips there, closest to the sea wall.

This was good.

The plan would still work without the slips there but the closer they could get to the impound lot, the better.

The barrier and fence started on their port side long before they got to the docks on their starboard, and Bruder sat and watched the yacht for movement.

Nothing.

Not even a plume of cigar smoke.

This was not fine or good, but he'd give it a while.

Bruder clenched his jaw when they idled past the four boats tied up along their starboard side.

None of these had cabin lights on.

Maybe they were empty or asleep.

Turley guided the boat toward the sea wall and spent what felt like an hour turning around, slowly spinning in place like a second hand, then reversing until he settled near the dock.

Valenti and Domm made the long step from the boat and tied them off, then came aboard again.

The light bleeding over from the impound lot and coming from the back of the fabricator's building was just below the threshold that would make Bruder feel exposed.

The upside: they wouldn't need flashlights.

They all sat and listened and watched, waiting for someone to shout a greeting or offer a beer or ask what the hell they were doing.

None of that happened.

After five minutes Bruder stood up and got to work.

CHAPTER NINE

Bruder pulled the propane tank and hoses out of one of the storage bins.

Domm started tugging his wetsuit on, breathing quiet curses when he struggled to wrap the neoprene over his upper arms and shoulders.

Turley stepped over to help him.

Domm had wanted to put it on earlier, outside the cove, but Bruder had told him to wait. If somebody blasted a flashlight into the boat, they might want to know why one guy was ready to go diving while the others were bundled up.

Valenti connected a long hose to the fuel bladder but left it coiled and shut.

When Domm was ready he eased over the starboard side and into the water between the boat and the concrete barrier.

The black wetsuit hood did a decent job of blending his shaved head with the dark water.

Bruder handed the soaker hose and bumpers down to Domm, then provided slack in the garden hose while Domm drifted toward the concrete barrier.

Bruder glanced over his shoulder and saw Valenti watching the sheikh's yacht.

Turley had an eye on the other boats docked at the fabricator's.

So far, everything was as they'd discussed.

Bruder pushed more hose over the side while Domm threaded the soaker hose and bumpers into one of the holes in the barrier.

The hole was in the same bay as the yacht, twenty feet or so off the wide stern.

Domm had to work with the gentle rise and fall of the water to feed the hose through and Bruder watched the water on the far side of the barrier.

At first there was nothing.

Then for too long there was nothing.

Then, through the fence, he saw a ripple of water spread away from the barrier.

He stood on the swivel chair to get a better look and spotted the end of the soaker hose snaking into the impound lot.

It looked like a wet log or a piece of floating trash.

Possibly a skinny alligator but he'd never seen one in person.

When it was in the right spot he snapped his fingers once and Domm drifted back to the boat.

He used a ladder and step built into the stern next to the engines to climb aboard, where Valenti helped him get out of the black wetsuit.

Domm toweled off and got dressed, including his radio and earpiece. He sighed from the warmth of the hoodie.

Bruder kept his eyes on the yacht while he stepped over to Turley.

"Anything?"

"Nothing moving. I've been looking for Dunbar's boat too, in case he docked here to keep an eye on the yacht. I don't think he did."

"Good."

"The hose is ready?"

"Almost."

Bruder picked up the propane tank and set it on the dock, then looped the remaining garden hose around the nearest wooden piling. He made sure none of it would catch on the Whaler when they took off.

He stayed on the dock with his hand on the tank's valve and nodded to Turley in the dim light.

Then he watched the yacht for any sign of cigar smoke.

***

When the first plume rose above the flybridge Bruder checked his watch: 2:17 in the morning.

He rubbed his rough thumb and forefinger together to let the others know it was time.

Turley unfolded himself from the captain's chair and peered up at the cloud of bluish smoke drifting inland, then pulled a flat black pistol out of one of the console storage bins, press-checked to make sure it was loaded, and stuffed it into the large right pocket of his sweatshirt.

Valenti and Domm did the same, the small sound of oiled mechanisms quiet enough to remain in the boat.

Bruder stayed with the propane tank and watched the smoke.

He normally had little patience for people who lingered too long over something they found pleasurable, like a sip of whiskey held while the eyes rolled back, the lips pursed, the head swayed...

Now, he had zero patience.

He willed the man up there to smoke the damn cigar and get it over with.

A dozen plumes and fifteen minutes later Bruder saw the stub arc out of the flybridge and drop into the water, trailing a faint ribbon of smoke.

He opened the propane valve a quarter-turn.

Fifteen seconds later he hit the remote igniter and all hell broke loose.

***

The propane caught with the same *whump*, sending a flash of orange light across the stern of the yacht.

It apparently wasn't enough to catch the attention of the man on the flybridge, so Bruder nodded at Turley who cupped his hands around his mouth and yelled, "Fire! Fire!"

A face popped up over the flybridge wall and looked down at them.

It was the same man they'd seen before, during the shift change, the same one Bruder saw the first time he'd scouted the yacht.

He wasn't wearing his black hat this time and had close-cropped hair and a lean face.

He turned from them to look down at the flames dancing on top of the water and Bruder saw his mouth drop open.

Turley yelled, "You got a fuel leak, man! You gotta shut off the fuel line!"

At the same time, Valenti yelled, "What did you do? Did you throw something in the water?"

Domm flailed his arms around.

"You gotta get out of there! Get out!"

It was all planned and had the effect they wanted—the man froze, looking from them to the fire and back, stuck in a loop.

He yelled down, "What? How? Where's the shutoff? What?"

After a few seconds of chaos Bruder cupped his hands and called out in a voice that cut through the racket, "You need to move that boat! Open the gate and we'll help you!"

"Shit!"

The man disappeared.

Turley started the boat while he and his crew kept hollering.

"Hurry up man! You gotta shut it off!"

"Move, move, move!"

"What did you *do*? What did you *do*?"

The man erupted from the rear of the salon with a fire extinguisher and rattled down a short set of stairs to the swimming platform, then jumped off the port side of the yacht onto the concrete barrier.

This, Bruder knew, was the tipping point.

The man had his back to them now and they kept yelling at him, questioning and ordering and accusing, and when he got even with the flames he stretched out over the water and blasted the extinguisher toward it.

Bruder opened the propane valve all the way.

The flames doubled, snapping back at the extinguisher foam, which wasn't going to do much from that distance anyway.

"Shit!" the man said again. "No! No!"

"That won't work, it's diesel!" Turley yelled, adding to the confusion.

Valenti said, "Everybody get back! Get down!"

"Open the fucking gate, asshole!" Domm yelled.

A woman screamed and Bruder looked back at the fabricator's docks and saw people standing on boat decks and heads poking out of hatches.

So far everyone was just watching, but sooner or later some hero was going to step up.

They needed to be moving before then.

He yelled, "The gate! The controls!"

The man glanced through the fence at them, pure panic stretching his face, then he dropped the fire extinguisher and took two steps toward the sea wall.

Then he took one step back, like he forgot the extinguisher and remembered he needed it.

"Leave it!" Valenti called. "Go go go!"

Domm yelled, "What the hell did you do? Were you smoking a *cigar*?"

They were doing a good job.

Bruder wanted the man in a spiral, terrified by the flames and the thought of the yacht burning or blowing up, yet distracted by the assumption he had started the fire with his cigar.

Right now, Bruder thought, the man's mind was already projecting into depositions and interrogations and charges being filed.

Humiliation and unemployment, maybe even jail time.

He got to the corner and sprinted toward the control box mounted on the railing.

Bruder told Turley, "Go."

As the Whaler pulled away from the dock Bruder dropped the propane tank into the water, along with the diving weights zip-tied to its handles.

The gas kept coursing through the hose and the flames didn't falter a bit, and putting the tank at the bottom of the cove would add one more hassle for whoever came along to figure out what the hell had happened here.

Turley idled to the corner of the impound barrier and cut to starboard.

By the time they got to the gate, the doors were almost fully retracted.

Turley goosed the engines and aimed to come along the starboard side of the sheikh's yacht.

The man was running back toward the ship, pointing at the flames.

"Can you put it out? Put it out!"

Domm yelled back, "Find the shutoff valve! The fuel's gonna blow!"

Valenti gave directions: "It's in the engine room!"

The directions were accurate but it didn't matter.

The man froze again on the concrete barrier, trying to

decide if he should stay there or get back on a boat that, as far as he knew, might explode.

Turley cut the throttle and skimmed along next to the yacht, the hull like a ten-foot white wall coming up out of the water.

Porthole windows slipped past their faces.

Bruder couldn't see the man on the dock but they all kept hollering to keep the panic going.

When the Whaler neared the yacht's stern Turley came out of the pilothouse with a black waterproof bag slung over his shoulder.

Domm passed him and took the helm.

Turley and Valenti stood near the starboard rail, yelling and fussing, but really just waiting.

They probably could have made the jump up to the railing along the yacht's starboard side, but then they'd have to shimmy to the rear deck or keep climbing, so they waited until the smaller boat passed the stern and just stepped onto the yacht's extended swimming platform.

The security man was still on the concrete dock.

He had the fire extinguisher again but didn't seem to know what to do with it.

Turley moved right, toward the five stairs up into the yacht's salon.

"Where are the keys? We gotta move this thing, bubba!"

Valenti acted just as confused as the security man.

"Which way is the engine room? This way? Over there? Come on, show me!"

Bruder yelled from the Whaler, "Hurry up! Move it!"

The man started to talk, then glanced at the flames, then stepped on board and told Valenti, "I don't know, they didn't tell me! I don't need to know that sort of thing!"

"Those assholes!" Valenti said. "Come on, we'll find it!"

Domm kept Turley's boat close to the yacht and got one more dig in: "I smell cigar smoke! Who's smoking cigars with all this gas around?"

The man looked at him, his mouth open and helpless, then turned to follow Valenti up the stairs to the salon.

Bruder stepped onto the swimming platform and followed them.

He carried the trash bag from the motel room and had the Glock 19 in the cross-draw holster and three spare magazines in a holder further around on his left side.

A half-dozen pairs of the zip-ties were looped together and stored in a thigh pocket, ready for wrists and ankles.

The radio was clipped to the back of his belt.

He didn't carry anything else.

On the way up the stairs he pulled his hood up and covered his mouth and nose with the gaiter.

Behind him, Domm turned the Whaler away from the yacht and flames.

The salon was wide with plush tan couches along both walls and low tables of blonde teak with splashes of color from artwork and silk pillows.

Indirect lighting made the space feel larger and more luxurious.

Turley and Valenti were both there, still and calm now, looking at the security man.

They also had their hoods and masks up.

Bruder closed in behind and tossed the trash bag onto the starboard couch, then pulled the Glock.

"Hands out to your sides."

The man turned, frowning, even more baffled in this stillness than he'd been by the fire and chaos. Close up, he was tan and looked in his mid-thirties.

He said, "What?"

"What's your name?" Bruder said.

"Huh?"

"My friend is going to check you for weapons. Just hold still."

Valenti ran his hands over the security man and found a Leatherman tool, wallet, and phone in his pockets.

Bruder said, "Where's the rifle?"

The man blinked.

"What?"

Turley snorted.

Valenti checked the wallet.

"Says here his name is Theodore Bevins."

Bruder said, "You look more like a Ted. Is that right?"

Ted nodded.

"Okay Ted, do you know how to pilot this ship?"

He shook his head, tense, then after a moment his shoulders slumped as he finally grasped the situation.

"You guys are stealing the yacht?"

"That's right," Bruder said.

He took Ted's phone away from Valenti and threw it off the back of the boat, then told Turley and Valenti, "Get started."

There was a narrow, curved staircase just outside the salon on the starboard side and Turley ran up the steps to access the flybridge, where the cockpit was.

Valenti went forward, past a table with seating for six and a large flatscreen TV mounted on the wall.

Another narrow staircase tucked into the far corner led below, and he went that way with his pistol out to clear the lower cabins.

Bruder was alone with Ted now, the Glock pointed at the deck.

He pulled out two of the zip tie loops.

"Ted, I know we don't need to tie you up. But it's for your own good. If you're tied up the other guys don't need to worry about you."

Ted stared at the gun and the restraints.

"Worry about me doing what?"

"Something stupid. I know you won't do anything like that, but again, the other guys..."

Valenti emerged from below and told Bruder, "All clear."

He hurried past them, back down the steps to the swimming platform and lifted a fiberglass hatch set between the staircases and disappeared into the engine room.

Ted stared after him, then turned to Bruder and said, "Just let me off and you won't have to worry about me at all."

Bruder shook his head.

"Can't do that. You're fine. You're safe. Just do what I tell you and you'll stay that way."

This was Bruder's call.

He and Turley had gone around on it with Turley wanting to get any potential problems off the yacht right away.

Bruder understood and agreed to a certain extent—if they kept Ted and had the yacht for too long, it became a hostage situation, even if they weren't treating Ted like a hostage.

Hostages meant media coverage and people in tactical gear getting ramped up to storm the ship, once they found it, and they'd be looking hard, because of the hostage.

It would have been better to truss him up and leave him at the impound marina, but Bruder had expected other people from the fabricator's docks to stand around watching, and he'd been right.

It was hard to carry a bound man around and make it look like something else, and once Ted got loose he'd alert everyone and they would close off the Gulf.

So Ted would stay on the boat and they'd drop him at the Dry Tortugas, if they got close enough, or off Key West after the job was done.

Bruder didn't tell Ted any of this—he just looked at him, and after a moment Ted put his hands out in front of him.

Bruder shook his head again and Ted gritted his teeth and put his hands behind his back and turned around.

Bruder secured the zip ties and guided Ted to the portside couch, then used more ties to bind his ankles.

He felt a rumble in the deck and the water off the stern

began to move, pushing the floating fire away.

Valenti closed the hatch and touched his radio mic.

Bruder heard his voice in stereo: "Fuel is half full; we're good for now."

He jumped onto the concrete dock and started untying the yacht.

"I might get seasick," Ted said.

Bruder looked at him.

"Then why are you on a boat?"

"I'm not. I mean, I am, but it wasn't supposed to go anywhere. We're just supposed to keep it safe until the transfer team shows up."

"Well, change of plans," Bruder said and the yacht began to move.

***

The yacht followed Domm and the Whaler through the open gate and Bruder marked the time: 2:38 in the morning.

Six minutes from propane ignition to control of the yacht and getting it underway.

They'd gone by fast.

He went to the swimming platform and stuck his head around the port side to check the clearance. Turley had the yacht to the left of center but still a good ten feet away from the gate and barrier.

He looked back and saw a man in his underwear trying to spray the propane flames with a water hose from the fabricator's dock.

He might manage it but Bruder had doubts.

A few more people stood on the docks and watched the yacht cruising away and Bruder stepped back into the salon, out of sight.

If all they saw was the yacht getting clear of the flames, they wouldn't think to call anybody about it except the fire department.

The yacht curled left and motored toward the cove's exit into Old Tampa Bay, where Turley took them out to the proper depth and cut right, heading south.

They picked up speed and caught up to Domm, who put the Whaler off the yacht's starboard stern.

Bruder slid the Glock into its cross-draw holster and looked at Ted.

"You aren't going to do anything dumb, are you? Like jump overboard?"

Ted didn't say anything, which Bruder took as confirmation he would not drown himself.

Bruder went up the narrow stairway and emerged on the flybridge, which had an exposed sundeck to the aft with a round covered Jacuzzi on it.

Padded bench seats were on both sides of the tub and along the stern rail and Bruder saw where Ted had set up his cigar smoking station.

The M4 Carbine was leaning against one of the seats.

Bruder checked it.

It had a full thirty-round magazine, no round in the chamber, and a tactical flashlight mounted on the rail. The flashlight had a mouse tail pressure switch for the hand holding the rail. Bruder pointed the gun at the deck and tapped the switch.

The beam came on, a white blade that left a spot when he blinked.

The whole setup would come in handy if they had to scare somebody away or got in a very brief firefight. He'd ask Ted about extra magazines.

He kept the rifle and stepped toward the bow, where Turley sat in a cockpit that looked like the interior of a luxury spacecraft. He had his hood and mask down now that they were clear of the cove.

Bruder left his on and surveyed the screens and dials and knobs and levers and hoped Turley knew what they meant.

He did recognize the black waterproof bag sitting on a table next to the console. It was open and had the police scanner peeking out from inside.

Turley glanced back and grinned, then patted the arms of the leather captain's chair.

"I could get used to this. Nice gun."

"Anything on the scanner?"

He shook his head.

"Somebody called about the fire, but nothing about a stolen yacht."

Bruder checked his watch.

At best, the fire department and police would get there and put the fire out and see the soaker hose setup, then smell or suspect the propane gas, and get everyone the hell away from the impound lot.

Somewhere in there they would call a contact number for the lot and somebody—maybe Julie—would scramble out of bed and rush to the marina.

Or call someone else and tell them to do so.

There was a chance that person would ask about the sheikh's yacht and the fire department and police would say, "What yacht?"

Which would either increase the panic from the impound person or leave them wondering what the tax dollars around here were paying for if the emergency services didn't know a yacht when they saw one.

Either way, Julie, or whoever, would get to the impound marina and find the yacht and Ted gone.

With all the running around and gas scare and potential for bureaucracy, Bruder put it between thirty and forty-five minutes before somebody figured out the yacht was missing.

Then another ten or twenty while they got in a boat and looked outside the cove to see if Ted had relocated it.

By that point, Turley should have it almost past the chokepoint and into the Gulf.

Bruder looked through the windshield, raked back on an angle like they were on a runway, and saw MacDill off the port side, land and sporadic lights off the starboard, and water straight ahead. He glanced down at the console but didn't bother trying to figure out what it was telling him.

"How are we on time?"

"On track," Turley said. "Having the tanks half full is a big help. I'm not nervous about pushing above cruising speed."

Bruder nodded and headed for the stairs.

"Holler if anything changes."

"Aye aye, *captain*."

He leaned on that last word, putting something icy in the undercurrent.

Probably sarcasm from getting ordered around while he was in the actual captain's chair, but also, maybe…bitterness, or he knew something Bruder didn't, like he was in on a joke with a punchline Bruder wouldn't like.

Bruder looked at the back of his head for a moment but Turley kept his eyes front and worked the control panel.

Bruder went down the stairs to the salon, where Ted scowled at the rifle.

"Any spare mags on board?"

"No."

"Don't lie."

"I'm not. The gun is mostly for show, to keep morons away. We're not supposed to have to use it."

"That's dumb," Bruder said.

He looked for a place to put the rifle, somewhere easily accessible but not out in the open.

Turley seemed the type who would enjoy carrying it around, and all it took was one passing boater to spot it.

The salon had some storage but the drawers and cabinets all looked too small.

He stuck the rifle behind a rank of throw pillows on the plush couch along the starboard side, near his trash bag full

of stuff, then poked and slapped the pillows back into place
and stepped back.

"Just toss it overboard," Ted said, being sly.

Bruder ignored him.

The pillows were good enough.

***

While Ted gave him a sullen look from the couch, Bruder
listened to the sounds of the yacht and tried to pick up
anything extraneous to that, someone moving around or
working.

He wasn't used to boat sounds and didn't know where
Valenti was and wanted to see if he could locate him by ear,
like if they were in a building.

No luck.

He stepped toward the stern rail overlooking the swimming
platform, but his view below was blocked by a large white
fiberglass panel hinged at the top like a hatchback door.

He touched the microphone button built into the earpiece wire.

"Two, where are you?"

Valenti came back: "Right in front of you."

His voice didn't come through the radio.

Valenti stuck his head around the side of the raised hatch
and waved.

Bruder checked Ted again—no trouble there—and went
down the starboard steps to the swimming platform.

"Just checking some things," Valenti said, motioning into
the engine room.

Bruder peered, and immediately inside the hatch he saw
a miniature stacked washer and dryer and some chrome
valves, and a rack with scuba tanks strapped in vertically
behind a bin full of masks and flippers and snorkels.

A narrow open doorway next to the laundry unit led deeper into the ship toward the bow.

Engine heat and noises came through the opening.

Bruder said, "Any problems?"

"Nah. Well, other than fuel. As soon as we clear the Gulf, Domm should leapfrog ahead and start ferrying more out to us."

"How far can we get?"

Valenti turned his face to the port side, south, the direction they'd be pushing into.

"Hard to tell the wind until we get out there, but it'll be working against us in some way. So, less than halfway to the Dry Tortugas without a refuel."

Bruder said, "Any idea when we'll hit the meet?"

"Man, no idea. Not until we're out there and underway."

Bruder nodded.

Another reason to hate boats.

"I'm taking Ted below."

"Who?"

"Ted. The security guy."

"Ah, right."

"You care which cabin he's in?"

Valenti shook his head and ducked through the doorway toward the engines.

"Nope. Makes no difference to me."

Bruder went up the port-side steps.

Ted was still there, slumped on the couch.

"I'm going to release your feet," Bruder said. "Then you're going to walk forward and down the stairs into the first cabin you come to. Then I'm going to secure you in there for the rest of the trip."

Ted's eyes were large.

"Why?"

"So you won't be a witness to anything else. Innocent bystanders have great stories to tell. Witnesses get killed."

Ted stuck his feet out.

***

They went through the salon and past a compact galley
on the port side with stainless steel everything, then down
the stairs.

The narrow hallway had two open doors along the sides,
almost straight across from each other, and one closed door
at each end.

Bruder pointed at the open door on the port side.

"In there."

Ted went in.

The cabin had a queen bed lengthwise along the hull wall
with a curtained window above it and a door in the stern wall.

Bruder stuck his head through the door and found a
claustrophobic bathroom.

He closed it and looked around the rest of the cabin,
ignoring Ted's sullen glare.

"You don't have to tie me to anything," Ted said. "I'll
stay here."

Bruder glanced down at him, then kept searching for an
anchor point.

"At first, yeah. Then you might start thinking about what
you're going to say to the guys you work with, and your
bosses, when they ask why you didn't do anything to stop
us. You look in good shape—what do you do, triathlons?"

Ted frowned, like he wasn't sure about the direction of
the conversation, then said, "I used to. Now it's extreme
races. You know, obstacles, mud, electric shocks. That
sort of thing."

"So it's even worse than I thought," Bruder said. "If that's
what you do for fun, eventually some part of your brain is
going to make you get up and cause trouble. So I do have
to tie you up, to save us both the hassle. Lay down."

Ted tipped onto his right side and Bruder pulled his hands
to the corner of the bed, where a part of the frame was

accessible between the mattress and the wall.

He used more zip ties to connect the ones around Ted's wrists to the frame, then went along the edge of the bed, feeling under the mattress and along the frame.

Then he checked the nightstand drawer, which was out of Ted's reach but still close enough for mild concern.

Ted said, "What, you think I stashed something in here in case I got hijacked and tied up?"

"I would have," Bruder said and kept searching.

When he was satisfied he went to the opposite corner of the bed and found a section of frame he could connect to.

"Ankles."

Ted hesitated, then stretched his legs out.

Bruder secured his feet together and connected them to the frame, leaving Ted angled across the bed, unable to get leverage or torque on his bonds.

Bruder considered covering his eyes but he was turned away from the window and the curtain was thick, possibly even blackout material, so he skipped the blindfold.

"Stay still and stay quiet. Sleep if you can, it'll go by faster."

"Wonderful," Ted said.

Bruder paused in the doorway.

"If you want, I can club you with the pistol. Then you can tell everyone you got knocked out and don't remember anything."

"I'll keep that in mind."

Bruder closed the cabin door and went back up the stairs.

***

Bruder's watch said 2:50.

Twelve minutes gone out of the hour they needed to clear the bottleneck.

He sat in the salon, feeling the vessel move and looking at the touches of extravagance but not really seeing or appreciating them.

This, for him, was the hard part.

There was nothing he could do to make the boat go faster and it didn't make sense for him to monitor the scanner— Turley knew the nautical lingo and locations and would know if people were moving into their path or wake.

Valenti had the mechanical and fuel stuff handled, at least for the moment.

So Bruder sat in the salon and looked around.

It was a nice boat from what he could tell, but unless it held some kind of sentimental value, he wasn't sure why the sheikh wanted it back so badly.

For someone with that kind of wealth, a yacht was like a car.

Maybe even a bike.

One is lost, just get another.

It could be a middle finger to the US government, taking back what they took from him, which made sense Bruder, though something like this was too flashy for him.

Cash, yes.

Freedom, sure.

But a yacht—you'd have to sail it around, showing off this thing the authorities tried to take away.

Asking for more trouble.

Maybe the sheikh was that kind of guy.

But Bruder kept thinking it was about more than the boat.

Now he paid attention to what he was looking at, scanning the teak woodwork and polished trim and plush couches, wondering if there was something he wasn't seeing.

A hidden compartment, maybe a hidden room.

He had no sense of space on the boat, so it was impossible for him to tell if a wall was closer than it should be or a room was too small.

How thick was the hull?

He had no idea and frowned in disgust at his ignorance.

There was no way he'd bring it up to Turley and the others. If they got it in their heads, they'd tear the place apart.

Bruder didn't care about the damage, but if they were busy looking for hidden loot instead of getting the boat to the Dry Tortugas, something would go wrong.

He got up and walked around the salon, lifting couch cushions and looking under the table and six chairs, then stuck his head in the compact galley and looked inside the stainless-steel cabinets and fixtures.

Nothing out of the ordinary.

One of the cabinets had an unopened box of crackers and Bruder ate some while he worked.

Forward of the galley was a small space fitted out like an office.

He looked in the cabinets and drawers and found office things, and none of the storage spaces had any hidden compartments.

He went back down the stairs and stood in the narrow hallway, looking left and right.

He went right, toward the bow, thinking that's where the master suite would be.

The forward cabin was filled with a wide, low bed and had shelves and storage along both sides.

Bruder tilted the mattress against a wall and found a short platform underneath instead of a standard frame.

He tapped it and heard hollow sounds but there were no hidden access points or locked panels.

He put the mattress back and ran his hands along the shelves and inside the storage drawers and cabinets.

The headboard above the bed was gray silk, upholstered to have an intricate pattern like a sunburst.

He poked at it until he was satisfied it wasn't hiding anything, then went back to the hallway and into the cabin opposite Ted's.

This one had two single beds attached to each wall with

a narrow lane between, leading into another tiny bathroom.

He checked under the mattresses and opened everything that had a door and turned in a circle in the bathroom, pulling and poking, frustrated by the knowledge he could be standing right next to what he was looking for, if it even existed.

As he searched, his mind wandered to what might be in a hidden stash on a sheikh's yacht.

Loose diamonds would be best. They took up less space, which could mean more of them, and would be easy to transport.

Cash or gold would be next.

Family jewels, not terrible, but the hassle of finding a buyer wasn't worth it.

Art?

He didn't even want to think about it.

At the bottom of the list, and what Bruder suspected was most likely, considering the sheikh and what he'd been up to: Documentation or proof of someone doing something they shouldn't have done.

Evidence to be used for blackmail or extortion, and would only be useful to Bruder if he needed to start another fire.

Unless it had something to do with McIntyre…

But Bruder didn't run in those circles.

Holding that sort of evidence only worked if people knew you had it, and that put a target on your back.

So he kept looking, in case the stash existed, and in case it happened to be something of value to him.

***

Bruder stood in the hallway again and, after a brief internal debate, opened the door to Ted's room and slapped the light on, startling the man tied to the bed.

He didn't say anything and ducked into the bathroom, found nothing, then went through the room again quickly while Ted blinked and frowned.

He shoved his hand under the mattress and slid it across the platform, paying closer attention this time.

He wasn't feeling for something as overt as a gun or knife or sliver of glass that could be used to slash and stab.

He was feeling for a seam, a countersunk screw.

A hinge would be like rolling over a speed bump.

He felt nothing but smooth wood under the mattress.

Ted continued to frown while Bruder went through the entire room again, then killed the light and closed the door without saying anything.

He went aft and opened the door into the last room, which turned out to be the actual master suite.

Bruder closed the door behind him.

A king-sized bed took up the middle of the cabin and he heaved the mattress up, then let it fall when he saw the same kind of platform beneath, offering no hatches or panels.

He smoothed the blankets to remove any sign of his actions and opened a door to the right of the headboard, discovering a tight closet.

He rapped a knuckle on the walls and didn't hear anything odd but had to shake his head—what was a closet wall in a yacht supposed to sound like?

He walked around the bed through an opening on the left side of the headboard into a compact bathroom with a glassed-in shower stall.

The medicine cabinet was empty and didn't budge when he tried to wiggle it.

The back panel was solid.

He stepped back into the cabin and looked around, his eyes landing on the headboard.

This one was also gray silk, but instead of a sunburst it was upholstered into squares.

He knelt on the smoothed bed and thumped each square, each one about three feet on a side, getting sounds of solid wall in return until a panel above the right side of the bed gave an interesting sound.

It was still solid, but…different.

He wedged his fingers in the seam and ran them around until he found the catch and released it.

The upholstered panel swung open on a silent piano hinge.

Behind it was a steel door, a little less than three feet square, flush to the wall.

It had a keyhole on the left side of the door but wasn't a true safe with a dial or keypad or other mechanism—which was good, since Bruder leaned on specialists whenever a job included something that complex and it couldn't be bashed or blown open for some reason.

He studied the steel door.

It made sense to keep the lock simple.

The sheikh must have figured no one would stay in this cabin except him, and if he had the only key, whatever was behind the locked door was secure.

It wouldn't have crossed his mind that a man like Bruder would have any time alone with it.

He checked his watch: 3:05.

They'd been moving for just under thirty minutes.

And since Bruder didn't know exactly how much time alone he had with the locked door, he got to work.

***

He tried his knife first, in case the door had any play and he could slide the blade through the locking mechanism.

He stuck the tip of the four-inch blade into the seam and pried, just a bit, but the door didn't budge.

If he kept going the only thing he'd get was a broken knife, so he put it away.

He closed the panel, then the door to the cabin, and went up the stairs to the salon and into the small space set up like an office.

The drawers had pens and sticky notes and rubber

stamps with ink pads and a pair of scissors.

He put the scissors in his pocket and, after some more rooting around in the drawers, found a box of paperclips.

He selected four based on their size and stuck them in the same pocket and closed the drawer, then turned and saw Valenti coming up from the swimming platform at the aft end of the salon.

Beyond him, off the starboard stern and across a few hundred yards of water, yellow light made a glowing dome above tall buildings.

That would be St. Petersburg, Bruder figured, already behind them.

He said, "We're ahead of schedule."

"Truth," Valenti said. "We're making good time."

"Nothing on the scanner?"

"Not that I know of. I've been leaning over the side of the yacht."

"Why?"

Valenti blinked and held up a roll of black electrical tape.

"The HIN. I used a couple strips of tape to change some of the letters and numbers. It won't hold up to anything more than a glance but I figured we'd take it."

"That's good," Bruder said. "How did the engine room look?"

"They've taken good care of her. The maintenance log seems tight, no red flags from what I saw. If we have to go full-steam ahead, I don't think anything'll blow."

He looked Bruder up and down, then added, "What are you doing?"

"Killing time and making sure Ted doesn't cause any trouble."

"Who?"

"The security guy."

"Shit, I already forgot. He seemed pretty shook up, I doubt he'll try anything."

Bruder was moving past him, toward the stairs to the flybridge.

"I'll make sure he agrees."

He went up the curving steps and found Turley singing to himself with a foot up on the console.

Bruder nodded at the scanner.

"What's the latest?"

"Still nada about us, bubba. I'm starting to think we just might make it."

He grinned at Bruder, gleeful in his mischief, then looked over at Valenti coming up the stairs.

"Hey, come try this captain's chair! It's amazing."

The two of them started fawning over the seat and controls.

"I'll check on Ted," Bruder said.

Nobody acknowledged him, so he went below and got back to work on the lock.

***

Bruder closed and locked the door to the master cabin.

He opened the silk panel and peered at the lock again, then straightened one of the paperclips into a tension wrench and used the scissors to bend and shape another clip into a lock rake.

He slid the tension wrench into the bottom of the keyhole and eased the rake in above it, then applied gentle pressure on the wrench while he manipulated the rake.

When the lock turned he checked his watch again: 3:25.

It had taken less than two minutes to get the lock open— about twice the time he would have needed if he'd had his tools and didn't stop a few times to listen for movement in the hall.

They'd been underway for almost fifty minutes now and the yacht had to be close to passing the choke points.

When that happened, he'd be able to relax a little.

He pulled the clips out and dropped them into his pocket

and opened the door.

Then he smiled, a thin line that spread and kept growing until his earpiece clicked and Domm's voice said, "We got a boat following us."

***

Bruder closed the steel door but left it unlocked and swung the silk panel back into place and left the master cabin.

He went up the stairs and kept going to the rear of the salon and looked out at the water.

The lights of St. Petersburg were still visible along the coast and he tried to use them as a backdrop to search the dark waters beyond the yacht's wake, but he didn't see anything.

He went up the stairs to the flybridge and tried again but still saw nothing.

Turley called from the captain's chair, "You spot him?"

"No."

Bruder felt the man move in next to him, then Turley pointed off toward the distant shoreline.

"There. No lights, so he's just a darker spot against the water."

"He?" Bruder said.

"Dunbar."

Bruder stared at the spot while Turley went back to the controls.

He gave up after a few more seconds of seeing nothing but water and shore and night sky and went to the helm, where Turley pointed at one of the screens on the console.

"That's him, right there."

Bruder looked at what he assumed was a radar screen, with them at the center.

A dark, oblong shape was at their four o'clock, just within the edge of the screen.

"How do you know it's Dunbar?"

"Who else would it be?"

"Cops."

Turley shook his head.

"Still nothing on the scanner about us. I think Dunbar and his crew were either tied up at the fabricator's in the cove, or anchored close enough to see the yacht leave."

"What are they going to do about it?"

"Well, that's the big question, isn't it? My guess, they'll trail along until they see a good opportunity to board us."

"They have to know we're armed."

"So are they. And you can bet your ass they have more than dinky handguns."

"We have the M4."

"Oh, yeah. Still..."

Bruder said, "Can we outrun them?"

Turley shook his head.

"Dunbar runs fast. If he's in the boat we already saw, he's got five Mercury Verado four hundreds pushing him around. And the faster we go, the sooner we'll need fuel, and hooking up with Domm for the transfer will slow us down. And that, just FYI, would be a good time for Dunbar to board us."

Bruder checked his watch.

They'd been moving for fifty-five minutes.

"How close are we to the Gulf?"

Turley leaned forward and pointed up through the slanted windshield.

"See that?"

Bruder looked and saw the underside of a bridge.

"That's the Skyway," Turley said. "We're in the Southwest Channel now. If we keep going at this clip, we'll be free and clear in another fifteen, twenty minutes or so."

"That's longer than we discussed."

"Yeah, well, tell it to the ocean. We were ahead, now we're behind. And the winds will pick up more once we're past the keys, so it might be a little longer."

Bruder stepped closer to the police scanner and listened.

Traffic stops and bar fights and a robbery at a gas station, but no yachts.

Bruder thought about it, then touched his mic.

"Number Three, bring the Whaler in close once we're past the keys. I need to get on board."

Domm came back: "Huh? What for? Number One, you good with this?"

Turley looked at Bruder.

"What are you doing?"

"I'm going to have a word with Dunbar."

"A word? About what?"

"About what's going to happen if he doesn't find something else to do."

"We're on a bit of a time crunch here, man. Once the word goes out on the scanner, they're still gonna come looking for us in the Gulf."

"We deal with it now or later, and later we'll be at a disadvantage. Maybe no fuel, Domm away getting more, no idea where Dunbar is. Right now, he's right there. If it's him."

"It's him," Turley said.

"You have a problem if I have to kill him?"

Turley's eyebrows went up and he rocked back a bit, taking it in.

"No, not at all. I'd appreciate it, actually."

"After I get off, you keep going. Just head south, we'll find you."

"Yeah, sure. You gonna take the rifle?"

Bruder shook his head.

"We'll leave that as a surprise, in case he doesn't get the message."

Turley looked around the cockpit.

"Where is that thing, anyway?"

"Tell Domm to come get me."

"Oh, right."

He touched his mic.

"This is One, yeah, I'm good with it. Come alongside, our man here is gonna have himself a palaver."

***

The yacht slowed a little and Bruder could hear Domm and Turley rattling boat information back and forth as the Whaler crept closer to the yacht's starboard side.

Valenti was on the swimming platform waving his hands around like he was on the deck of an aircraft carrier.

He glanced over at Bruder standing on the stairs leading up from the platform to the salon. He didn't ask any questions or offer advice, but the glances told Bruder Valenti thought he was sailing to his own funeral.

When Domm got the Whaler close enough Bruder reached out and grabbed the rail and pulled himself over.

He held on while Domm swept away from the yacht, then squeezed between the rail and the pilothouse and dropped down to the deck near the swivel chair he'd been using.

Domm glanced over his shoulder. His hood and mask were down, like Turley and Valenti.

Bruder's were still covering his head and face.

Domm said, "Ballsy, I'll give you that. Now what?"

Bruder went into the pilothouse.

"Take me to Dunbar."

Domm sucked a tooth.

"You know, I'm all for a good fight every now and then, but we ain't exactly equipped for a shootout."

"There won't be one."

"Look man, he wants the yacht. You give him a chance to take the two of us out, or just put this boat out of commission, he'll do it."

"We'll see."

"We'll see?"

Bruder shrugged.

"Just get me over to him."

CHAPTER TEN

Domm brought the throttle almost all the way back and Bruder watched the yacht pull away, heading between Egmont and Passage Keys and toward the Gulf.

He didn't like slowing down or being off the boat—and away from the stash he'd found—but knew this had to get done if he wanted to finish the job.

There was no sense in letting Dunbar, or any problem, nibble and distract from the task.

Better to turn and face the issue and get rid of it as soon as it showed up.

He told Domm, "Give me your gun."

"Huh?"

"Your job is to get us away from Dunbar if I start shooting. You don't need your gun for that."

Domm frowned but pulled his Glock 17 out and handed it to Bruder.

Bruder press-checked and saw a round in the chamber, then ejected the magazine and found it missing just the one chambered round.

He slid the magazine into place.

Between his Glock and Domm's he had thirty-three rounds without reloading—he'd loaded one round into his Glock's chamber and replaced it in the fifteen-round magazine.

He stuck Domm's gun in his waistband next to his magazine holder and waited.

If he needed any of the spare mags, they'd officially be in a shootout and things would have gone to shit.

Domm started to look anxious, cranking his head from the screens on the console to the darkness off the stern and back again.

After a few minutes he locked onto the screens.

"Here he comes."

"Turn all the lights on," Bruder said.

Domm shook his head but hit some switches and the boat turned into a floating lantern.

Bruder stood between the swivel chairs and watched the water and still saw nothing, then the nothing formed into a gray shape a few hundred yards away coming in fast off their starboard stern.

Bruder waved his left hand over his head.

Fifteen seconds later the gray shape burst with illumination—orange running lights along the hull, white floodlights over the deck, blue LEDs from within the pilothouse, even lights beneath the water for snorkeling or diving or night swimming, Bruder guessed.

If the sheikh's yacht looked like a spaceship, Dunbar's boat was a sports car.

It was longer and taller than the Whaler, with an open flybridge above the pilothouse, a small deck on the bow and one twice as large at the stern.

Bruder counted five muscular-looking outboard engines hanging off the back.

He saw three men on the boat, one in the pilothouse and two along the port rail of the stern deck, closest to the Whaler.

Domm kept the boat going just above idle speed and Dunbar's boat pulled alongside with ten yards between the vessels.

Bruder looked across at a man in his forties wearing cutoff camouflage pants and a bright blue tank top. He had shoulder-length hair held back with a bandana and was tanned and lean, almost sinewy, and wore a lopsided, ear-to-ear grin.

"What's up, fellas? Domm, is that you, you ugly bastard?"

Domm looked over and gave him the finger. The muscles on his head rippled from the way his jaw was clenched.

"I thought so. Where's Turley hiding? On the yacht?"

Bruder asked Domm, "That's Dunbar?"

Domm nodded.

Dunbar looked at Bruder.

"You, I don't think I know. Hard to tell with the mask on."

"I'm the guy taking that boat."

"You mean the yacht?"

These people, Bruder thought.

"That's right."

"Where you taking it?"

"Doesn't matter. You don't want any part of this. Back off and find something else to steal."

Dunbar's crooked grin didn't falter.

"But I like that one. It used to belong to a sheikh, did you know that?"

Bruder shook his head.

"It's the Lab's now."

The grin twitched.

Bruder didn't want to bring McIntyre and the Labyrinth into it, but if it sent Dunbar packing, he'd gladly drop the name.

Dunbar said, "The Lab? Don't they have enough yachts?"

"Find something else," Bruder told him again.

Dunbar turned and said something to the man beside him, who looked like a darker and taller version of Domm.

The man had his hands below the railing, hidden from Bruder's sight.

Dunbar nodded and called to Bruder, "Sorry, bro. I already got a buyer lined up."

"Tell them it sank."

"You didn't let me finish. You hand the yacht over, I'll cut you guys in on...ten percent."

"No."

"You don't even know what the ten percent is."

"I don't care."

Dunbar laughed.

"Domm, where'd you find this robot? He's programmed to be a straight-up dickhead."

"We're leaving," Bruder said. "Turn around and forget whatever ideas you had about the boat."

"Two million," Dunbar said. "That's what my buyer is paying."

He waited for Bruder to say something, then gave up and turned toward the pilothouse.

"Domm, who's on the yacht? Just Turley and Valenti? So four of you. What'd you do with the security dude? Ah, doesn't matter, he doesn't get a cut. Unless he's in on it...but hey, let's go with fifty grand each, just for handing me the keys."

"No," Bruder said.

Dunbar said, "Domm, does he speak for all of you?"

Domm didn't say anything.

Dunbar shook his head but he was grinning again.

"You don't like that deal, how about this one? We shoot up you and that Whaler, then board the yacht and take it anyway. How's that sound?"

Bruder pulled the two Glocks and pointed them at Dunbar.

The man next to Dunbar brought his hands up, holding a fully automatic SWD Street Sweeper shotgun with a twelve-round rotating cylinder.

He pointed it at Bruder.

"I think we got better cannons," Dunbar said.

"I'll still put enough holes in you and your boat to cancel the job. Then Turley sails away and you got nothing but trouble, if you're still alive."

"Really? Right here in in the bay?"

Bruder didn't say anything and Dunbar's eyes flashed across the water.

"You ever hear the quote, 'Beware the fury of a patient man'?"

"Don't be patient. Be gone."

Dunbar grinned for a while, then said something over his shoulder to the man in the pilothouse and the boat pulled away and started to drop back.

"I'll see you again real soon," Dunbar called.

The spotlights and underwater lamps on his boat went out but the running and pilothouse stayed illuminated—no reason to run dark anymore.

Bruder watched it drift away, then handed the Glock 17 back to Domm, who said, "Well, that was exciting. Back to the yacht?"

"Yes."

"You gonna tell Turley about the two million? The fifty grand each?"

Bruder looked at him.

"It doesn't matter if it's two million apiece. We're doing the job."

Domm shook his head.

"He don't like leaving money on the table."

Bruder didn't say anything.

He watched the yacht grow larger and closer and thought about how he'd never get on a damn boat again when this was over.

***

Turley's voice came over the radio: "So how'd it go? Do we have peace?"

"For now," Bruder said, "but he isn't going anywhere."

"I expect nothing less from that leech. Now, I was watching through the binoculars up here—did I see guns getting waved around?"

"Just a show, to see what they brought along. Any word on the scanner yet?"

"Nothing about us. I'm shocked."

Bruder glanced back and saw Dunbar's boat still pulling away.

"Let's transfer the fuel while we have eyes on him."

"You're the boss," Turley said and Bruder caught that undercurrent again.

He frowned out at the yacht and picked up on Domm looking at him.

Finally Bruder said, "What?"

"You didn't mention the two mil."

"I already told you—it doesn't matter."

Domm shut up and steered the boat.

The yacht slowed and Domm got the Whaler alongside, working through the mild wake from the larger vessel.

The boats were just beyond the two keys, Egmont and Passage, and Bruder could already feel the change in the wind.

He didn't want to think about how there was no land in front of him until Texas or Mexico.

When the timing was right Bruder tossed the loose end of the fuel hose to Valenti, who left a few coils of slack on the platform and carried the rest into the engine room.

The coils still on the Whaler were near Bruder's feet and he stepped away after a sour look at them.

After some jerking and gurgling the fuel bladder started to shrink.

"Fold up them corners," Domm yelled.

Bruder added weight and pressure to the material and yanked the corners toward the center as the fuel drained.

When it was light enough he picked it up and turned it upside down and held it by the four corners, letting everything drain toward the hose connection.

Valenti emerged and tossed the hose back over.

"Good to go!"

Bruder stood holding the empty bladder and Domm told him, "Just leave it there, I probably gotta go fill it up again anyway."

"Why?"

"Because if the shit hits the fan we don't want an empty fuel tank to be the reason we get caught."

Fair enough, Bruder thought, and dropped the bladder and waited for the ocean to cooperate before making the jump from the Whaler onto the yacht's swimming platform, where Valenti caught his arm.

Before Domm peeled away he looked at Bruder and hit his mic.

"Hey guys, be sure to ask Mr. Kline here about the two million dollars."

He winked and cranked the Whaler to starboard, picking up speed.

Valenti said, "What two million dollars?"

***

Bruder first checked on Ted, who hadn't moved and may have been asleep when the cabin door opened.

He blinked in the shaft of light cutting across the bed, then Bruder shut the door again and went all the way up to the flybridge where Turley and Valenti waited.

Turley said, "So?"

"First tell me about the scanner."

Turley grinned.

"The propane tank is causing all kinds of trouble—they

think it's a gas leak and called the propane services to see where all the tanks are."

Bruder was pleasantly surprised.

"Nothing about the yacht?"

"I guess nobody from the impound is there yet. It's only been an hour or so."

"Seventy-three minutes," Bruder said.

Turley shrugged.

Bruder asked both of them, "How long until we get to the Dry Tortugas?"

Valenti said, "Based on this weather—which could change—I'd say eleven hours, maybe up to thirteen if we have to do another refuel."

"Let's not have to do that," Bruder said.

Turley's hand waved, impatient.

"Sure, whatever. So tell me the story."

"Dunbar wants the boat and says he has a buyer lined up."

Valenti looked at Turley and said, "Told you."

Bruder went on: "The buyer is offering two million, and Dunbar said he'd cut this crew in on ten percent."

Turley's lips moved.

"That's fifty grand each."

Bruder waited to see how they'd handle it.

Valenti asked him, "How much are you getting from McIntyre?"

"That's between me and him."

"More than fifty grand?"

"No."

The truth was actually better than lying. If he told them he was making more than fifty, and they weren't, they had no reason to finish the job.

"So this is a better offer," Turley said.

"Wrong."

Turley and Valenti shared a frown.

Bruder said, "The job is about more than money. I'm

getting a shitty ten grand to do all of this, but McIntyre and I have an agreement about something else."

The cockpit was silent for a few moments.

Valenti said, "What's he got on you?"

"Doesn't matter. What matters is, we're delivering this boat to the sheikh's men at the Dry Tortugas."

Turley winced.

"Ten grand, though? We're each getting twice that."

"Good for you. I don't care."

"Well," Turley said, "I care about the difference between twenty and fifty grand."

Bruder took a deep breath in through his nose.

"You guys know McIntyre is with the Lab, right?"

"Sure," Valenti said. "But we don't really operate in the same orbits. We piss him off, what's he gonna do? He won't even be able to find us."

"That's what I thought too," Bruder said.

Valenti got it: "Ah."

Turley was still stuck.

"So who's gonna make up the loss for us?"

"What loss?" Bruder said.

"The extra thirty grand we're missing out on—each—by not working with Dunbar."

"There is no loss. That offer doesn't exist. Forget about it."

"Too late for that, bubba."

Bruder said, "It's never too late to act smart. No matter how stupid you've been acting."

Turley's eyes went flat and Valenti pushed off the side of the cockpit to stand between them with his hands out.

"Ho, now. Everybody just hold up."

"Get this straight," Bruder told them. "If you mess with the job, you won't get anything. Not the twenty you have coming, let alone this fantasy of another thirty. You'll be at the bottom of the Gulf collecting crabs."

"Is that so?" Turley said.

"Believe it. We do what it takes to get to the Dry Tortugas, you get your twenty grand. I'll even give you my ten to stop your pissing and moaning. Then you can go do whatever the hell you want. But until then, do the job. And don't mention Dunbar again unless he's trying to board us."

Turley stared at him and Valenti's eyes moved back and forth, trying to keep track of both of them.

Finally Turley said, "You get rid of us, who's gonna steer the yacht?"

"I'll figure it out."

Turley scoffed.

"The hell you will. A gorilla like you, you'd sink this thing inside an hour."

"Then I'll drop anchor and tell McIntyre to send another crew. Somebody with sense, this time."

The two men shared a look then, like they hadn't considered the possibility of being replaced.

"Tell you what," Turley said. "You call McIntyre and tell him the price went up. Fifty grand each or I might just turn this wheel one degree too far and we end up in Havana."

Bruder knew how it would play out, but this was a good way to end the conversation without shooting anybody.

He shrugged.

"I'll let you know what he says."

***

Bruder pulled one of the pre-paid phones out of the motel trash bag and went to the swimming platform to make the call.

Penza answered right away.

"Get McIntyre up," Bruder said.

"He's awake, smart-ass."

A moment later McIntyre came on, sounding bright and chipper at four in the morning.

"A fire! Quite blunt, but effective. Well done."

Bruder scowled at the ocean.

"You had somebody else watching."

"Well, yes. From the business next door, I believe they manufacture sails or something."

"Did your lookout happen to catch the other crew looking to steal the yacht?"

McIntyre hesitated.

"This is the first I'm hearing of it. It was you who set the fire, wasn't it? Do you have the vessel?"

"I'm standing on it. Turley and his guys know the other crew, somebody named Dunbar. He's offering these boys fifty grand each to give him the boat."

"A mutiny," McIntyre said, like he relished the chance to use the word. "Clearly that's not an option. Let me guess— they want more money from me."

"Right."

If McIntyre came back and matched the price, everything ought to be fine.

"Are they listening right now?"

"No."

"Say I agree to pay them each fifty thousand, and after you deliver the yacht to its rightful owners you put the three of them out of my misery."

"No."

"Let me guess again: Now *you* want more money."

"Wrong. I'm not a mechanic. I won't do any killing unless it's the only option."

McIntyre's voice came through in a sneer: "Don't tell me you have *standards*, Mr. Bruder."

"Of course I do. For this particular standard, I don't commit triple homicide without a damn good reason."

"So if they were to try and kill you…"

"McIntyre, if I get the sense you're pitting us against each other just to cut your loose ends, I'll sink this boat and come looking for you. You've been in my trunk once.

It can happen again."

The man on the other end chuckled.

"I doubt it, but I do need you to deliver that vessel. Can you fend this Dunbar person off and keep Turley and his men from turning on you long enough to do so?"

"Another twenty or thirty grand for each of them would help."

"Ah, now it's my turn to have standards. No."

Bruder grimaced.

"You can afford it."

"Yes," McIntyre said. "But I won't be held hostage. I hired you to do a job—what are you prepared to do to complete it?"

Bruder said, "We'll be at the Dry Tortugas in eleven hours, unless a hurricane shows up. The sheikh's people will be there?"

"I'll make sure of it."

"And they'll have the money."

"Indeed."

"Tell them to bring fuel too. Diesel, for the yacht."

"Noted."

"Good."

Bruder ended the call and tossed the phone into the yacht's wake.

When he turned around Turley and Valenti appeared at the salon rail.

They looked down at him with their hoods and masks on.

Ted was between them with wide eyes.

Valenti had his gun out, pointed at Ted.

Turley's gun was pointed at Bruder.

He said, "Did you toss the phone already?"

Bruder frowned.

"Yeah."

"Shit. Okay, screw it. We've been talking. There's a new plan."

***

Bruder said, "Put Ted back in his room."

Nobody moved.

Ted looked from Bruder, down on the swimming platform, to the two men next to him. The cords in his neck were taut and his upper chest pumped in and out.

Bruder said, "Whatever you guys cooked up, he doesn't need to hear it."

"It don't matter," Turley said.

That lingered over everyone.

Bruder raised his left hand, palm-out.

"Everybody stop. Ted, you're fine. I'm gonna take you back to your room."

"No you're not," Turley said. "Ted's going for a swim. Well, a sink."

Bruder needed to stall.

"Slow down. What's the new plan?"

Valenti said, "First we get rid of the dead weight. Come on, Teddy."

He pointed Ted to the starboard stairs and held his upper arm down to the swimming platform.

They'd cut the zip ties off his ankles, and Ted gritted his teeth and braced himself like he was ready to take a punch.

He gave Bruder a look that switched between pleading and accusatory, like he'd lied about him being safe and was the only person who could make it true again.

Valenti said, "Right to the edge there, buddy."

He still had his pistol pointed at Ted's back but it was rising and his left hand came up to cover that ear, protection from the sound of the shot.

Bruder took a step and reached out and yanked Ted forward, chucking him off the back of the platform into the water churning off the stern.

"You idiot!" Turley yelled.

Valenti fired two shots into the water, probably hitting nothing, then brought the gun around on Bruder, who caught the barrel in his right hand and used his left to club Valenti on the side of the neck.

Valenti slumped and Bruder hit him again, a short chop to the temple, and the gun came free in his right hand as Valenti fell to the platform.

He held the gun by the top of the slide and didn't try to get it in an operable position.

He just looked up at Turley, who hadn't fired for some reason.

Now Turley yanked his mask down.

"You idiot," he said again. "You fucking moron!"

Bruder cut him off.

"You know who cares about a stolen yacht? Maybe ten people. You know who cares about an executed civilian? Everybody."

Turley said, "If we'd shot him, maybe he never gets found."

"Even worse," Bruder said. "They never stop looking for him, or us. Use your head, Turley."

Turley's eyes bugged.

"Use *my* head? He was a witness!"

"A witness to what? Four guys in masks stealing a yacht. That's it. Then we leave him at the Dry Tortugas with no idea where anybody went. What's the problem with that?"

Now the apoplectic look slid into a smirk.

"We aren't going to the Dry Tortugas anymore, that's what."

Domm's voice came through the radio: "What was that? Who's shooting?"

Turley kept staring at Bruder and answered: "Three, this is One. The package is overboard, check our wake. If you find it, finish the job."

"Copy that," Domm said.

Bruder cursed himself for not seeing it coming.

They'd been talking on another radio channel, or had another set.

Turley told him, "Give the gun back to Valenti."

Bruder looked down at the man, limp on the swimming platform.

"He's not ready for it yet."

"Then give it to me."

Bruder considered the situation.

Turley didn't have the attitude or posture of a man about to pull a trigger.

The pointed gun was a security measure, a fence, meant to keep Bruder from coming any closer.

As to why Turley hadn't tried to shoot him yet, Bruder didn't know.

He said, "I'll keep it for now. Where are we going?"

"That's up to McIntyre."

"I think he'll say Dry Tortugas. Just a guess."

Turley shook his head.

"No. Call him back, tell him the price went up again."

"Again? He didn't even go for the extra twenty grand apiece."

"Twenty grand?"

"Yeah. I would have told you, but you decided to point guns at me."

"No, fuck twenty grand. The price is two million."

That floated past Bruder's head and disappeared in the wind behind him.

He said, "Two million."

"That's what Dunbar would get, so that's the market value. McIntyre or the sheikh pays, I don't care."

"And you can't get in touch with McIntyre," Bruder said.

"Yeah, thanks to you and your goddam no cell phone rule. But how about I grab one of yours and you give me the number?"

"No."

Turley touched the hilt of the knife on his belt, a narrow fishing blade that looked fragile but Bruder had seen it slice just fine.

"We could get it out of you," Turley said, "but it would be better for everyone if you just go along with us. Take your cut out of the two million."

"You're dreaming if you think that money will happen."

"If McIntyre wants us to give this thing to the sheikh, the price is two million. Otherwise, someone else will pay it. Dunbar is proof of that."

Bruder was done arguing with nonsense.

He looked out at the water and the Florida coast.

"Shouldn't someone be steering?"

"I got the alarm on, we're fine," Turley said. "Call McIntyre."

"I need another phone. In the trash bag."

Turley glanced over his shoulder and moved that way, then came back.

"Nah. I give you the bag, you might throw the whole thing overboard. Then we got no way to call him. Come up here, slow. And put that damn gun down."

Valenti was starting to moan and squirm.

Bruder dropped the gun on his stomach.

"Add yours," Turley said. "Use your left hand."

Bruder clenched his jaw and used his left thumb and forefinger to pull the Glock out of its holster.

It landed on Valenti with a soft thud.

Bruder stepped over him toward the starboard stairs.

Turley tracked him with the pistol.

Bruder started up the steps, waiting for a good time to kill him.

***

Turley stepped back from the stairs and Bruder filled the emptied space, then moved to the starboard couch and sat down next to his trash bag.

He reached for it and Turley said, "Set it on the deck and kick it over to me."

Bruder did and leaned back against the pillows and M4 behind them. He spread his arms across the back of the couch.

Turley crouched and rooted around in the bag, coming out with one of the phones still in its clear plastic shell.

He lobbed it onto the couch next to Bruder.

"Call him."

Bruder picked up the package and turned it over in his hands.

Just like with the previous phone, the packaging had a crimped edge all the way around with no perforated entry points.

"I need to use my knife to open it."

Turley thought about it.

"Nah. Slide it back."

Bruder sent the phone back across the deck.

Turley crouched and moved the gun to his left hand so he could pull his knife with the right.

He put one foot on the phone to hold it still and went to work on the plastic.

"I've seen those videos, the ones where the guy with the knife gets to the guy with the gun before he can shoot. What is it, anything inside twenty feet? You seen those?"

"No," Bruder said.

He was thinking about the M4 pressing against the small of his back, behind the throw pillows, and which way the barrel was pointing.

He replayed the scene, stuffing the gun back there while Ted pouted, and decided the barrel was on his right side.

Probably.

What he did know, for certain: The gun was not ready to fire.

He'd have to get it out, point it in Turley's direction, pull the charging handle, make sure the selector was off Safe, then pull the trigger.

Before Turley shot him with the gun already loaded and aimed at him.

It wasn't something he practiced.

Turley made a mess of the shell, ragged cuts and shards of plastic sticking out everywhere, and finally got the phone out.

He slid it between Bruder's feet.

Bruder reached down with his left hand and glanced up.

Turley was rising, putting his knife away and still had the gun in his off hand.

Bruder heard a muffled cough from the swimming platform, Valenti coming around.

This was the time.

He fumbled the phone forward and had to reach out, letting his right hand drop from the back of the couch into the pillows.

He felt the top of the rail cover, the casing around the barrel between the front sight and upper receiver, and the flashlight mounted to its side.

His finger followed the wire to the mouse tail switch, and as he sat up with the phone he yanked the M4's barrel around and hit the switch.

The tactical flashlight cut through the salon like a laser as Turley was moving the pistol to his right hand.

"Hey!"

The beam slapped across his face and he recoiled from the assault, covering his eyes with his left forearm and firing wildly.

The first bullet hit the couch to Bruder's right and he dove left, keeping the flashlight on Turley's face while he tried to get a round in the chamber.

Turley swept the pistol across the salon, shooting and shooting and shooting, and Bruder felt an impact on his right side.

The M4 wasn't cooperating and Turley kept shooting, so he hurled the rifle and lunged for the stern rail and vaulted onto the swimming platform below.

Valenti was sitting up, frowning at all the racket, and his head lazily tracked Bruder's landing, then his arm as he reached for one of the pistols.

Bruder's fingers touched the grip and another shot came and it felt like someone jabbed him on the right side of his neck with a live wire.

He had his back to Turley and didn't have time to turn and knew more bullets were coming, so he dove off the swimming platform and plunged into the black water and sank.

PART THREE

PART THREE

CHAPTER ELEVEN

When they threw the security guy off the yacht Dunbar was watching through binoculars from the flybridge.

He saw the man get tossed off the swimming platform, then someone—he thought it was Valenti—fired twice into the water.

The sound of the shots drifted by a moment after the flashes.

His lopsided grin spread and called down to his guys, "Watch out, we might have a night swimmer out here."

Hendrick said, "Should we grab him?"

"Nah, just try not to hit him."

"I'll try."

Hendrick was Dominican and built like a linebacker but had never watched football, let alone played it.

Dunbar watched the yacht, a few hundred yards off his port bow, through the binoculars and saw people moving around on the swimming platform but couldn't tell what was happening.

Domm and the Whaler were to the right of the line between Dunbar's boat and the yacht, acting like a buffer.

A moment later the Whaler cut hard to port, toward the yacht's wake, and a spotlight mounted on the exterior of the pilothouse came on.

They were scrambling, looking for the security guy, so whatever shenanigans were happening on the yacht likely weren't part of the plan.

Dunbar kept smiling.

He always smiled when he was on the water—he couldn't help it.

He was certain he'd been born in the wrong era. He was meant for a time when the oceans were unexplored and a man could make his fortune discovering new lands and taking an occasional merchant vessel, either for king and country or just for the hell of it.

He wasn't sure if he believed in reincarnation, but a woo-woo girl with toe rings he'd been engaged to for a few weeks had told him he'd been a French corsair during the Napoleonic Wars, harassing and demoralizing the British navy long after the French lost the war at sea at the Battle of Trafalgar.

Dunbar thought she might be full of shit, because a line like that would work on any man with a boat, but he chose to believe it anyway.

He liked the name corsair, or privateer, to describe what he did, which was intercepting and boarding vessels of all sizes and claiming them and their contents as his own.

Authorities preferred the title *criminal*, or the slightly more acceptable *pirate*, which also made him smile.

A couple centuries ago they would have issued him a letter of marque and redemption and sent him out to raid enemy ships.

And there was money to be made in the same line of work, mostly off the coast of Africa, but a lot of those ships had armed escorts and Dunbar preferred targets that did not shoot back.

So far Turley and his crew hadn't done so, but the guy Dunbar had talked to, the one with Domm—he seemed the type.

When he was aboard the yacht, Dunbar planned to ask Turley who the hell he was getting mixed up with, hardasses like that who didn't have fun out on the water.

He watched the yacht cruise along, the Whaler slicing back and forth behind it, searching with no luck.

The Whaler was a good boat, reliable.

If Turley and his guys didn't play nice, Dunbar thought, maybe he'd give it to Hendrick, add it to his privateer fleet.

Dunbar had christened his current boat *Cooper's Hawk*, and it had started out as a Scout 530 LXF before he and Hendrick and Fulton did all the custom work on her.

Now, she was practically a stealth bomber on water.

He didn't care if Domm and the others knew where he was, and if he wanted to disappear for a while and come back at them without warning, he could do so.

But for now, he'd—

A bright white light flashed inside the yacht's salon, followed by strobes of orange.

More gunshots.

Dunbar held the binoculars steady.

A man came over the stern rail and dropped to the swimming platform, then another man—Turley from the shape of him and the way he moved—appeared at the rail and fired down toward the platform.

The man down there dove into the water and Turley fired after him a few times, disappeared into the salon, then came back with an M4 Carbine.

"Oh, shit," Dunbar said, his grin nearly painful.

Turley aimed at the water off the stern, then worked on the rifle to get a round in the chamber.

He brought the gun back up to his shoulder but didn't fire.

Another man rose from the swimming platform with his

hands out, like he was trying to calm Turley down, and the two of them had words before Turley carried the rifle up to the flybridge and into the pilothouse.

The man on the platform turned and looked at the water and Dunbar recognized Valenti.

So the man who'd gone overboard was most likely the hardass.

Domm and the Whaler picked up a more frantic pattern.

Dunbar figured he'd been tasked with finding both of the castaways, or told to forget the first guy and find the second.

Fulton watched from the bow, then called up, "What the hell is going on over there?"

"It's a circus," Dunbar said with delight.

The Whaler was falling behind the yacht.

The spotlight played across small waves and chop and Dunbar almost felt sorry for Domm, trying to find something the size of a volleyball in a constantly shifting seascape.

And if the volleyball didn't want to be found, all it had to do was drop below the surface.

After a minute or so the spotlight died and the Whaler roared ahead, catching up to the yacht, both of them cruising south into the Gulf of Mexico.

Dunbar brought the binoculars down and scanned the water, thinking about what to do next.

He called down to Hendrick, "Kill the lights."

***

Dunbar told Fulton, "Watch the water, get the hook ready."

Fulton nodded.

He was twenty-five and made his taxable income up in Alaska on crab boats, then came down to work with Dunbar in the off-season and make some real money.

Dunbar climbed down into the pilothouse and looked at the radar and sonar screens.

The sonar was designed to find fish, which they used it

for occasionally, but it could also show sunken boats, cars, planes, and people, if you knew what to look for.

The boats and cars and planes sometimes had what could loosely be called treasure.

Dunbar told Hendrick, "Gimme...fifteen degrees to port and cut back to five knots."

Hendrick worked the controls.

Fulton called from the bow, "You want me to push or pull?"

Meaning, were they drowning or saving these guys?

"Depends on who we find," Dunbar said.

***

They cut back and forth across a grid in the long-faded wake of the yacht, which was just a spot of light to the south now.

Dunbar went back and forth from the sonar and radar to the rails, scanning the surface for anything that didn't look like water.

Eventually he gave up on the screens and stayed at the rail, trusting his eyes more than the machines.

After ten minutes Fulton carried the extending hook over and said, "How long you want to keep doing this?"

"I don't know yet. Can you still see the yacht?"

"Barely."

Dunbar kept his eyes on the water, skimming.

"Well, we can catch up to it any time we want, long as we know the direction. Knowing Turley, they're headed for the Keys, maybe Miami or Fort Lauderdale. We'll catch up before then."

"Not Havana?"

Dunbar shook his head, then crouched to peer just over the rail.

"Cubans don't like Turley. He's the fake kind of macho."

Fulton frowned down at him but didn't ask for more details.

"What about the—"

"There!"

Dunbar pointed and yelled to Hendrick, "Hard to port, aim for shore and kill the throttle, all the way!"

The boat pivoted almost in place and slowed in the chop.

Longboat Key was about five hundred yards straight ahead, a narrow strip of land with Sarasota Bay on the far side, then Bradenton to the north and Sarasota to the south.

Much closer than all of that, Dunbar saw a small object in the water that didn't reflect light.

He barked orders to Hendrick and moved in on the shape, putting it along the port side.

"Lights," he said, and the boat lit up like it had for the meeting with Domm and the hardass.

The object was a head, turned away from the boat, with arms out to the sides flapping at the water in slow motion, like they were fading.

"Snag him," he told Fulton.

Fulton got the hook under the man's armpits and tugged him toward the boat.

When the man was close enough Dunbar and Hendrick leaned over and hauled him up and over the rail, not worried about how their fingers dug in or what they might be pinching.

Dunbar took his hands away and found blood on them.

The man blinked up at them, but it might have been his eyelids fluttering in and out of consciousness.

Dunbar got a better look at the sweatshirt the guy wore and found two holes, one just above his right collarbone and another on his right side.

He lifted the fabric and saw a matching exit wound below the man's ribs, rimmed with ragged white flesh and welling with blood.

To get at the one higher up, they'd need to cut the shirt off.

The guy had a cloth gaiter around his neck and Dunbar pulled it up over his mouth and nose, then examined the results.

The gaiter was soaked and the man started to gag, so Dunbar tugged it back down and grinned at him as he passed out for good.

"Welcome aboard, hardass."

***

Before Bruder opened his eyes, his mind felt the movement of water and he remembered going over the stern of the yacht and he thrashed awake to keep his head from going under.

His arms shot out to pull at the water but his right arm wouldn't work and he keeled that way, tilting to his right and holding his breath, waiting for the impact.

He landed on something soft and dry, and when he opened his eyes he was on a bed in a cabin that looked like a blend between a miniature hotel suite and a hospital room.

The lower walls had a tan covering with texture; the upper stretches had padded cabinet doors with stainless hardware.

Recessed light cans in the ceiling were turned low but there was enough light to see the man standing in the doorway at the foot of the bed, leaning against the wall.

Bruder tried to sit up but his right arm still wouldn't cooperate and a lance of pain streaked across his right shoulder all the way down to his hip.

He gritted his teeth and used his left arm to push off the bed until he was upright with his legs splayed out in front.

His hooded sweatshirt and the shirt underneath were gone, along with the radio.

His right arm was bent at the elbow and strapped across his stomach with Ace bandages and his shoulder was wrapped in gauze and white tape.

He looked below the forearm and saw more tape and gauze on his right side, below the ribs.

His pants and shorts felt clammy. The quick-dry pants had streaks of white salt starting to appear, and while his belt was still in place the holster and magazine holder were gone.

The four-inch folding knife was still clipped inside his right pocket, so whoever took the other gear apparently wasn't concerned about him running around the boat on a stabbing spree.

He moved his left foot and the boot felt heavy.

"This ain't the first time you been shot," the man in the doorway said, flicking a finger at the scars on Bruder's chest.

"The yacht," Bruder said.

His throat was raw and swollen from Gulf water.

The man stepped back into a small room, which had stairs leading up to the deck, and opened a drawer. He pulled out a bottle of water, cracked the top off, and handed the bottle to Bruder.

Bruder drank half and tried again: "Where's the yacht?"

"We haven't officially met yet," the man said. "I'm Raleigh Dunbar."

"Yeah, I know."

Dunbar leaned against the corner again and crossed his arms.

"Maybe you think so, but forget whatever Turley and those clowns told you. And by the way, who the hell are you?"

Bruder finished the water.

"Kline."

"Kline, huh? And you were running the show on the sheikh's yacht before things went sour?"

"I thought so."

Dunbar's tilted grin flashed.

"Yeah, that's Turley for you. Though Domm's no peach either. Valenti...he's a pro, but if the other two want to go one way, he won't fight it."

Bruder poked his left fingers around on his right trapezius muscle and the constant dull ache there turned into a burning pain.

He did the same along his right side and the pain there

was similar, but not as intense.

"Both wounds are through-and-through," Dunbar said, "so you got four holes. He didn't hit anything but meat though, no bones, which makes you a lucky man."

Bruder grunted.

Dunbar said, "You remember who shot you?"

"Yeah."

"Good. I just want to make sure you know it wasn't me."

"Where's the yacht?" Bruder said again.

Dunbar pointed over Bruder's head, almost straight across the cabin.

"About three and a half miles that way."

Bruder looked over his shoulder at the wall.

"That's the bow?"

"Correct."

"So you're chasing them."

"I'm following them. If I wanted to chase them, it would be over already."

"I need to get back on that boat."

Dunbar nodded.

"Then what?"

Bruder stared at the wall and thought about it.

"Kill Turley, probably."

"You kill him, you gotta do the others too."

Bruder tested his shoulder and grimaced.

Dunbar said, "Which means you'll have no one to work the yacht. No offense, but you don't have the demeanor of a sailing man."

"Good for me. You want a job?"

Dunbar's eyebrows went up.

"You got two million dollars?"

"No."

"Then I'll pass. And you ain't a sailor, but you do seem capable of other sorts of work. So if you help us snatch that yacht, I'll cut you in on a share."

It was a non-starter.

He needed to deliver the yacht to the Dry Tortugas and the sheikh's men and get McIntyre off his back, no matter what Dunbar's offer was worth.

He said, "Who's offering you two million?"

"Don't you worry about that. Just sit tight and think about your options. When you're ready, come topside and let me know if you want in on your share or if I need to chuck your ass back in the drink."

Dunbar was still grinning when he turned around and left.

CHAPTER TWELVE

Turley was at the helm of the yacht with a beer and the phone he'd opened in the salon before Kline went full asshole and tried to kill him with that flashlight and carbine.

The beer came from the fridge in the galley, not as cold as he liked but it would do in the moment.

They were making decent time, with Captiva Island coming up off the port bow and the local police channels saying nothing about the yacht.

The channels back around Gandy and St. Pete were probably burning up with yacht talk, but that wasn't his problem anymore.

He'd been working the phone numbers of people who might know someone interested in buying a stolen yacht, but at five in the morning most of those people were either drunk or passed out.

Valenti came up the stairs with an ice pack from the yacht's first aid kit pressed to the side of his head.

His eyelids seemed heavier than usual, like he still hadn't come all the way back, but maybe he was just tired.

He said, "Any luck?"

Turley glowered at the phone, useless so far, laying there on the console.

"Carson said he'd trade us a plate of nachos for her, then laughed and dropped the phone."

"What a dick."

"I'm thinking Mexico," Turley said.

Valenti sat down and moved the ice pack around his forehead.

"Mexico. Cancun?"

"For starters. We fill up in the Keys, we should be able to make it."

"The Whaler won't," Valenti said.

They both looked off the starboard bow, where Domm was shadowing the yacht.

Turley said, "Yeah, well...We can tow it after it runs dry or Domm can stay in the Keys with it. Or fuck it, we leave it behind."

"Then we'd be all-in on this baby," Valenti said. "We'd have no getaway boat."

Turley assured him: "We're all-in."

Valenti sat back and iced his head.

"We'll need to stay away from the Dry Tortugas."

"Well, duh."

"And what about Dunbar?"

"I haven't seen him back there. Neither has Domm, line of sight or radar."

Valenti said, "What, he just gave up?"

Turley pulled from the beer and let it sit in his mouth while he tipped his head back and thought about it.

Valenti interrupted him.

"He said he already has a buyer."

"Yeah, I know. But ten percent? Assuming he isn't full of shit?"

"It's better than nothing."

"And worse than the full two mil," Turley said.

"Assuming we can find a buyer."

Turley rapped his knuckles on the side of the beer bottle. "Maybe we can get Dunbar to tell us who his buyer is."

"I'm gonna file that under 'Unlikely'."

"Yeah...Okay, worst case, we offer to cut him in on the deal. The same terms he offered us, ten percent."

Valenti was giving him a look.

"What?" Turley said.

"Worst case, I think, is Dunbar and his guys attack us and try to take the yacht."

"Well, they try that shit, we'll kill them. That's a given, so I wasn't including it in the list of scenarios."

"Best case being we never see him again."

"You got it."

Valenti nodded and they sat there for a bit, waiting for something else they hadn't thought of to manifest.

Then Valenti said, "So, Cancun. Then what?"

"I'll call around some more. There's gotta be some king-pin down there who wants a luxury yacht."

"Kingpin...the cartels?"

"Why not?"

Valenti was quiet until Turley turned to look at him, then Valenti said, "Aren't they sorta tied in with the Lab?"

"Who knows?"

"McIntyre's gonna be pissed."

"Well, he can get over it or die pissed, that's up to him."

Turley knew he was being dismissive of things that would likely come back to bite him in the ass, but his approach to life was to deal with those things when they showed up, not before. Because if they never showed up, what was all the fuss about?

He kept going, convincing himself: "McIntyre should have agreed to pay us more money. Actually, he should have paid us more money in the first place, not that bullshit twenty grand apiece. Then none of this would be necessary."

"Well, maybe it still isn't."

Turley looked at him again.

Valenti said, "What if we do the meet with the sheikh's guys and tell them the price went up? Cut McIntyre out of the loop and deal with the buyer directly."

Turley frowned, thinking about it.

"So, what, we just putter around in this thing while they get the cash together?"

"Nah man, we have them make a transfer to an account. One call, the money's in."

"What account?"

"We set one up," Valenti said. "Offshore somewhere."

Turley crossed his arms.

"You're being very vague for how confident you sound."

"Well, how hard can it be? Banks want money, right? We start calling around to see who wants to accept a two-million-dollar deposit. Here, gimme that phone."

Turley handed it to him.

"Oh, see?" Valenti said. "He got the ones with internet minutes. I'll just look up how to open an offshore account."

"I will be one hundred percent shocked if it's that easy."

Valenti grunted, already working the phone.

Turley went back to the wheel, feeling good about the plan. Or plans, really.

No matter what they decided to do they'd have to hit the Keys for fuel, so he relaxed at the helm and watched the water and felt the yacht responding to his touch.

She was worth the two million, at least, and that's what he'd get for her.

***

The sun was a pink smudge off the port side when Bruder came up from the cabin into the pilothouse, facing aft.

The helm was on his left, and a large man with burn scars across his ear and neck nodded at him but didn't say anything.

Bruder recognized him as the one holding the Street Sweeper during the nighttime meeting and it was fine with him if nobody mentioned it.

A two-seat bench meant for the co-pilot was on his right, but he shuffled past it toward the bow into a small lounge area with a forward-facing couch that almost spanned the boat's width.

He eased onto that and grimaced when his side complained.

It was chilly out in the morning air with no shirt and damp pants and he started to shiver.

Dunbar moved along the port rail like he was walking across a dance floor and dropped into one of the rear-facing seats across from the couch and grinned at him.

"How we feeling?"

"Fine. The yacht's still ahead?"

"Just over the horizon, my verbose friend."

Bruder stood and looked through the pilothouse windshield. He saw boats, but nothing that looked like the sheikh's yacht.

He eased onto the couch again and asked Dunbar, "Where?"

"Like I said, about three miles ahead. She's on our radar. I'm not exactly sure what kind of gear they have on board, so we're playing it safe and hanging back. You didn't happen to notice the make and model of her radar system, did you?"

"No."

His body started to rattle against the bench.

Dunbar said, "You cold?"

"Yes."

It didn't cross his mind to lie or try to act tough about it—he was cold and being cold was going to affect his ability to work.

Dunbar went below and came back with an aqua sweatshirt with a dolphin on it and a fleece blanket.

"You can't put the sweatshirt on yet, but let's drape it over your shoulders and wrap the blanket over it."

They did that and Bruder sat back. When his left arm stopped shaking he began to unwrap the bandage holding his right arm like a sling.

"What's the rush?" Dunbar said.

"I need to know what works and what doesn't."

He got the arm free and flexed the hand, which was fine, then the wrist and elbow.

The elbow caused some grief because it made him move his shoulder, and as soon as he did that his right trapezius muscle twitched and sent a bolt of pain through the top of his head.

Dunbar winced.

"No fishing for you, buddy."

"You have a police scanner on board?"

"The yacht is officially hot," Dunbar said, answering the real question. "Word is out for authorities to be on the lookout."

"Did they say where?"

Dunbar's grin widened.

"The Gulf of Mexico. Which is about the size of Texas, Oklahoma, Arkansas, and Louisiana combined. You can probably throw in Mississippi too."

"But they have to know it's along the coast somewhere."

"So are a lot of other boats."

"Yachts?"

Dunbar shrugged.

"All kinds and sizes."

Bruder looked out at the water. Between them and the shore he counted at least twenty vessels, big and small, most of them doing some sort of fishing, or trawling, or whatever they called it.

Above and closer to shore a few small planes and a helicopter moved around, but none of them showed urgency.

He said, "What about the security guy?"

Dunbar blinked.

"What about him?"

"Any talk about him crawling onto shore? Or a body being found?"

"Oh, not that, but they did mention a possible hostage situation."

"Yeah," Bruder said, still looking at the water. "What happens to a body out here?"

"A dead body?"

Bruder nodded.

"Uh, well...just about everything. If he got caught in a current, it could pull him into the loop, which would dump him out toward the Bahamas. If something didn't chew him up before then."

"Sharks?"

"Sharks. Freighters. Maybe some barracuda. Lots of stuff out here will take a test bite, given the chance."

"What if he was alive?"

"If he's a decent swimmer, and Valenti didn't hit him with either of those shots he threw off the stern, he could make it to shore. Assuming a shark didn't get after him. You think he made it?"

Bruder thought about his brief time in the dark water, getting rolled by the swells and knowing his blood was leaking out, sending a signal to things he'd never see coming.

Ted probably hadn't been shot, but his hands were bound behind his back.

Was he a good enough swimmer to overcome that?

"If he did," Bruder said, "we'll hear about it eventually. He might know the yacht turned south. Then they'd point the search this way."

Dunbar nodded but didn't seem too worried about it.

Bruder said, "Is the Whaler up there too?"

"She's a little tougher to track. We got a lot of boats her

size out and about, so she and Domm blend in. But they're around the yacht, no doubt."

"For now. Turley can't risk someone identifying the yacht, so there's a good chance Domm will need to ferry fuel out at some point. That would be a good time to take the yacht back."

"Where were you headed?"

Bruder flexed the fingers on his right hand, making sure they weren't going to surprise him at the wrong time by not working.

"Dry Tortugas. The same place we're going once I'm back on board."

Dunbar found that amusing.

"And who's meeting you there? The people who don't have my two million dollars?"

"That's right."

The way Bruder saw it, there was no reason not to tell Dunbar the plan. He'd either be a part of making it happen, or dead, so it didn't matter if he knew.

"And these people," Dunbar said. "They're with the Lab?"

"No."

"So you were bluffing when you said that before."

"No. I'm delivering the boat for a guy who's with the Lab. The people at the meet belong to the sheikh."

Dunbar's grin widened.

"Oh, shit. You stole it just to give it back to him?"

"Something like that."

"What's your cut?"

Bruder didn't want to get into that conversation.

"It doesn't matter. You help me deliver the yacht, I'll make it worth your time."

"You already said you don't have two million dollars."

Bruder did have that, actually, but he wasn't giving any of it to Dunbar.

The man at the helm turned around and watched the

conversation.

Another man, somewhere in his twenties with a beard and tattoo sleeves on his arms, came down from the flybridge where he'd apparently been listening.

He stood in the starboard opening of the lounge, holding onto a rail along the roof, and waited for Bruder to continue.

"Look," Bruder said. "You guys pulled me out of the water and patched me up, and I appreciate that."

"We're nice guys," Dunbar said.

Now Bruder smiled, a tight line across his face.

"You want the yacht, and you think I can help you get it. But I'm delivering it to the Dry Tortugas. You want to help, great. You decide to get in the way, I'll have to do something about it."

"Like what?" Dunbar asked.

He seemed genuinely curious.

"Pay you seventy grand to change your mind."

Dunbar said, "Seventy grand?"

"Right."

It was Bruder's payment plus what Turley and his men had coming before they'd started making bad choices.

Dunbar said, "The coffee hasn't kicked in yet, so my math might be off...but that's about one-point-nine-three million shy of what we should be getting."

"True. But if you take it, you don't have to deal with me."

Dunbar laughed hard and long, then wiped his eyes.

"My man, you should see yourself. All banged up, on another man's boat in the Gulf of Mexico, surrounded by dudes with guns—yet still talking shit. But what you're telling me, really, is that we should finish what Turley started, then dump your body in the water."

They stared at each other while the other two men looked on, ready for whatever came next.

When he was done thinking it through, Bruder said, "Anybody know the current price of gold?"

***

Bruder said, "There's a stash in the master cabin of that yacht. Shallow, felt-lined shelves holding three hundred ten-ounce bars of gold. Twenty-four karat from the look and feel of them."

Dunbar squinted at him, then said, "Bullshit."

Bruder shrugged.

The one with the tattoo sleeves said, "How much is all that worth?"

Bruder had a figure in mind but let Dunbar run with it.

He said, "Three hundred bars, ten ounces each...the rate right now is what, around fifteen grand per bar if we're selling legit."

"Which you can't do," Bruder said.

"I can't? I got a guy."

"Yeah, everybody has a guy. You won't be able to take this stuff anywhere near a dealer. You'll see why when you lay eyes on it."

Dunbar was intrigued.

"Okay, so figure the gold is worth three million, straight-up legit. We'll probably get two point five?"

"Tops," Bruder said. "But don't count on it. Two is more realistic."

"That's the same we're getting for the yacht," the tattooed one said.

Dunbar shook his head.

"Nah. I can get more than two for the gold."

He looked at Bruder.

"So is that why you got hired to steal the yacht? To get this gold back for the sheikh?"

"I think it's both. But the gold is more important."

"Then why didn't this Lab guy..."

"McIntyre," Bruder said.

"Why didn't McIntyre just hire you to sneak on board

and steal the gold? Why bother with the whole damn ship if it's not the priority?"

"Because I don't think he knows about it. And if he does, he knows better than to tell a guy like me where a bunch of gold is hidden."

Dunbar grinned.

"Yeah, that tracks."

"Here's the deal," Bruder said. "You get me back on the yacht and help me deliver it to the Dry Tortugas. We split the gold four ways, and you drop me off somewhere I can rent a car and drive away from all this damn water."

"What about Turley and the others?"

"I don't care what happens to them."

Dunbar looked out at the water and Florida coast and the sun, now wholly above the horizon, and rubbed his chin.

"Your pal McIntyre and the sheikh are gonna be pissed about the missing gold."

"What gold?" Bruder said, and Dunbar's grin widened.

***

Dunbar brought a carafe of coffee up from below and put a mug in Bruder's left hand and filled it.

"So that's Hendrick at the helm, and this young buck is Fulton."

Bruder nodded at Hendrick again and reached out to shake Fulton's hand, wincing when his shoulder complained about it.

"I would have introduced myself sooner," Fulton said, "but I thought, you know. We were gonna kill you."

Bruder said, "Yeah, hello. You guys know how to get back on the yacht?"

"We do," Dunbar said. "I can't guarantee there won't be any shots fired, so we need to pick our spot wisely. Once we get south of Marco Island it's all Everglades along the coast. There'll still be boats around, of course, but we won't have to worry about anybody on land, in case Turley heads for shore and we have to follow."

"How close is Marco Island?"

Dunbar looked at the shoreline.

"We'll pass it in about thirty minutes. But here's the thing—Marco Marina is the last fueling station until the Keys. If Domm is gonna make a run, he'll do it at Marco. My guess is, Turley will take the yacht in a little closer, run along the Everglades until Domm catches up again. That way they get to conserve fuel for both vessels."

Bruder said, "How good is your guess?"

"It's what we would do."

"So thirty minutes."

Dunbar nodded.

"We get close enough to see if Domm makes his move, then we make ours."

"They'll be ready for something like that," Bruder said.

"Yeah, probably. But it won't matter."

Bruder flexed his hand again.

"What kind of weapons do you have?"

"The Sweeper," Dunbar said, "and some handguns."

"That's all?"

The crooked grin flashed.

"You fell for the bluff, my friend."

"I don't care about that. Why don't you have more firepower?"

"Because if the Coast Guard or some Grouper Trooper stops for an inspection, we have to chuck everything over-board. And I don't like throwing money into the drink."

Bruder said, "Grouper Trooper?"

"Conservation officer," Fulton said. "A fish cop."

Bruder nodded.

"I can hold a pistol. Anything more than that, I don't trust the shoulder."

"Yeah, about that," Dunbar said. "I talked to the guys, and

we aren't comfortable with you having a weapon just yet."

"What?"

"You understand. We go through all the trouble to get you on board, then you shoot us in the back or take a hostage or something."

"Why, is that what you would do?"

Dunbar winked.

"Just hang out and enjoy the show."

Bruder didn't say anything, letting his silence indicate agreement.

CHAPTER THIRTEEN

Turley was going to miss watching the sunrise from the helm of the yacht.

Everything was so smooth, so responsive, and clearly engineered to be used by a professional.

He wondered if it would be worth it to get a job as a captain of one of the yacht charters, lead a crew of three or four hot young people and steer vessels like the sheikh's around the world while wealthy people lounged around and partied and made fools of themselves.

He pictured it, and each time he got as far as some fat pasty guy barking an order at him and Turley punching him in the mouth in front of his wife and kids.

So...probably not.

But he'd enjoy it while it lasted, which was how he approached just about everything without really analyzing the pattern.

They cruised south at twenty-two knots, seven miles off the coast, hovering between the inshore fishing boats and pleasure craft and those headed for deeper waters and offshore or deep-sea fishing.

It kept them out of sight from shore and most sailors, and even though being this far out used more fuel, the anonymity was worth it.

Valenti came up the stairs using the burner phone Kline left behind when Turley tried to kill him.

"Yeah. Okay, good. Let me know."

He ended the call with Domm, who was on the Whaler with the last burner from Kline's trash bag. There hadn't been much else in the bag—sandals and a change of clothes and some protein bars and a map of Florida, which made the three of them laugh.

Kline was nothing but a tourist in their world, and he'd been roughly ejected from it the moment he tried to step outside his lane.

Valenti looked off the stern and saw nothing but water, then sat next to Turley and enjoyed the view for a moment and said, "He's gonna hit the Marco Marina and fill everything he's got. If they have any other tanks for sale nearby he'll grab those too, long as it doesn't take too long or make him look too sketchy."

Turley snorted.

"Him trying not to look sketchy is about the sketchiest thing I've ever seen."

"Maybe I should have gone in," Valenti said.

"Nah. He's fine. And you need to be here to advise me on yacht transactions."

"Oh, I'm your advisor now?"

"That's right. I got a call back from Mills, he's in Cabo right now. The way he told it, he's working logistics for a chemical company based around there."

Valenti said, "Logistics?"

"Moving product."

"Ah."

"He might have a line on a dude who's been looking at the yachts in the harbor at Cabo San Lucas, talking about how he's gonna get himself one."

Valenti said, "Cabo? We can't take this thing through the Panama Canal, man. My tape job on the hull won't hold up to that kind of scrutiny."

"No, no, if that guy wants it, it's his problem how to get it there. I say Cancun is the closest we can take it."

"Agreed."

"See? My advisor."

Valenti shook his head.

"So, Cancun…Shit, it would be so nice to just swing in somewhere and fill up. Maybe we could run into Hemingway Marina in Havana. Some hoops to jump through, but we'd be going from Cuba to Mexico, so we don't have to worry about the whole Cuba back to the States stuff."

"Yeah. I think—"

Turley had glanced down at the radar, and he frowned and looked over his shoulder and saw Dunbar's boat flying across the water toward them.

***

Dunbar was at the helm and Bruder could feel a difference from when the bigger man, Hendrick, had been piloting the vessel.

Dunbar stayed on his feet and worked the controls and everything just seemed smoother, even though they were roaring across the water now and Bruder's head rattled from the sound of the five huge engines hanging off the stern.

He had the sweatshirt on after a tussle filled with grunts and curses and needed to hold onto the back of the bench to keep from sliding around.

Hendrick was at the bow, crouched below the rail wearing a Kevlar vest and holding the Street Sweeper shotgun.

Fulton emerged from below and stood in the lounge to don his own Kevlar vest, showing Bruder a seam in the heavy black canvas with orange fabric inside.

"These things inflate if they hit the water. Keeps you from sinking. Pretty slick."

"Not if someone is shooting at you."

Fulton laughed and pulled on reinforced demolition gloves and safety goggles, then stuck a rubber mouth guard in. He racked a round into the chamber of a Colt 1911, a pistol that could knock somebody clean overboard, and slid the gun into a chest holster.

He checked the radio clipped to his belt and the bud hooked over his ear—a setup almost identical to what Turley and his crew used—then climbed up to the flybridge again carrying a long pole with a hook on the end.

Dunbar hadn't bothered to share their plan, a routine they seemed to know well and had done before, so Bruder did as he'd been told—he sat and watched, waiting for the moment when he could do more without getting in the way.

The yacht had appeared ahead and rapidly sprouted up from the water until it was right there, a couple hundred yards away, leaving a churned-up wake behind but seeming to stand still compared to Dunbar's boat.

There were more vessels within sight but nothing close enough to cause trouble, and no sign of Domm and the Whaler, just like Dunbar's radar had shown.

He aimed straight for the yacht's stern and through the windshield Bruder saw two men scrambling around, running the stairs from the flybridge to the swimming platform and back.

He smiled, then ducked when a gunshot cracked from the yacht.

It was loud and sharp, the M4 Carbine, and Bruder risked another look and saw Valenti peeking over the stern rail of the salon with the rifle.

Dunbar glanced back at Bruder with the grin tilting across his face.

"You might want to get below!"

Bruder stayed where he was but knelt on the deck behind one of the aft-facing chairs and yelled, "Don't put any holes in that boat!"

Any noticeable damage might lead to the sheikh's men demanding a full inspection before anyone was allowed to leave, and an inspection would reveal the missing gold.

Dunbar gave him a thumbs-up, hardly reassuring.

Valenti fired again and Bruder heard the shot but had no idea where the bullet went, with all of the noise and motion happening around him.

He'd never fired a gun from a moving boat at another moving boat. It was probably the same as shooting at anything—easy if you knew how to compensate for the factors—and Valenti probably had practice.

Then one of the windshield panes grew a ragged hole with cracks spiderwebbing away from it and the sound of the shot rolled over the boat.

"Lucky bastard!" Dunbar yelled. "Rotten son of a bitch cocksucker!"

Hendrick rose and fired two fast shots above the yacht, flat punches that drove Valenti below the stern rail.

The yacht was a hundred yards ahead now and Dunbar moved levers and the boat sprang forward, tapping another reserve of power Bruder didn't know existed.

Dunbar made erratic adjustments to the wheel to keep Valenti guessing.

The hull skipped over some waves and slammed through others, leaving walls of spray behind, and Bruder grabbed the chair in front of him and held on, bracing for impact with the yacht.

Hendrick braced himself in the bow and fired some more, and he either had terrible aim or was using suppressive fire to keep Valenti from sticking his head and M4 back up, because every shot was wide or high.

They were close enough for Bruder to see the interior roof

of the yacht's salon and smell the diesel fumes coming off her, and at the last moment Dunbar peeled off the starboard corner and ran alongside the bigger vessel, near enough for Bruder to step from the rail to the swimming platform if he'd been ready for it, which he wasn't.

He caught a glimpse of Valenti's head popping over the stern rail.

The man watched them blow past, his eyes as wide.

Movement made Bruder look up in time to see the hooked pole catch a vertical post on the yacht's flybridge, then Fulton jumped from Dunbar's flybridge onto the starboard wall of the yacht's, hanging from the pole.

Bruder was too close and low to see if anyone was up there, but Turley had to be.

Dunbar took the boat ahead and cut across the yacht's bow to get away from Valenti and any plans he might have to poke the M4 around the side and start shooting.

Before his view got cut off, Bruder saw Fulton brace his feet against the flybridge's exterior like a mountain climber and pull himself up the pole, then he disappeared over the rail.

Dunbar raced ahead and torqued through a tight turn to go back at the yacht on its port side.

He called to Hendrick, "Get ready!"

Bruder pulled himself up by the chair and tested his right arm again.

It still hurt, but it would have to do.

***

Dunbar moved controls and Bruder heard the engines drop from a roar to a growl.

The yacht plowed toward them and Dunbar leaned his body a fraction of a second before the boat followed, as though he was controlling her by willpower alone, and when the bow closed in on the yacht's swimming platform Hendrick kept scanning with the shotgun and put one foot on the *Hawk's* rail.

Bruder moved to the port side and did the same, only with empty hands and more bandages.

Dunbar was watching Hendrick and didn't catch on until it was too late.

Hendrick judged the speed and distance, his head bobbing, then he hopped over the rail and landed on the swimming platform.

A second later Bruder landed behind him, accompanied by Dunbar yelling, "Hey!"

Hendrick turned and scowled at him but didn't point the shotgun.

"I'll take port," Bruder said and stayed low as he went up the narrow steps toward the salon.

Hendrick went starboard and led with the shotgun, turning sideways to fit up the stairs.

Bruder peeked over the top step and didn't see anything except too many places to wait and hide, and an empty casing from the M4 rolling around.

He dropped back down and yelled, "Valenti! It's Kline! Give it up!"

Maybe his voice and name would be enough to stun Valenti—even Turley, if he was still alive—into surrender.

Nothing happened and no one said anything.

Muffled shouts and a thump came from the flybridge above them.

Bruder leaned back and found Hendrick doing the same, waiting to catch his eye.

"Stay out of the way, asshole."

The voice was lighter than expected but it didn't diminish the point.

Hendrick went into the salon and poked the shotgun into every hiding spot before he got to the corner before the galley and the compact office and stairway heading below.

He said, "Valenti, don't make me come in there for you. Come on, man."

Bruder watched and waited.

After a few seconds Hendrick peeled around the corner and went into the galley.

Bruder pushed to his feet and followed, then stopped when Hendrick yelled, "Coming out!"

"I'm right here," Bruder said.

Hendrick gave him a quick scan and moved around to the office.

He didn't yell at or shoot anyone, then he moved to the side of the opening leading below with a sour look on his face.

Bruder understood—anything could be waiting for him down there, and the most likely candidate was Valenti with all the slack taken out of the trigger.

His jaw muscles rippled and he took a deep breath, then put his foot on the first step down.

"Wait," Bruder said, and Hendrick looked at him.

"How many rounds you got left?"

"Twelve," Hendrick said. "I reloaded."

He spoke loud enough for Valenti to hear it, wherever he was.

Bruder kept his voice lower: "Move back and wait for him to show. I'm going up; maybe Turley can talk him out."

Hendrick frowned, but after a moment's consideration he stepped back and knelt in the galley doorway, protected on both sides with a good view of the stairs.

Bruder turned and, on his way toward the stairs, checked the deck in case Turley had left his Glock there after their scrap.

No luck.

So he went up the steps to the flybridge, empty-handed with no idea what he was going to find.

***

Turley heard Valenti firing the M4 and he looked back to see if it had any effect on Dunbar's boat.

Not so far.

He cursed and went back to the controls, pushing the yacht as fast as she could go.

He didn't care about fuel conservation anymore—it wouldn't matter if they were dead or not in control of the yacht.

When they'd spotted the *Cooper's Hawk* coming at them, Turley had a brief thought about just stopping and turning the yacht over for the fifty grand Dunbar had promised.

But he didn't know if the offer still stood, and once Dunbar was on board it would be too late to negotiate.

So he banished the idea from his mind, because of that and because screw Dunbar and his fifty grand—why take a slice when you could get the whole pie?

He used the cell phone to call Domm, who said, "Hey, buddy."

"Where are you?"

Domm picked up on the tone and may have heard Valenti firing again.

"At the marina, filling up. What's happening? What's wrong?"

"We got Dunbar on us."

"Ahh, shit!"

"You need to get out here!"

"Uh, hold on…it took me, what, forty minutes to get here, but I wasn't in a huge hurry. But it sounds like you're hauling ass, are you going south?"

"Domm!"

"Shit, okay, I'll be there as soon as I can! They got the fucking no wake zone here!"

Turley said, "Call me when you're moving, I'll give you

the coordinates."

He hung up on whatever Domm said in reply and tossed the phone into a console cubby.

When he turned to look for Dunbar his stomach twisted—the other boat was right *there*, chewing up the yacht's wake, and he could see Hendrick crouched in the bow with a mean-looking gun.

Some idiot, maybe Fulton, was on the flybridge dancing with a long boat hook, pounding his chest and pointing at Turley like something out of a *Mad Max* flick.

Turley flinched when Valenti fired again and he thought he saw Dunbar's windshield take the bullet, then the *Hawk* shot forward and swooped to his starboard side.

Turley went hard to port but Dunbar stuck with him, and Turley was stretching up over the console and looking down at the bow as the *Hawk* cut across, making Turley spin to starboard out of reflex and he didn't hear Fulton until the man clambered over the rail and spilled onto the flybridge deck.

Turley went for him and Fulton came up swinging, leading with an uppercut that started at the deck and nearly took Turley's head off.

He felt the breeze as he leaned back and the gloved fist zipped past his face, then he dove in with a hard left and felt the Kevlar take the blow.

"Cheater!"

Fulton laughed and jabbed with his left.

With his right, he reached for the .45 strapped to his chest.

Turley pounced again and used his size to pin Fulton's hand against the vest, ignoring the short, ineffective punches from the other hand.

He lifted the kid off his feet and dumped him on the deck, landing with his full weight and crowing with delight when he heard the air rush out of Fulton's lungs.

He slammed his forehead into Fulton's nose and mouth

a few times, knocking a mouthpiece loose, and only stopped when he felt blood on his face though he didn't know whose it was.

Fulton had gone slack and Turley rose up, bringing the .45 with him. He hesitated, thinking about putting a hole in the deck of the flybridge, and that was enough time for Fulton to recover and slap his hands around Turley's gun wrist.

Fulton shoved the arm up and Turley fired out over the water, his finger twitching on the trigger again and again as he tried to bring the arm back down.

Turley heard people shouting below and realized he'd been tunneled in on Fulton. He wondered if Valenti had been firing the whole time, then he tried punching Fulton in the ribs with his left hand and hit the Kevlar again.

"Fucker!"

Turley looked up at the console where his pistol was, too far away to reach, then in a moment of clarity he remembered the Glock stuck in his waistband, the one he'd taken off Kline.

He quit thumping the Kevlar and used his left hand to fumble the pistol out. It was upside-down in his hand and he worked to flip it around and almost had it, his finger snaking into the trigger guard, when a large hand clamped over his like a shark's mouth.

He looked up into the grim face of Kline, who was supposed to be crab food somewhere between Captiva and Naples.

Turley had enough time to say, "Oh—"

Then Kline's other hand came around in a fist shaped like a brick and Turley's world went black.

***

Bruder plucked the Glock 19 out of Turley's floppy hand and stuck it in his belt, then held his torso up while Fulton reclaimed his .45.

He ignored the pain streaking from his right shoulder and side while he dragged Turley across the deck and used the last zip-tie from his pocket to secure his wrists behind his back.

Bruder left him face-down near the Jacuzzi.

He asked Fulton, "Can you steer this thing?"

Fulton lifted his safety goggles onto his forehead and blew blood and snot out of his nose over the rail.

"Yeah, I can."

"Keep us going. Domm's out here somewhere."

Fulton looked over at Turley and shook his head.

"Bastard's stronger than he looks. Thanks for the help."

He stepped to the helm and waved down at Dunbar, who was still circling the yacht.

Bruder called over the stern rail to Hendrick in the salon, "Tell Valenti Turley's done. It's just him left, give it up."

He heard Hendrick relaying the message to Valenti, wherever he'd stowed himself, then had a thought and yanked the radio off Turley's belt and pulled the earpiece out from under his shirt.

He stuck the bud in his ear and keyed the mic.

"Valenti, it's Kline. You hear Hendrick?"

There was nothing for a moment, then Valenti said, "If I'm talking to you, Turley must be dead."

He sounded disappointed, but not frightened. The hum from the yacht's engines was louder from his end and Bruder placed him in the stern cabin.

"Not yet," Bruder said, "Don't make us come find you."

"Yeah, okay. I'm coming up."

"Hold on."

Bruder went down the stairs to the salon.

He passed the couch and saw blood on the cushion, realizing it was his from the gunshot wound in his side.

He made a note to do something about it when this was over, moved on and stood around the corner of the galley, close to the stairs going below but protected.

Hendrick was still in the galley, watching the stairs.

Bruder told him, "Be ready."

Then he hit the mic.

"Valenti. Push the rifle out of the stairway, butt-first."

"Okay, give me a minute."

Bruder watched the stairs over the sights of the Glock and waited.

Hendrick whispered, "Is he coming or not?"

Bruder told the radio, "Valenti, let's go."

"I'm coming up the stairs now."

"Rifle first."

Bruder let the mic switch go and wrapped both hands around the Glock.

His right arm started to shake from the effort of holding the gun up.

They waited another ten seconds and Bruder was reaching for the mic again when he caught movement to the right.

He turned and saw the edge of the fiberglass hatch to the engine room rising on the far side of the salon's stern rail.

Bruder yelled to Hendrick, "He's there!"

They both ran to the rear of the salon in time to see Valenti slide off the swimming platform in a small inflatable life raft, the sort that expands instantly with the pull of a cord.

He had the M4 trained on the salon and opened fire and Hendrick went down.

Bruder caught the spray of blood and dropped with him as more bullets smacked into the ceiling.

He had no way to communicate with Fulton or Dunbar, but Dunbar had to see the life raft. A moment later the sound of the M4 changed and Bruder peered through the stairway opening and saw Valenti firing at Dunbar's boat a couple hundred yards off the yacht's port side.

He was taking his time, placing his shots, and Dunbar veered away.

The life raft was drifting back rapidly.

Bruder yanked the Street Sweeper from beneath Hendrick's body and braced it on the stern rail, but the engine room hatch was in his way.

He went from kneeling to a crouch and rose, bit by bit, until he could see the raft beyond the barrel.

He didn't know if the loads were slugs or shot—he'd find out the same time as Valenti.

He pulled the trigger once and the shotgun kicked and pain exploded on the right side of his body.

Black spots appeared and expanded across his vision, but he thought he saw a small geyser of water sprout in front of the life raft.

Despite the pain Bruder was pleased—he had slugs.

He switched the Sweeper to his left hand and shoulder and aimed higher, feeling awkward but not completely unfamiliar because of the off-hand training he did. He was ready to squeeze and hold the trigger until Valenti and the raft were both leaking but froze when he heard a thump and running steps above his head.

A body flew over the stern rail of the flybridge and plummeted in front of him, hitting the water twenty feet behind the yacht.

It stayed below the surface as the life raft grew smaller.

Bruder yelled, "Fulton!"

No answer.

If that was Fulton in the water, Turley was loose on the yacht again.

Bruder clenched his teeth and braced the shotgun again, only to be driven down by a round from the M4 thumping into the fiberglass above his head.

If Turley came down the stairs, he'd have a clean shot at Bruder pinned behind the stern wall.

So Bruder made the decision and stood up, firing three quick shots from the Sweeper toward Valenti, then ran up the stairs to the flybridge, ready to blow Turley in half.

***

Bruder went up the curving stairway and dove next to the Jacuzzi, hoping the couch along the stern was enough to block him from Valenti's sights.

Fulton was sprawled on the deck near the helm.

Which put Turley in the water.

Bruder turned and risked a glance over the couch.

Turley was on his back, kicking his legs to propel himself toward the raft.

His hands were still zip-tied behind him but he didn't seem panicked about it.

Bruder eased the shotgun barrel over the back of the couch and the cushion to his right erupted in scraps of foam stuffing.

The crack from the M4 arrived a split-second later and Bruder got on the other side of the Jacuzzi.

He checked the Sweeper's drum and found eight shots left and tried to recall how many times Valenti had fired.

He didn't know for sure, but the thirty-round magazine was still half full, at least, and Valenti knew how to shoot.

The yacht cruised on at full speed, putting more distance between the two groups with every second.

Pretty soon, the shotgun would be worthless while the M4 would still be lethal.

He had the Glock and Fulton had the .45, both just as useless at long range.

"Fulton! Turn us around!"

Fulton groaned and rolled onto his stomach.

Another engine sound rose from the starboard side and Bruder risked a look and saw Dunbar next to the yacht, skipping over the waves.

He waved his hand forward.

"Keep going! You're clear ahead!"

Bruder told him, "Go back and kill those two!"

Dunbar shook his head.

"He's got range on me! We got the yacht, fuck 'em, let 'em float away!"

Bruder fumed.

He didn't want to yell back and forth about how Turley and Valenti and Domm—once he showed up—knew about the meet at the Dry Tortugas and might screw everything up again.

Those three had made it clear they wanted the man they knew as Kline dead, and Bruder knew he wouldn't relax until that threat was gone.

He peered over the Jacuzzi.

The life raft was just a yellow spot about the size of a penny now, and Valenti was pulling Turley over the side.

He told Dunbar, "They killed Hendrick!"

Maybe that would change his mind.

Dunbar looked stricken, but he recovered quickly and shrugged.

"He knew the deal. Where's Fulton?"

Bruder looked at the dwindling raft again and decided the shooting was done.

He went over and thumped Fulton in the ribs with his boot.

"You're bad at this. Get up."

Fulton pushed onto his hands and knees and spat blood onto the deck.

Bruder shook his head.

The kid was nothing but mistakes and blood.

Dunbar yelled up, "How's the fuel?"

Bruder looked at the console until he found the gauge with a fuel symbol.

"Half!"

"Good—we go another ten miles, then stop. You need to show me the gold."

CHAPTER FOURTEEN

Both boats dropped anchor and Dunbar took a small inflatable dinghy from the *Hawk* to the yacht.

Bruder met him on the swimming platform, where he and Fulton had carried Hendrick's body.

Dunbar looked down at the mess made by Valenti and the M4.

"Damn shame. It was fast though, huh?"

"He was dead before he landed," Bruder said.

"Well that's good, I guess."

He looked up at Fulton, who leaned on the salon rail with toilet paper sticking out of his nose.

"I got brought some chain over, weigh him down and we'll let him go."

"Okay."

Dunbar said, "Who busted you up, kid? Turley?"

Fulton nodded.

Dunbar glanced north but there was nothing behind them but water rising and falling.

He told Fulton, "Keep an eye out for their Whaler. I highly doubt they'll come around, but Turley's as dumb as he is tough."

Bruder saw what he was doing, pumping Turley up a bit to let Fulton feel better about getting his ass handed to him, and he approved.

He also didn't see any point in mentioning it happened twice.

He said, "Where are we right now?"

Dunbar pointed off the port side toward the rising sun.

"About twenty miles that way is the southern tip of Florida, the Everglades National Park."

He turned ninety degrees and pointed south.

"Big Pine Key, thirty...five miles or so."

"We're safe stopping here?"

"Until and unless."

Bruder frowned.

"Until and unless what?"

"Somebody shows up on the horizon."

Bruder didn't like it, but there was nothing he could do about it.

Dunbar said, "Okay. Let's see the booty."

***

Bruder put one knee on the bed in the aft cabin and opened the hinged panel.

The unlocked steel door eased ajar, following the panel, and Bruder pushed it all the way open and stepped back.

Dunbar pursed his lips and let his eyes wander over the stacks of gold bars.

"My my," he said. "That's three million dollars' worth of gold, huh?"

"It would be, if not for this."

Bruder pulled one of the bars out and showed it to him.

"Custom made. It would take about two seconds for a dealer to flag them."

"Depends on the dealer," Dunbar said. "May I?"

Bruder handed him the bar and Dunbar ran his thumb

over the image of a man's face and the Arabic letters.

"Oh, shit. This is the sheikh—it's his face on these."

"Yeah, I figured," Bruder said.

"Well, no wonder he wants them back. You think he'd pay full price to get them?"

Bruder shook his head and took the bar and put it back on the hidden shelf.

"Not worth the risk. We make the split and get what we can for them. I know a guy who can melt them down, if you need it."

Dunbar's voice was distracted while he gazed at the bars: "Nah, I got my own guy, but thanks."

"We'll do it three ways, with Hendrick gone. A hundred bars each."

"Mm-hm. Well, you get your third. Fulton gets one quarter of my two-thirds, being the junior member."

"That's between you and him," Bruder said.

Dunbar crossed his arms and reached up to tug on his bottom lip.

"And you're not worried about catching hell for taking this?"

"It won't be a problem," Bruder said.

"Because I'm wondering, if we keep the gold *and* sell the yacht...my man, that's a payday right there. That puts me in the black for years."

"Stop wondering," Bruder said. "The only way we keep the gold is if we deliver the yacht as expected. Nobody can trace the gold to us unless we're stupid about it. This boat, on the other hand..."

"Yeah, I see it."

Dunbar was disappointed but not dumb.

They shook hands on the deal and Bruder closed the steel door and panel.

They climbed up to the salon and found Fulton waiting for them.

"He's ready."

***

Hendrick's body was on the swimming platform with a chain wrapped around the midsection and a few diving weights attached to the chain.

"I found the weights in there," Fulton said, pointing at the scuba gear just inside open the hatch.

Then he pointed at a money clip and knife and phone on the deck near the opening.

"That's all he had in his pockets. I thought about poking some holes in him, you know, so he doesn't gas up and float, but I think he's got enough already."

Dunbar nodded.

Fulton said, "I didn't count the cash, but he has some cards and an ID stuck in there. Did you know his real name is Bordeaux?"

"No it isn't," Dunbar said. "Anybody want to say anything?"

Bruder was silent and Fulton just shrugged.

Dunbar looked down at the body and said, "You were a hard worker, and I never had to explain anything to you twice. You, uh...you knew how to get things done."

He paused and looked out at the water like he was waiting to see if anything else came to him.

"Okay, then."

He and Fulton heaved the body over the side and Bruder caught a glimpse of the bottom of the big man's feet before he disappeared.

They all watched the water for a moment—Dunbar and Fulton looking down while Bruder scanned the horizon—then Fulton used a bucket to scoop some water and rinse the blood off the swimming platform.

Bruder assumed some of it was his from the shoulder wound and was glad to see it go.

He asked Dunbar, "How long until we can get to the Dry Tortugas?"

Dunbar turned his face to the west and seemed to sniff the air.

"Five hours, give or take."

"Give or take what?"

"An hour. It's the ocean, man."

"We don't need more fuel?"

"Shouldn't."

Bruder shook his head.

He was done with all of these mystic variables of the sea.

And he still didn't like the idea of Turley and his crew out there, knowing where the rendezvous was supposed to happen.

He said, "What if we change the site for the meet? You can do a spot out in the open water, right? Just some coordinates?"

Dunbar shrugged.

"Sure. As long as the other crew has the same info."

Bruder pointed at Hendrick's phone.

"Is that thing clean?"

"I bought it yesterday," Dunbar said. "It's clean."

Bruder picked it up.

Fulton stowed the bucket and said, "So is somebody gonna tell me the deal with that gold?"

"You're looking at a share of about five hundred large," Dunbar told him.

"For real?"

"Have I ever lied to you about money?"

Fulton said, "So, that's with us selling the yacht?"

"No," Dunbar said. "Forget the yacht."

He nodded at Bruder, like he deserved credit for honoring their deal.

Fulton said, "Wait, so that's just money from the gold?"

Bruder cut in.

"Yes, dammit. Now get moving."

Fulton got into the dinghy and Dunbar pushed him off

toward the *Hawk* so he could trail the yacht and keep an eye out for trouble.

Before he started the small motor Fulton said, "Wait, can I see the gold before I go?"

Bruder and Dunbar both said, "No."

***

After Valenti hauled Turley over the side of the life raft, sputtering and coughing, Valenti picked the M4 up again and aimed at the yacht.

It was a few hundred yards away and he could still hit it, but with the raft bobbing and the yacht doing its own thing, he'd be extremely lucky to hit Kline up on the flybridge.

He tracked over to Dunbar, zipping around on his jacked-up Scout, and knew that would be a waste of ammunition too.

Dunbar took his boat alongside the yacht and Valenti waited for one or both of them to turn and come back around toward the raft, but they kept pushing south.

Turley said, "Shit," and spat over the side to work the salt water out of his mouth.

The raft was made for four normal-sized people to huddle together. With Turley splayed out and Valenti leaning on the inflated wall with the rifle, it was a tight fit.

Turley said, "Little help here?"

He rolled to the right so Valenti could slice the zip ties.

When his hands were free Turley touched his jaw, where a nasty-looking bruise was starting to purple.

"Goddam Kline. Tell me you still have that phone."

Valenti pulled it out of his pocket.

Turley called the only number in the recents list.

Domm answered with, "Where the hell are you guys?"

Turley could hear the Whaler's engines singing in the background.

"We're in a goddam yellow life raft, about the size of a kiddie pool."

"Huh?"

"Just head back out to the line we were on, about twenty miles out, and come south."

"What the hell happened?"

"Just get here!"

Turley killed the call and almost threw the phone off the boat, then collected himself and gave it back to Valenti, who said, "I'm pretty sure I hit Hendrick."

"Good. I beat the hell out of Fulton but he's too stupid to be hurt for long. Fucking Dunbar. Fucking Kline."

Valenti let him seethe for a while, then said, "So when Domm gets here...what then?"

Turley said, "What the hell do you think?"

PART FOUR

CHAPTER FIFTEEN

Dunbar got the yacht underway and Bruder took Hendrick's phone into the salon and eased onto the couch next to his bloodstain.

His right side hurt from hip to ear, and when he checked the dressings he found blood seeping through both but nothing leaking beyond the tape, so he left them alone.

He looked at the salon's ceiling above the aft opening and the holes from Valenti's suppressive fire. The ceiling was made of narrow, smooth fiberglass planks, cream colored, and there were four holes spread across two of the planks.

He turned, grimacing from the pain, and moved couch pillows around looking for holes from when Turley shot at him. There were three he could see and he set the pillows over them, poking and squeezing until the holes in the pillows were hidden as well.

Good enough.

He knew there were at least two more holes in the boat: in the stern fiberglass below the rail, and the couch on the flybridge.

Maybe Dunbar knew how to cover them up.

Not permanently, just enough for him to hand the boat over and cruise away without any of the sheikh's people pointing them out.

As for his blood on the couch cushion…

He frowned at it.

The spatter was all on the bottom cushion and took up an area about the size of a dinner plate. The drops were dry and maroon with the smallest among them starting to brown.

His DNA wasn't on file anywhere as far as he knew and he doubted the sheikh would bother to have it sampled and analyzed—more likely he'd just have the couch replaced—but Bruder didn't like the idea of McIntyre having access to it, even if he didn't know whose it was.

He picked at one of the spots with a fingernail and it flaked, leaving a faint shadow behind that might disappear with a wet cloth.

He looked at the fabric with new appreciation—it was some sort of water-resistant marine material—then lifted the phone and dialed McIntyre's number.

Penza answered.

"Yes?"

"It's me," Bruder said.

"Hold on."

McIntyre said, "How soon?"

He was all business now that authorities were out looking for the yacht. He probably had the sheikh hounding him, maybe even people from the Lab asking if he knew anything about what was happening.

Bruder told him, "We're changing the location. The Dry Tortugas are out."

"Tell me why."

He didn't want to get into the whole Turley/Dunbar thing, so Bruder just said, "We need to pick a different spot. It's not secure."

"According to whom?"

"Me."

"Well, your information is wrong. We've been monitoring law enforcement activities from Key West to the Dry Tortugas and they aren't on alert. There is a storm coming through, but you'll just have to deal with it."

"Pick a different spot," Bruder said through his teeth.

"I don't expect you to care, but you should at least acknowledge how much work and planning has gone into this prior to your involvement. You telling me to pick a different spot would be like a janitor telling Houston to pick a different moon when the rocket is already in flight. The expectation is you will meet the recipients at the Dry Tortugas, and that expectation will be fulfilled. Now I ask you again: How soon?"

Bruder managed to keep his temper by squeezing the phone like it was McIntyre's windpipe.

"Five hours."

"That's too long."

"I agree. Let's pick someplace closer, and sooner."

The phone was silent while McIntyre processed it.

"Five hours it is. I'll tell the people who will meet you. Call me when you're sixty minutes out."

"Right."

"A man was found along the shore of Longboat Key."

Bruder waited for more information.

"Apparently," McIntyre said, "he was a security contractor tasked with protecting the yacht."

"Is that so?"

"Before he was found, there was some speculation about him being involved with the theft. But now he's told the authorities about four masked men who stole the yacht and were preparing to execute him when one of the men threw him overboard."

Again, Bruder waited.

Ted had made it, which was fine with him.

McIntyre said, "What do you have to say about this?"

"Did he say where the boat was going?"

"If he did, it hasn't been conveyed to my sources."

"I guess that's good."

"Good? It is far from good. Who let him live?"

"I'll ask around," Bruder said and ended the call.

***

Turley and Valenti bobbed around in the open Gulf waters for over an hour before Domm spotted them.

They watched the Whaler a mile away, vectoring around on some grid only Domm could see, and they waved and hollered and Turley yelled worthless directions through the phone and wanted to shoot the M4 as a signal but Valenti talked him down from that ledge.

When the boat suddenly pointed straight at them and they could see the white spray blasting off the hull, they relaxed and waited. Even though it was still before nine in the morning the sun was already pressing down on them, and the salt water Turley had swallowed combined with the yelling had left his throat raw and voice hoarse.

Domm cut the throttles back when he was a hundred yards out and idled the rest of the way, swinging the starboard side toward the raft.

He pulled Turley up first, then Valenti, then hauled the raft on top of the fuel bladder on the stern deck and found the valve to start it deflating.

He didn't say anything while Turley and Valenti drank a bottle of water each.

Turley was reaching for another when Domm finally said, "So, anybody wanna fill me in?"

"Well," Turley said, "Kline is still alive."

Domm gaped.

"What? How do you know?"

"Because he helped Dunbar take the boat."

They gave him the quick version about the attack, and

Kline being alive and still an asshole, and how they got away.

It would have been a fun story to tell if it didn't end with them losing the yacht.

So far, anyway.

When they got the yacht back, Turley knew, this would be a legendary tale told for years over drinks and crab legs.

Domm shook his head and said, "Dunbar and Kline, working together, huh? Pricks. What do you think they'll do?"

Turley sat in the captain's chair and gave a sour look at the console with its chipped corners and faded varnish.

It was his boat, yeah, but it wasn't the yacht.

"Turley," Valenti said.

"I know, shut up."

To Domm, he said, "We talked about it on the raft—we had a lot of time to talk, thanks to you—and I can't see Kline giving up on delivering it to the sheikh's people."

"Dunbar said he has a two-million-dollar fish on the line," Domm said.

"Doesn't matter. Not to a guy like Kline."

Domm nodded and said, "That's exactly what he told me, when we were coming back from the meet with Dunbar. That it didn't matter how much the payout was, he was doing the job."

Turley was chuffed by this validation of his theory.

Valenti said, "I don't buy it. If he isn't swayed by the money, Dunbar and Fulton will just kill him or throw him overboard and go find their buyer."

Domm said, "What about Hendrick?"

"Valenti thinks he shot him," Turley said. "From the raft, too."

"Oh yeah? Nice."

Turley went back to Valenti's point: "I hear you about Dunbar; he's ruthless when it comes to money. But look—I shot Kline twice, I think, maybe more than that. He left blood all over the couch and the swimming platform, then jumped off the yacht in the middle of the night. Domm, you couldn't find him. The next thing I know, he's grabbing my wrist like a goddam vice and I wake up with my hands zip-tied behind me."

"So, what," Valenti said, "he's going to scare Dunbar into missing out on the two million?"

"That, or kill him. I'm telling you man, Kline's some kind of savage cyborg. So however they work it out, the yacht is headed for the Dry Tortugas. We'll find it there or somewhere along the way. My only question is, will it be a ghost ship, or will Kline be the lone survivor, up there trying to figure out how to steer a ninety-foot yacht?"

He looked at the unopened bottle of water in his hand, then put it back in the ice chest and pulled out a beer instead.

"And either way, it don't matter. We're taking that damn yacht back, wherever we find it."

***

After the phone call Bruder went into the galley, where he'd seen club soda in one of the cabinets, and used it to scrub his blood off the couch cushion.

Again, he was impressed. The liquid didn't penetrate beyond the surface, and though it left a dark wet spot on the fabric the blood seemed to be gone.

He'd check it after it dried.

If the blood was still there he'd douse the cushion in diesel fuel, set it on fire, and throw it overboard.

And if anybody asked him where it went, he'd just shrug.

He yelled at Dunbar to come down from the flybridge and pointed at the holes in the fiberglass ceiling planks.

"What can you do about those?"

Dunbar looked up. The holes were small but had ragged edges with fine splinters like tiny shark's teeth.

He said, "As in, fix them?"

"Right."

Dunbar made a show of patting his pockets.

"You know what? I left my spackle in my other shorts."

"There isn't some sailor's trick for plugging holes?"

"Yeah, the trick is, don't get any holes in your boat."

Bruder looked at him, unamused, and Dunbar went on: "I mean, there are ways to keep water from coming in through the hull, but as far as this sort of thing, like finish carpentry...nah."

"Fine. What's on the police scanner?"

"Nothing."

"Nothing?"

"The model you guys brought on board has a range of about twenty-five miles, and we're running thirty-five north of the Keys, which is as close as I want to get. The one on my boat has a longer range but Fulton hasn't said anything about it, so it must be nothing. And unless they're talking about us in the Keys, we won't hear anything useful."

"So we're deaf and blind, unless something shows up on the horizon or we happen to move within range of someone talking about us."

"Pretty much," Dunbar said. "But cheer up—everybody else out here is just as deaf and blind as us. Well, except the Coast Guard and Navy."

He climbed the stairs to the flybridge and a few moments later the stereo came on.

Dunbar sang along, loud enough to be heard over the speakers, and Bruder shook his head and went below.

He went through the cabin where Ted had been trussed up and into the bathroom.

In his search for the stash he'd seen a stack of tiny, wrapped bars of soap in one of the drawers and he carried four of them topside, then used his knife to slice chunks and slivers off, working them with his fingers and thumb and shoving them into the bullet holes when they were soft enough.

He scraped and smoothed and stepped back to look at the ceiling.

In the right light—preferably zero—it would work.

He did the same to the hole below the stern rail but didn't bother trying to do anything with the couch on the flybridge other than putting a pillow over the hole in the cushion.

When all that was done his side and shoulder were griping enough to force him back to the galley, where he raided the first aid kit and swallowed a thousand milligrams of Ibuprofen and checked in on the couch cushion.

It was nearly dry, leaving no trace of his blood behind.

He welcomed the good news and went below to collect the gold.

***

While Turley finished the beer and looked at charts and maps Domm topped off the Whaler's fuel from the replenished bladder.

He hadn't used much during the crazed search from the station to the life raft, but it was better to do it now before things got unpredictable again.

Valenti tightened straps and made sure nothing was going to shift around and cause trouble.

He asked Turley, "Straight to the islands?"

Turley frowned at one of the maps and shoved it aside.

"Yeah. I don't see any point in trying to find them out here. They're limited by the max speed of the yacht, but even if we track them down they got Dunbar's *Hawk*. Whoever's on that can buzz around us like a hornet."

"I got the M4," Valenti said. "Sixteen rounds left."

"And they got the Street Sweeper, and the pistols, and whatever else Dunbar has that we don't know about. Nah. We go where we know they're going. We just need to get there first."

When everything was set he pointed the Whaler a few

degrees south of west and pushed the throttles until they were skipping across the waves at forty-four knots, just shy of fifty miles per hour.

The boat got less than a mile per gallon at that speed but Turley didn't care.

Valenti and Domm held on to whatever was within reach, their shirts snapping in the wind, and watched the horizon to the south.

After fifteen minutes Domm yelled and pointed at something, a gray shape on the edge of the water that could have been the yacht, so Turley veered west until the shape disappeared.

Then he got back on course for the Dry Tortugas, knowing they would get there first.

***

Bruder had six pillowcases from a stack of linens in the master cabin's closet.

He figured the three hundred bars totaled about one hundred ninety pounds and didn't trust the pillowcases to carry more than thirty pounds each, if that.

Before he started pulling and counting he stood next to the bed and looked at the golden stacks inside the hidden panel.

He wanted to make sure he was seeing all the angles and outcomes with a clear head.

To do so, he projected the worst possible scenario and weighed it against the benefit of the gold.

He played it out in his head:

The worst possible scenario would be the sheikh and McIntyre showing up to take ownership of the yacht and both of them heading straight for the hidden panel to ensure its integrity.

That, Bruder knew, was so unlikely it shouldn't be considered.

The sheikh wouldn't venture into U.S. waters and risk getting snatched up, and McIntyre's whole world was built around paying and leveraging other people to do this sort of work for him.

So that was out, Bruder decided.

He ran through what he saw as the worst, yet still probable, outcome: The sheikh's people hand over the cash and take the yacht and sail away, probably back to Cuba.

Somewhere along the way, they notice the bullet holes or the sheikh orders one of his men to make sure the safe is secure.

If it's the bullet holes, it's only a matter of time before someone thinks to check the safe.

If the man has a key, which Bruder assumed he would based on worst-case outcomes, the missing gold is discovered.

The sheikh calls McIntyre screaming about shootouts and thievery and demands the return of his gold and probably someone's head on a pike.

McIntyre has no idea what he's talking about but promises satisfaction.

He calls Bruder to find out what the hell is going on, but Hendrick's phone is at the bottom of the ocean somewhere between the Dry Tortugas and Key West.

Then what does he do?

Reassure the sheikh it must have been the United States government who confiscated the gold?

That would be ideal—redirect the ire away from Bruder, and if McIntyre ever happened to find him again, Bruder would simply deny any knowledge of the gold.

But he wasn't searching for ideals.

He figured McIntyre would seethe about the possible cross and send his hunters after Lola and Kershaw and Gator, and, of course, Bruder.

That would be the worst case.

And the question was, was it worth almost nine hundred thousand dollars in gold?

Then he caught himself.

He couldn't be thinking clearly—maybe it was the gunshot wounds or being stuck on a goddam boat for so long.

In looking at worst-case scenarios, he'd skipped right over the most likely outcome.

He was assuming McIntyre planned on letting him walk away from this in the first place.

Bruder shook his head for being a damn fool and started counting bars.

CHAPTER SIXTEEN

When all the gold was out Bruder closed the metal door and spent five minutes re-locking it.

His right shoulder didn't like the position and he had to grit his teeth through it, sweating while he moved the tiny paperclips around.

When the lock finally turned he shut the silk panel and nudged the pillows around and tugged the blankets until his tracks were gone, then carried the sacks up in twos, using just his left hand, and set them in front of the refurbished salon couch.

After the last pair he went up to the flybridge and found Dunbar tilted back in the captain's chair with his mouth open.

"Wake up."

"I'm not sleeping," Dunbar said, "just relaxing. You should try it."

"How long to the islands?"

Dunbar grinned like Bruder had stepped into some trap he'd set, then said, "Two hours. We're just past Key West, over there to the south."

Bruder looked and didn't see anything except Fulton and

the *Hawk* a few hundred yards away.

"How much do you trust him?"

Dunbar said, "Who, Fulton? He's solid. Why?"

"If we move the gold onto that boat now, will he start thinking about how much faster he is?"

Dunbar frowned, like the thought of Fulton running off with the gold had never crossed his mind.

"Nah. I mean…nah. He wouldn't do it. I don't believe he'd even consider it."

"Why not?"

"He's just a dumb kid."

"You're not convincing me," Bruder said.

"Well, he knows I'd find him and kill him."

"Dumb people think they can disappear if they have enough money."

Dunbar gazed over at the *Hawk* and had an epiphany.

"Oh, I know where his mother lives. He'd probably assume I'd go after her to track him down."

"Would you?"

"I mean…I'd go ask her. Maybe talk tough, but I don't think I'd do any lasting damage. She's a sweet old lady."

"So he knows you'd go light on her."

"Yeah, maybe," Dunbar said.

He sounded discouraged by his own morals, then brightened, saying, "But I guarantee he'd assume you'd kill her. So yeah, if he thinks it through…he takes the gold, I tell you where his mom lives, you give her a hard time…he decides not to take the gold. But again, I don't think it crosses his mind in the first place."

"Call him in," Bruder said.

***

They moved the sacks of gold from the sheikh's yacht to the *Cooper's Hawk* and Fulton stowed them below.

Bruder watched him for any sign of mischief, a gleam in

his eyes, but saw nothing.

Dunbar was right—he was just a dumb kid who did what he was told and had a good time doing it.

Bruder decided he'd work with Fulton again if the opportunity came around.

He collected the remaining shells for the Street Sweeper, another two dozen to give him thirty-two total, and figured if he needed more than that he would officially be at war.

Dunbar sent the *Hawk* away again and Bruder said, "We're still two hours away from the rendezvous?"

"Unless they shrank the ocean while we've been stopped, yeah."

"Close enough," Bruder said.

"For what?"

But Bruder ignored him and went to the rear of the flybridge and called McIntyre.

Penza answered.

"Yes?"

"Hurry up," Bruder said.

"Hold on, prick."

McIntyre came on: "You're making good time."

"We're two hours away. Where are we meeting these people, and how are they handing over the money?"

McIntyre was quiet for a moment.

"We agreed you'd call at one hour out."

"I feel a tailwind picking up, we'll be fine. Here's how it will go: We stay on the yacht until the sheikh's people come along the starboard side and hand over the money. If it looks good, we exit the port side onto our boat and we're gone. Whatever happens to the yacht after that is up to sheikh."

"That's what you and Mr. Turley devised?"

"Sure."

"Put him on the phone."

"Why?"

"Because you don't know a damn thing about boats and

water and I need information about those things to identify a meeting location."

Bruder thought about it and decided there wasn't a logical reason not to fill McIntyre in.

"Turley isn't on the yacht anymore."

"What did you say?"

"We had a disagreement, he's not here."

McIntyre was silent, processing it, then said, "What about the others? Mr. Valenti and Mr. Domm?"

"They aren't here either."

"Well this...this is unacceptable!"

Bruder just waited.

McIntyre said, "What the hell are you trying to pull?"

"Nothing. I'm trying to deliver this goddam yacht, like we agreed."

"*You're* steering it?"

"No."

"Then who is?"

"I found somebody else."

McIntyre made some noises, starting and stopping, too flabbergasted to finish any of them.

Bruder told him, "This doesn't change anything on your end. The money's the same and the delivery is the same. You need to know a good place to meet?"

"That's what I said, yes."

Now he was somewhat back in control of himself and trying to make up for the lost ground.

Bruder pressed the phone against his chest and called to Dunbar, "Where's a good place to do the meet?"

Dunbar had been eavesdropping, amused by Bruder's end of the whole thing, and he started rattling off coordinates.

Bruder interrupted him.

"Just write it down."

McIntyre's voice barked against Bruder's chest: "Who is that? Who are you speaking to?"

Bruder ignored him.

Dunbar handed over a slip of notebook paper and Bruder recited the information into the phone, then said, "You get all that?"

"Be quiet," McIntyre snapped.

Bruder could hear mumbling. He pictured the three of them, McIntyre and Penza and Reed, bent over maps spread on the low table inside the Miami suite.

When McIntyre came back on he said, "That's north of the Dry Tortugas."

"Okay."

"You need to be south."

"Well why the hell didn't you say so?"

"Put whoever you're working with on the goddam phone!"

Bruder told Dunbar, "We need to be south of the islands."

Dunbar shook his head and consulted the yacht's maps and charts, then gave Bruder another slip of paper.

They went through the routine again.

After a while McIntyre said, his voice chilly, "I'll share this information with the right people and call you back with confirmation or rejection."

"Tell them about the procedure for when we meet," Bruder said.

"No, I'll ask them what they want to do, then tell *you* the procedure. And I *will* talk to whoever is steering the yacht before we end this call."

Bruder ended the call and turned the phone off.

***

It took just under ninety minutes for Turley to get the Whaler north of the Dry Tortugas.

He turned the engines off and gazed south and liked where they were, the top point of a triangle created by the boat, Loggerhead Key to the west, and Garden Key to the east.

The Loggerhead Key Lighthouse was a hazy vertical shape on the horizon that leaped into sharp view when he used the binoculars.

Beyond the island, to the south, he saw a low line of dark clouds and frowned.

The wind was blowing from that direction, getting pushed by the front coming up from the Caribbean.

He hoped it would come apart before it got too close, but if it didn't, everyone out here on a boat would have to deal with it, not just him and his crew, so he panned around and spotted the low bulk of Fort Jefferson on Garden Key.

He'd been to the fort a few times as something to do with women who enjoyed that sort of experience, or tagging along with other women who had the day trip all planned out and wanted him to come after spending the night together.

The large ferry from Key West docked on the south side of the island so he couldn't see it, but he knew it was there and would leave around three in the afternoon with the day-trippers.

He assumed there would be campers staying on the island, staking their claim on the primitive spots with no electricity or water and wandering around the island and fort until sunset, when they were supposed to behave around the campsites.

And there were park rangers stationed at the fort along with service and maintenance people, maybe a dozen total, which Turley knew because his brain couldn't help looking at the hexagon-shaped fortress with its moat and forty-five-foot-high ramparts and thinking about how he would break in or out of the place.

It had started as a naval station to combat Caribbean piracy and was converted into a military prison during the Civil War, and Turley initially had a hard time wrapping his mind around how miserable it was living in what was now a vacation destination.

But the ranger tour guide set it straight pretty quickly, taking them through the arched brick casements and tower bastions and showing them the cisterns—where the residents had survived on rainwater that was hopefully potable after filtering through pillars of sand—and the moat that had filled with human sewage because the tides weren't strong enough to flush the water out.

So for the rest of the tour, Turley thought about how he would have escaped paradise if he'd been one of the poor sons of bitches locked up there.

Now he looked at the fort through the binoculars and knew Dunbar wouldn't be dumb enough to get close to that many people, so he swept the glasses along the horizon further to the east, toward Key West, then back again until he went past Loggerhead Key and was looking almost due west.

Nothing so far.

But he and Valenti and Domm knew the yacht would come into their triangle, sooner or later, and when that happened they'd pick the time to strike.

***

When Bruder put the phone away Dunbar said, "Was that your Lab guy?"

"Yeah."

"Didn't want me to talk to him, huh?"

"You don't need the hassle. Getting south of the islands isn't a problem?"

"Not usually, no, but look here."

Dunbar pointed at a radar screen showing a line of greens and yellows and reds along the bottom edge.

"That," he said, turning and using the same finger to point at a line of dark clouds on the southern horizon, "is that."

"A storm?"

"Might be a squall; I can't see enough of it yet."

"What's the difference?"

Dunbar said, "If it's a storm, we ride it out and can make the handoff if the waves aren't too crazy. If it's a squall, I might want to seek shelter in the anchorage area off Garden Key. Let it pass, then we do the trade."

"Are there any people there?"

"On Garden Key? Yeah, there's a big-ass fort there, tourists, campers..."

"Can they communicate with the rest of the world?"

Dunbar frowned.

"Well, there's no cell reception there...but the rangers might have an emergency line or a satellite phone."

"Rangers?"

"Yeah, park rangers. It's a national park."

"Then forget it. We aren't going near it."

"My man, a squall isn't really negotiable."

"We can't have any eyeballs on the yacht this close to the trade. Once we hand it off, I don't care who sees it."

"But you aren't thinking it through," Dunbar said. "For one thing, if we try to hang around the islands during a squall, there's a decent chance we get shoved onto a reef and the yacht is done for anyway."

"So stay away from the reefs."

"Says the guy who doesn't know shit about boats. And you didn't let me finish—if the storm is bad enough for us to seek shelter, nobody on the island is going to be out on the beach looking around anyway. I'm talking rain, wind, thunder and lightning."

Bruder thought about it.

"You said there's a fort. Can they see us from there?"

"I mean, they might be able to see it's a *boat*, but not any ID numbers or anything. Then we clear out as soon as the weather allows, before anybody is on the beach again."

"This is only if the storm is bad enough."

"Right," Dunbar said. "Well, even if it *might* be bad enough. Because if we wait too long to find out, it'll be too late."

"Goddam ocean," Bruder said.

Dunbar grinned.

"Ain't she a beauty? The other option is, we wait up here until the storm passes, then run south of the islands and do the meet. But that could be hours."

Bruder shook his head.

"No. We get it over with. I told McIntyre two hours."

"Okay. So we cruise on, and if I don't like the look of things, we're ducking into the cove."

"Fine. Tell Fulton. And have him do a sweep ahead."

"For what?"

"Coast Guard. Navy. Turley."

"Turley? His tail is firmly tucked, my friend. I'm not looking forward to the next time I see him, but it won't be today."

"Just tell Fulton," Bruder said.

Dunbar spoke into the radio. They weren't bothering with earpieces anymore and Fulton's voice came back, acknowledging the command, and the *Hawk* pulled ahead, skipping over the waves and sending curtains of spray off the bow.

Bruder looked to the south and the line of clouds edging toward them.

The base along the front was darker gray, almost black, and despite his complete ignorance of nautical things, Bruder knew that wasn't good.

He turned the phone back on, willing McIntyre to call so he could get this damn job over with.

***

"Here we go," Valenti yelled, looking through the binoculars.

"You see it?"

Turley was taking a break from lookout duty, resting his eyes and head in the dim light of the cabin. Kline's punch had done more damage than he'd first realized; when he talked his jaw kicked off to the side and his right ear reverberated like he was underwater.

Turley didn't know how many concussions he'd sustained during his rough and tumble life, but he believed this added one more.

He climbed up the narrow stairs and squinted until he got his sunglasses on, then had to pull them off again when he took the optics from Valenti, who held a karate-chop hand out toward the southeast horizon.

"About a hundred forty degrees, just on the edge."

"Yeah. Yeah, I see it."

The yacht, and Kline, the bastard.

They'd pulled the Whaler further north, expanding the triangle until the Dry Tortugas were about five miles away. After a semi-heated debate, they'd agreed Dunbar and Kline wouldn't sail straight into the islands, instead looping to the north, and if the Whaler stayed put they'd spot the other crew for sure.

It had been the right call.

The yacht was maybe two miles north of the Dry Tortugas, putting it right on the horizon for Turley.

"What about the *Hawk*?" Domm asked. He was laying between the swivel chairs, using the fuel bladder as a pillow.

"No sign so far," Turley said. "But the yacht is just a speck. The *Hawk* would be half a speck, maybe less. Just like us, if anybody on the yacht is looking."

Domm frowned without moving anything else.

"You're sure it's them?"

"It's them," Valenti said.

"Do I need to get up?"

Turley shook his head and brought the optics down, seeing only open, empty water without them.

"Not yet. When we make our move, if the *Hawk* is there and Dunbar and whoever's left of his crew decide to bolt, we let 'em go. Dunbar will get what's coming but it doesn't have to happen today. We care about the yacht, and Kline."

Valenti looked over at him.

"How much do we care about Kline?"

"Yeah," Domm added. "Do we care two-million-dollars' worth? If he bails with Dunbar and leaves the yacht behind, we ain't chasing him, right?"

"He won't leave the yacht," Turley said. "We're gonna have to kill him to take it back."

He brought the binoculars up again and his mouth spread in a wolfish grin beneath them.

"No, let me rephrase that. We *get* to kill him."

Valenti sat at the table inside the pilothouse and hefted the M4. He'd taken an instant liking to the rifle and touched it whenever he could, re-checking the magazine and peering down the sights at gulls while he muttered, "Bang... Bang...Bang."

Now he said, "Those clouds are gonna be trouble."

"For them," Turley said. "It's looking like a squall line to me. Everybody on the yacht will be worried about the south, waiting for the shit to start coming down."

He took his time looking at Valenti and Domm, making sure they were paying attention and fully appreciated his guile.

"When we come in from the north, we'll be on 'em before they know it."

***

When the phone rang at twelve noon Bruder was looking at the lump on the horizon, which was apparently the fort Dunbar had told him about, and the wall of darkness above it stretching east and west as far as he could see.

The sun was almost straight over the yacht, cooking down on them, but he could already feel a cooler breeze getting shoved in front of the storm like a plow pushing snow.

Bruder said, "Yeah."

He expected McIntyre but Penza said, "Stay on the line."

Bruder shook his head at these guys playing power games when no one else was around to care.

McIntyre came on.

"The coordinates you provided are approved. The second set, south of the Dry Tortugas."

"Great."

"At one-thirty you're meeting six gentlemen in a forty-six foot Skater."

"What's that?"

"A boat," McIntyre said, his voice dripping with condescending patience. "It's a powerboat, and will be bright red. I doubt you'll be able to miss it."

"These boys are coming up from Havana?"

"That's my understanding, yes."

"Did anyone mention the storm?"

"As a matter of fact, they did."

He sounded amused now, like he wanted Bruder to make an attempt at changing the rendezvous so he could shut him down.

"It's quite vicious, apparently. But these men expressed no concern—do you have anything to add?"

Bruder didn't take the bait.

It was either possible or not to make the switch and he wasn't the person to decide.

He asked Dunbar, "Ninety minutes from now, you good with the coordinates?"

Dunbar went to the port rail of the flybridge and stared at the dark clouds.

He inhaled the breeze, analyzing it, then looked at some charts showing water depths around the islands, then another map with the rendezvous point marked.

It was about twenty miles due south of the Dry Tortugas, away from any ferry or recreational boat traffic between the islands and the Keys.

McIntyre said, "Well?"

"Be patient, we're working."

Bruder heard McIntyre muttering to Penza, or Reed,

or both.

Something about wanting to strangle somebody.

Finally Dunbar said, "Well, hell. I guess. But I reserve the right to seek shelter if things go completely sideways. You tell him that."

"Tell me what?" McIntyre said.

Bruder said, "We'll be there. Give me the number for the guys on the powerboat."

"Not a chance. You will continue to communicate through me."

"That's moronic."

"It's necessary. You've already proven me correct in your inability to operate without adult supervision. Why on earth would I remove your leash now? *That*, my simple friend, would be moronic."

Bruder chewed the inside of his cheek.

"These guys have the cash?"

"They do. And I'm tempted to have them just hand your share over, since Turley and his men are no longer involved. But I know how important the money is to you."

Bruder hung up on him.

He'd lost count of how many times it had happened but knew McIntyre was keeping track.

CHAPTER SEVENTEEN

The yacht was headed southwest to loop around the Dry Tortugas when the radio crackled and Fulton's voice came through.

Bruder got up from the flybridge couch with the bullet hole in it and grimaced. His shoulder and side were stiffening and didn't want to do anything, let alone quickly, so he worked them through small movements as he walked to the helm.

Dunbar was saying, "Okay, keep in touch."

He put the radio down and looked to the south, where the world had turned into a curtain of black clouds.

His permanent lopsided grin was gone.

Bruder asked, "What did Fulton say?"

"He's just south of the islands and can see the squall line coming at him. The temperature dropped about fifteen degrees on him, which is bad. He's gonna hang there and let me know how it goes."

"And if it gets worse?"

"He can break out of it with the *Hawk*, scoot north and take shelter before the storm catches up to him again. Same with the sheikh's crew in the Skater—it won't be comfortable, but that thing will plow through just fine. We can't do it in this beast. If we get caught in the storm, we're stuck there. And I won't let that happen."

Bruder believed him.

In his experience, when someone as laid-back as Dunbar suddenly got serious, it was wise to pay attention.

Bruder opened his mouth but Dunbar cut him off.

"Before you start barking at me, my decision at that point isn't about saving the yacht or keeping the gold. It's about survival. The sea doesn't give a damn about what we're trying to do. If she gets riled up, the only thing we can do is find a corner and hunker down until she's spent. You can be as grumpy about it as you like, but it won't change anything."

Bruder waited until he was sure Dunbar was done.

"I was going to ask if he saw any sign of Turley."

"Oh. No, he didn't mention that. But everything I said still stands."

"Yeah, I figured."

"So if I make the call to abort, I don't want to hear—"

"Dunbar, shut up about it. You made your point."

"Okay, well…I hope so. And I hope whoever we're meeting has half a brain and won't sit out there waiting for us if shit gets biblical. You can call your guy, right? And he can relay the news?"

"I can call him," Bruder said. "What he does with the information is up to him."

Dunbar shook his head and grumbled, "If they get rolled, nobody's gonna be around to hand the yacht off to, so…It's whatever…I guess I get to keep it…"

Bruder let him stew.

A couple miles to the southeast, the whitewashed light-house on Loggerhead Key stood out like a glowing finger against the storm front.

Dunbar wanted to sweep around the islands rather than cut through, saying he didn't want to drop speed to dodge the reefs or risk running into traffic if the ferry decided to break for Key West before the storm hit.

All Bruder cared about was getting to the rendezvous on time, and Dunbar had assured him they would be there early.

If the storm didn't send them scuttling into the Garden Key anchorage.

He continued to stretch and roll his shoulder and neck and twist and lean his trunk while the yacht cruised on.

The skin around the bullet holes was tight and hot.

He'd checked for any infection and found none, so it was just standard gunshot wound pain. He knew things wouldn't get worse unless he broke them open and started leaking again.

So he worked slowly and deliberately until the sharp pain grew dull and began to throb. He'd take the additional discomfort if it meant more freedom to move.

When the yacht curled due south with the lighthouse off the port side, Dunbar told him, "We'll be there in less than an hour."

"Good."

"I hope they brought fuel. Pushing into this headwind has cost us."

"That's their problem," Bruder said.

Dunbar didn't respond to that, so they stood in silence and watched the black storm grow in front of them like they were sailing toward a landmass of sheer cliffs.

After a while a speck appeared at the base and Dunbar stood up.

"Give me the binoculars."

"You have them."

He looked down at his chest and brought them up.

"Shit."

"What?"

Fulton's voice broke through the radio, hollering nonsense with background noise that sounded like he was inside an industrial dishwasher.

Dunbar grabbed the handset.

"Bad copy, bad copy, say again."

Fulton screamed, "Shelter! Get to shelter!"

***

Bruder held on while Dunbar tilted the yacht to port until they faced due east and pushed the throttles all the way.

The Loggerhead lighthouse was just to the left of the bow and didn't seem to be getting any closer, but when Bruder looked down at the water it swept past like concrete on the highway.

He turned to the starboard rail and saw the *Hawk* slicing through waves at an angle to the yacht, aimed at the same spot from the south.

Beyond it, the wall of black clouds rippled with constant lightning.

Bruder used a wide stance and handholds to get to the helm.

"Tell Fulton—»

"Not now," Dunbar said.

He kept looking over at the squall line.

Bruder noticed the beads of sweat on his forehead and upper lip.

He repeated, "Tell Fulton to radio back about what he finds in the anchorage."

"It doesn't matter what he finds, that's where we're going."

"Not if he finds a Coast Guard boat with the same idea, seeking shelter from the storm. Or DEA. Anybody with a line into police channels."

"Yeah? What are we going to do instead?"

Dunbar was only half-listening as he checked gauges and screens and made adjustments.

"Start thinking about that," Bruder said.

He grabbed the radio off the console and turned away.

"Hey!"

Dunbar lunged for it but didn't want to leave the helm.

"Asshole!"

Bruder watched the *Hawk* while he used the radio.

"Fulton."

"Yeah!"

The engine noise from the smaller boat was obnoxious.

"Tell us who else is in the cove when you get there."

"Yeah, okay!"

"Gimme that back," Dunbar said.

Bruder clipped the radio to his pocket, opposite the one with Hendrick's cell phone.

Dunbar said, "As soon as I drop anchor, you and me are gonna sort this out."

"No we aren't. After we hand the yacht off, maybe, if you're still set on it."

Dunbar glared at him, then the lopsided grin twitched at the corner of his mouth and he shook his head.

"Goddam. You're a piece of work, you know that? Possibly the biggest prick I've ever met. And the most infuriating part is, you don't give a damn if I like you or not."

Bruder shrugged and pointed at the weather radar.

"Can you see how big the squall is yet?"

"No, I can't, which means it's big. You'd better call your guy, make sure the people we're meeting are still on the right side of the surface."

***

When McIntyre came on the line Bruder said, "Are you watching the weather?"

"Yes, dammit. Don't tell me you're scared of it."

"We're going to the anchorage off Garden Key until it passes. No discussion."

After a string of profanity, McIntyre said, "I'll call you back."

Bruder waited.

The phone rang five minutes later.

"The men you're meeting are in the storm right now."

McIntyre's voice was flat with furious acceptance.

"And?"

"And they say it's bad. So they're going to meet you in the anchorage."

"I thought they didn't want to get that close to enemy territory."

"They're making an exception," McIntyre said. "They'll be there in less than an hour."

"Tell them we'll leave the yacht anchored and come alongside in another boat to collect the money."

"No, you will stay with the vessel until they allow you to go."

"Not a chance," Bruder said and killed the call.

***

Turley frowned beneath the binoculars when he saw the yacht make the sudden turn to port.

"What the hell are they doing?"

Valenti was at the helm.

"Let me see."

They switched places and Valenti peered through the optics.

When he found the yacht, cruising broadside to the Whaler now, he said, "Dunbar doesn't like the look of that storm."

"Pussy."

"Or maybe he convinced Kline to scrap the meet and sell the yacht to the highest bidder."

Turley scoffed.

"No way. Kline is McIntyre's bitch, through and through."

The words came through a sneer of disgust.

Domm had the second set of binoculars, smaller and less powerful.

"He's heading for Garden Key, right? The anchorage? I

think we can catch him before he makes it."

Turley worked the throttle and wheel to keep the yacht on the horizon as his eyes flicked around, judging angles and the storm and what he knew of the reefs surrounding the islands.

"Nah, screw that. We're done chasing. Switch again."

Valenti took the helm and Turley jabbed a finger at the map they'd been using.

He traced a route, looping above Loggerhead Key and cutting between islands to come at Garden Key and Fort Jefferson from the north.

"If we come down this way, we either make it there first and cut them off or we come in behind and trap them in the cove."

Domm said, "What if they just ram us?"

"They can't, the yacht is too slow. We'll just zip around and come at them from another direction."

"Yeah, but the *Cooper's Hawk* is around somewhere," Valenti said, "and it's faster than us. What about that?"

Turley slammed a fist down on the map.

"Look, do you guys want to do this, or do you want to keep coming up with reasons not to? Because there's always a reason not to. I thought we were the kind of crew who doesn't give a shit about those—what we care about is doing it anyway. Am I wrong?"

Valenti blinked, stunned by the outburst.

"No, man, we're just working out the plan."

"The plan is to force our way onto the goddam yacht, kill Kline and anybody else who tries to stop us, and get paid. Whatever comes up while we're doing those things, we fucking handle."

Valenti and Domm shared a look.

They'd had short, quiet discussions about Turley's behavior ever since the life raft.

They weren't sure if he was concussed from Kline's fist, or

freaked out from jumping in the ocean with his hands bound behind his back, or just sore about losing the yacht and the big payday and was now looking at everything through the lens of getting vengeance and the money at all costs.

Whatever it was, it had him acting short and pissy.

Bottom line, they didn't fully trust his decision-making process.

But he was the man in charge, and things had mostly worked out for them in the past when they relied on aggression more than strategy...

To Valenti, it seemed like they'd switched places with Dunbar, and not just the situation of being on the yacht vs. chasing it, but with their overall behavior.

They were the pirates now.

And Turley's plan wasn't bad, it was just...aggressive.

Something Dunbar would do.

But now *he* was the one constrained by Kline and his tunnel vision.

Valenti smiled at the thought of the two of them kneeling on the swimming platform, wondering how things had changed so quickly and violently, then putting a bullet into each head and tipping them overboard.

Turley told Domm, "Look, he's grinning. He gets it. How about you, big man?"

Domm just held his hands out, like he was confused by the question.

"Was there ever any doubt?"

"Hell no!" Turley whooped. "Now move, I know the way through."

Valenti stepped away from the helm once more and Turley cut the Whaler hard to port, aiming for a point between the Loggerhead lighthouse on the right and a low smudge of an island on the left. That was the northernmost island of the Dry Tortugas, and if it had a name nobody on the Whaler knew it.

Valenti glanced at Domm again, who shrugged and press-checked his Glock for about the tenth time.

Whatever happened, they were all-in.

***

Fulton met the yacht southeast of Loggerhead Key and came along the starboard side as both vessels cruised north.

Behind them, the squall was a tsunami of black clouds, rolling and flashing, and even though Dunbar said it was a few miles away, to Bruder it looked like he could touch it if he leaned off the swimming platform.

The air had turned thick and hazy and yellow, and when Bruder looked down at Fulton from the flybridge it made him think of old war footage.

The wind and waves getting pushed ahead of the storm were growing, and Fulton had to work to keep the *Hawk* a safe distance from the yacht.

Bruder used the radio: "See the powerboat?"

Fulton shook his head, then fumbled the radio while he tried to keep hold of the wheel.

"Nothing. It's black as night in there, raining like hell."

Bruder watched him chuck the radio into a nook and grip the wheel with both hands again.

Dunbar's grin flashed.

"If it's a Skater, those poor bastards probably don't have a roof. Probably gonna draw straws to see who has to drive the thing back to Havana while everybody else parties on this beauty."

He took a moment to gaze around the cockpit, running his hands along the edge of the console.

"Yeah, I'm gonna miss you, baby. Two million would have been a bargain for a sweetie like you. But hey, maybe we'll meet again."

He snapped out of it and told Bruder, "Hey, I need that radio back. No more macho bullshit."

Bruder handed it over.

Dunbar told Fulton, "All right my man, just clip your radio somewhere you can hear it, no need to reply. And sneak in behind me, I'm gonna lead you through these shoals."

The *Hawk* dropped into the yacht's wake and followed it through a series of turns and curves that seemed random to Bruder, but Dunbar was sweating again and working the yacht and screens and charts like a mad scientist, so Bruder left him alone and went to the stern rail of the flybridge to keep an eye on Fulton and watch for the powerboat.

He could make out sand and grass on Loggerhead Key to the west, along their port side, and there were other low humps of land off the starboard side.

To the northeast, in the direction they were generally heading, a dark shape on the horizon had to be Garden Key and Fort Jefferson.

It made Bruder frown, being so close to land yet not able to stand on it for a while.

After a few minutes of staring off to the south he thought he saw something, a spot at the base of the squall that didn't change shape like the water and clouds.

He was working his way toward the cockpit for the binoculars when Dunbar said, "Oh, shit."

Bruder froze just past the Jacuzzi.

Dunbar's tone made his hand move toward the Glock.

He said, "What?"

Dunbar pointed through the windshield to the northeast.

"I think that's Turley."

CHAPTER EIGHTEEN

"It's them," Bruder said.

He had the binoculars up, looking through the yacht's windshield, and recognized the Whaler.

Two shapes moved around outside the pilothouse.

Valenti and Domm, Bruder assumed.

"How far are they?"

"Less than a mile," Dunbar said.

"It looks like they aren't moving."

"Nah, just bobbing on the waves. They know we're heading for the cove—my guess is they'll come in behind and brace us. Or set up a one-boat blockade. Bastards. You were right, we should have circled back and gotten rid of them."

"We didn't, so it doesn't matter."

He lifted the Street Sweeper and tested his right arm with it.

Pain flared when he brought the stock into his shoulder, and he knew from experience it would only get worse when he pulled the trigger.

But he also knew, if he was pulling the trigger, he'd have

other things to think about.

So he kept the shotgun close and brought the binoculars up again.

"There's another possibility," Dunbar said.

"A good one?"

"They wait for us to get closer, then open up with the M4."

Bruder shook his head.

"They want the yacht. If they happen to shoot you, there's a good chance this thing crashes into a reef or something. Right?"

"That might happen whether I get shot or not."

Bruder's mouth was a grim line beneath the binoculars.

"So they'll wait for us to drop anchor, then attack. Maybe try to negotiate."

Dunbar said, "After everything that's happened?"

"Yeah, you're right. We need to kill them first."

***

Turley kept the Whaler a few hundred yards away, rocking and tipping on the growing waves, as the yacht curled around Bird Key Bank toward the Garden Key anchorage, followed by the *Cooper's Hawk*.

Beyond the vessels, the brick ramparts and towers of Fort Jefferson loomed.

Even without the binoculars Turley could see Kline standing on the yacht's flybridge, staring over at the Whaler.

Turley gave him the finger and asked Valenti, "You think you can hit him from here?"

Valenti frowned.

"I thought we weren't shooting until they drop anchor."

"I know, I'm just pissed. Look at that asshole. I tell you what, if we take him alive, I might keelhaul his ass."

Valenti laughed like it wasn't a serious threat.

Turley lifted the binoculars and checked the *Hawk*.

"That's Fulton back there, so we were right, Dunbar's

on the yacht. Good. Domm, you know what you're doing?"

"We get Fulton first, I take over the *Hawk*. If he stays cool, I stay cool. If he tries to get in the way, I drop him."

"And then?"

"Check the boat for anything good. Then sink it. If the storm don't do it for me."

He cast a wary eye on the dark clouds, which looked poised to roll over them at any moment.

Turley said, "You do that, me and Valenti take down the yacht. No prisoners."

He was nattering to himself, getting ready, pumped up for what was coming.

The yacht and *Hawk* cruised southeast, skirting Bird Key Harbor, and would soon cut due east and enter the Tortugas anchorage.

Turley watched them, smiling at how concerned Kline was about them, standing at the stern rail of the flybridge now so he could keep staring.

Fulton's face kept coming around as well, twisting forward and backward at the bottom of Turley's view.

"They're in," he said. "Let's go get our yacht, boys."

He pushed the throttles and the Whaler fought against the wind and waves to move south.

Water sprayed over the sides and Domm and Valenti got low, holding on, then Domm yelled, "Hold up! What the fuck is that?"

Turley followed his finger to the south and saw the thing coming at them, a mile out and closing fast, like a red missile shot out of a cannon.

It gave him an immediate bad feeling, which he tried to ignore, but Valenti picked up on it too.

"You think that's the sheikh's guys? Here for the yacht?"

"It doesn't matter," Turley said and shoved the throttles all the way.

***

Bruder glanced at the high walls and corner bastions of the hexagon-shaped fort as Dunbar took the yacht around the ruins of some dock pilings sticking out of the water like a clear-cut forest in a swamp.

The fort was enormous and ominous, like an ancient gladiator coliseum converted to a death camp.

The rampart along the cove was two hundred yards long with an arched entryway near the center, accessed by a wooden bridge spanning a wide moat.

A goddam moat, Bruder thought.

He could see how, years ago, anyone trying to force their way through that gate would get decimated by crossfire from the corner bastions.

The boardwalk continued away from the bridge toward shore and ended at a boathouse and wide dock off the yacht's port side. Before they passed the boathouse, the yacht cruised by a half-dozen short docks sticking out from the beach with small personal watercraft tied off.

"Finally, some good goddam news," Dunbar said.

"What?"

Dunbar pointed at the empty dock.

"The ferry from Key West isn't here. They either left early or canceled the day trip, probably because they aren't morons and actually checked the weather before they got started."

He shot Bruder a sidelong glance and had to shout over the growing wind, but the waves were a mere light chop compared to what they'd come through prior to the cove.

Bruder scowled.

Dunbar was apparently feeling saucy again now that they were in the anchorage and the ferry wasn't around, even though Turley and his crew still lurked.

Bruder said, "We had to steal it this morning before you

screwed everything up."

Dunbar shrugged.

"Eh, fair enough."

"You see any rangers?"

"No, nobody. Again, they aren't the morons here."

He used the radio and told Fulton, "I'm gonna go as far into the northeast corner as I can. You move to the south. Give them two angles to worry about."

"Copy that."

The *Hawk* peeled away into the southeast corner of the anchorage and sliced through a rapid turn until the bow was pointed toward the cove's entrance.

A low mass of grassy land stretched from the fort to the east, and Dunbar cut the engines and coasted toward the sandy beach before reversing and turning the yacht to get it pointed in the same direction as the *Hawk*.

"I wish this damn thing had a chase gun," he muttered, and dropped anchor about twenty yards from shore.

Bruder touched the Glock 19 tucked into his belt and picked up the Street Sweeper, which he figured was close enough, and got ready.

***

Bruder stood along the port rail of the flybridge, where he could see Fulton and the *Hawk* and, if he leaned out a bit and looked forward, the entrance to the anchorage.

The outer approach to the cove was blocked from his view by some trees and low buildings and he kept looking from there to the squall line pushing in from beyond the *Hawk*, which looked like a fragile toy beneath the storm.

"We got about five minutes," Dunbar said, looking at the flashing clouds. "Maybe less."

As if the weather heard the challenge, a fat raindrop smacked against the windshield.

More followed, cracking off the hull and roof like the

sound of a distant and growing firefight.

The storm was going to do whatever it wanted, so Bruder turned his full attention to the entrance.

The Whaler appeared thirty seconds later, blasting through the chop around the field of broken pilings and heading straight for the yacht.

Bruder wedged the shotgun's stock into his right shoulder, clenching his teeth against the pain, and kept the barrel pointed at the deck.

Dunbar had his pistol out and his voice was higher than normal when he said, "Is that idiot gonna ram us?"

He darted toward the stairs, then hurried back to peer through the windshield.

The Whaler was a hundred yards away, then fifty.

Bruder went to the starboard side and leaned over the rail and aimed the Sweeper at the left side of the windshield, where Turley's face would be, then the boat swerved to his left and exposed the port side, where Valenti and Domm were crouched.

Valenti fired first and Bruder felt the bullet snap past his ear.

He dropped below the rail and moved in a crouch toward the port side, yelling at Dunbar, "Get on the radio. Tell Fulton to open up on them."

Two more shots barked out, less sharp, and Bruder knew it was Domm's Glock, keeping their heads down.

The sound of the Whaler's engines moved away.

"They're going for Fulton, tell him," Bruder said.

Dunbar yelled into the radio, "Heads up, they're coming for you!"

Fulton yelled back: "Somebody else is coming in!"

Dunbar peered over the console through the windshield.

"Wait, hold on, wait...What is that?"

Bruder kept below the rail into the cockpit and looked.

A white rooster tail of water arced above the trees and

buildings along the southern point of Garden Key.

A moment later, a long red boat shaped like a bullet tilted around the bend, skimming past the pilings before settling back to level and rumbling into the cove.

Bruder saw six men in the exposed cockpit, two seated in the front with a row of four behind, all of them strapped in and wearing black balaclavas and tinted safety goggles.

All six heads turned toward the yacht as the powerboat cruised closer.

They didn't seem to mind the rain, which was rapidly growing from sporadic drops into a constant drumming.

Dunbar said, "Turley's fucked, he's outnumbered now."

"Let's make sure," Bruder said.

He went back to the port rail and risked a glance.

Turley had taken the boat across Fulton's bow without firing any shots, and now it looked like the three men weren't sure where to point their guns—at the *Hawk*, the powerboat, or the yacht.

Bruder stood up enough to point at the Whaler, yelling down to the powerboat, "They're trying to steal the yacht!"

He didn't care who killed Turley as long as the job got done.

Then Dunbar said, "What if they don't speak English?"

Bruder rose and fired one shot from the Sweeper in the general direction of the Whaler.

It hurt like hell and didn't hit a damn thing, but it also didn't require translation.

The men in the powerboat ducked and came up bristling with gun barrels, short mean-looking submachine guns with integrated suppressors.

The boat leaped into a tight right turn and shot toward the Whaler, which scampered recklessly to the south, where Bruder could see mounds of sand peeking between the waves.

Dunbar said, "Oh, he's gonna get beached out there. It's—"

The Whaler suddenly jolted to a stop and tipped to the

right.

A heavy crunching sound carried to the yacht on the wind.

The powerboat ended the brief charge, like a bull satisfied by a fleeing clown, and turned toward Fulton and the *Hawk*.

Bruder took the radio from Dunbar and said, "Fulton, keep this line open. Let me talk to them."

"Yeah, good."

He was out of breath, a live wire.

"Watch that Whaler, they still have the rifle."

"Yeah, yeah, I know."

Bruder scanned Turley's boat with the binoculars.

It was hard to see through the rain, but from what he could tell no one was on the deck or in the cockpit and the craft had a growing and unnatural tilt to the starboard side.

Bruder panned down to the powerboat and Fulton.

The four men in the back row of the cockpit were standing now that the boat was idling.

They seemed to be talking as they turned and pointed at various boats, nodding in agreement about something.

The radio clicked and Fulton's voice yelled, "Hey guys! Welcome! Thanks for saving our asses!"

"Of course," a man's voice said.

Through the binoculars, it looked like it was the man in the back row on the port side.

He had a gravelly accented voice, maybe British, and clearly understood English.

The sound of the rain was in stereo and made the conversation hard to hear.

Bruder pressed the radio to his ear and the accented voice said, "And who might you be?"

Fulton said, "Uh, I'm with the guys on the yacht. We're the ones delivering it to you."

"Ah, you are with Mr. Bruder?"

"Who?"

The man shot Fulton in the head.

***

The sun disappeared, swallowed by the squall line, and Bruder stared through the binoculars and said, "McIntyre, you goddam rotten son of a bitch."

He'd given these men the Bruder name, and they were here to kill him.

He dropped the optics and brought the shotgun back up.

Dunbar gaped across the water as the powerboat curled around the *Hawk*, now a ghost ship, and started idling toward the yacht.

"They shot him."

"I know," Bruder said.

"They shot him."

"Dunbar."

"It's a setup," Dunbar said.

"We need to get off this boat. Right now. Let them take it and get the hell out of here."

"The cash…"

Bruder was already at the top of the stairs.

He turned and said, "Dunbar, there is no cash. There never was. We still have the gold on the *Hawk*, but we have to go. Now."

He went down the stairs to the rear of the salon and kept going to the swimming platform.

Rain hammered his head and the wind pushed him toward the starboard edge.

He looked down.

Even with the sun gone the water was clear enough to see the bottom—rocks and sand and green patches—but he had no idea how deep it was.

He glanced back and saw the powerboat picking up speed, leaving the *Hawk* in its wake.

Bruder slipped over the side of the platform and held the shotgun over his head with his right arm so he could pull at the water with his left.

The salt water and exertion instantly got to the bullet wounds and he gritted his teeth and swam toward the shore.

He tried to keep the yacht between himself and the men in the powerboat as he kept pulling, and when he looked back he expected to see the sleek red hull creeping around the yacht's stern so the guns could chop him up.

The rain and wind and waves worked to confuse the sound of the powerboat's engines but when he slipped below the surface the rumbling became clear and ominous.

Bruder fought against the water and pulled.

When his feet scraped the rocks and sand he churned onto the beach and ran backward, spitting salt water and stumbling.

He'd been on boats for the last twelve hours and his legs weren't used to solid ground—it came up to meet his boots too soon and didn't move when they made contact.

He felt punch-drunk while he staggered through the sand up a gentle slope, searching the edges of the yacht for any sign of the men McIntyre had sent to kill him.

Something else felt off, a nagging alarm in his head, and it confused him until he touched his waist and found the Glock missing.

His hand moved around and the knife was still clipped in his pocket but the gun was gone, fallen out in the water or during his sprint up the beach, and he peeled his eyes off the water to search the ground nearby.

The storm forced him into a crouch to identify the shapes at his feet and he started to backtrack, touching grass and rocks with his free hand, waiting for one of them to be the smooth shape of the gun.

He glanced over at the water and caught a red blade appearing at the yacht's bow.

Apparently, the men in the powerboat didn't trust the depth closer to shore and were skirting around to get their angle on him.

Bruder dropped to one knee, knowing the front of the boat was ridiculously long with the cabin toward the rear, so he had time, but a man crouched on the fiberglass nose shouted and fired a three-round burst at him.

Bruder didn't know where the bullets went, but they missed him, and he cursed and ran away from the water and nearly fell when his feet got tangled in some low scrub brush about fifteen yards inland.

He went to his belly and crawled with the shotgun across his forearms into thicker bushes, then froze.

Rain and wind pounded the tiny leaves above him and made sound irrelevant.

He rose just enough to check the beach, squinting through the downpour.

The yacht was all he could see now, and even that was just a large white shape in the darkness and chaos of the storm.

He was too exposed and knew he had to move.

Wherever the hell Dunbar was, he was on his own.

Bruder was pushing to his hands and knees when a flash and gunshot exploded directly above him.

He dove down and chewed sand, then shook his head, realizing it was just lightning and thunder.

He rose again, scanned the water and saw nothing but a curtain of rain and darkness, and started to move.

***

Turley peeked over the Whaler's stern rail.

He couldn't see a damn thing except rain and waves, so he had nothing to point the M4 at.

Valenti crawled up from below and hissed a warning when Turley stood up, but Turley said, "It's fine, they can't see us."

So Valenti stood up too and touched the gash on the side of his head, where he'd smacked into the edge of the map table when the boat hit the shoal.

His fingers came back with blood on them, but it was less than the last time.

Turley said, "How bad is it down there?"

"Yeah, she's done."

Domm squeezed through the cabin hatch and crawled across the deck until he saw the other two men looking down at him.

He got to his feet said, "The good news is, the rock coming in through the hull is keeping us from sinking."

Turley sucked a tooth and looked toward the yacht and fort, which were somewhere out there beyond the wall of rain, along with the goddam powerboat, moving like a shark in the cove.

Dunbar's *Hawk* was out there too, and they'd all seen the guys in the black masks straight-up execute Fulton right before the rain shut off the rest of the world.

That incident had told Turley the men in the powerboat sure as hell wouldn't bother to listen to whatever he had to say.

He couldn't see Bush Key either, but knew it stretched away from Fort Jefferson to the east and spread out, then turned south and became Long Key.

He pointed to the north, then the east, and said, "If we swim for it, we'll hit beach within a few hundred yards."

"What about the *Hawk*?" Domm said. "We get on board and get gone. Fulton won't mind."

Turley shook his head.

"Did he drop anchor? That boat could be anywhere in the anchorage, and we end up chasing it until we drown. Besides, we get on that boat, we're in the same spot we were before I wrecked this one. Those powerboat fuckers are prowling around somewhere, and even the *Hawk* won't outrun them."

Valenti said, "The yacht's lost, man."

"Huh?"

"It sounds like you're coming up with reasons to go after it again. Or Kline."

"Do I need to? I mean, they're both right *there*."

"Yeah, and the yacht is the reason the powerboat guys are here. Those are the sheikh's men. Gotta be."

"I know it, dummy. And they think we're sunk or stranded. We come at them from shore, we'll get the drop."

Valenti had a dubious squint.

"On Kline, too?"

"If the bastard's still alive. Those guys shot Fulton, why not wipe everybody out?"

"Maybe Kline set Dunbar and his crew up," Domm said.

"Maybe. Who gives a shit? We get to shore and take a look. We sure as hell can't stay here."

He stared at the two of them.

Finally Valenti said, "I vote east. The powerboat won't come cruising through these rocks looking for us. Not in this storm."

Turley waited for someone to mention how *nobody* should have been in the rocks, but they kept their mouths shut about it and Domm started passing out snorkeling gear.

Valenti brought plastic bags up from below and he and Domm sealed their pistols inside, just in case, and Valenti wrapped one around the barrel of the M4 and secured it with tape.

"Don't turn that goddam flashlight on," Turley said.

"I know, I know. Here."

It was an awkward moment when Valenti handed his pistol to Turley, who'd lost his on the yacht, but they didn't linger on it and got busy donning snorkeling gear.

They slipped over the port rail into the waves and fought their way east toward shore.

***

Bruder used the rain like a smokescreen and ran what felt like west through the grass and low scrub toward the fort.

He watched the water on his left for movement and color and listened for shouts of warning but the rain was everything.

Even the lightning flashes, which seemed constant, didn't illuminate anything other than the waterfall surrounding him.

His boots slapped against wet brick and he faced front and tried to stop, then fell backward to keep from dropping into the moat.

He reached between his feet and felt the worn, sandy edge of the brickwork, and leaned forward and pushed his hand over the edge and down. When his elbow bent over the edge and he still didn't feel water, he pulled back.

He could drop over the edge and hide in the moat, blocked from view and targeting from the powerboat, but he had no idea how deep it was and the thing was designed to keep people from climbing back out, so he dismissed the idea.

He stayed low and followed the moat to the left, back toward the water. After a dozen steps it curved to the west and he followed it, knowing he was moving along the face of the fort now toward the bridge and entryway.

The rampart was an ominous presence on his right, invisible in the downpour but large enough to change the shape and sound of the wind. Lightning flashed and he may have caught a glimpse of the corner bastion, but it could have been a low thundercloud.

The face of the fort was about two hundred yards long, he recalled, and the gate was near the halfway point.

So he just needed to go the length of a football field without any trouble.

He stayed low, the pain in his side and shoulder forgotten, and kept the shotgun pointed toward the invisible cove on his left.

A sudden, crouching shape appeared in front of him and he swung the shotgun toward it, dropping to one knee and tensing on the trigger until he realized it was a brick post. He closed in and saw it was part of a foundation securing a sign declaring this as Fort Jefferson.

He moved along the front of the sign and didn't see the two men until they were within ten feet, creeping east away from the dock toward his last known location.

It was smart—the powerboat had dropped them off as a blocking force and probably had others coming in from behind him, further out on the beach.

They didn't react to him and Bruder kept still, just a dark shape against the dark shape of the sign.

The Sweeper was pointed low, at the sand, and he eased the barrel up a sliver at a time.

Knee high.

Stomach.

Chest.

Lightning flashed and the two masked faces turned and looked right at him and Bruder fired.

The one on the right reeled backward like the earth had been yanked out from under him.

Bruder fired again at the one on the left, who was already tumbling and rolling toward the shore.

Bruder didn't wait to see if he'd been hit or try to pursue him.

He ran forward until his boots hit wood.

In the wind and rain and thunder he heard a man yelling, "The bridge! He's at the bridge!"

Into a radio, or to other men nearby.

Bruder turned right and sprinted across the bridge toward the fort.

Then he was through the arched entryway and into a dark, forty-foot long brick tunnel with water pouring down like a curtain at both ends.

He wiped the water away from his eyes and walked about
ten feet in, then found a nook in the brick wall on the left and
tucked himself in.

He turned and crouched and aimed the shotgun around
the corner toward the entrance, taking slow, even breaths
to keep the gun steady.

There, he waited.

CHAPTER NINETEEN

Turley led the way north on Long Key and watched for more land curving to the west, which would be Bush Key, and would lead them toward the fort.

He had the pistol in front of him, tracking wherever he looked, even though he couldn't see more than ten or fifteen feet at any given time.

It was hard to stay straight. The wind shoved him around and drove rain into his back hard enough to sting through his shirt, and Long Key was only ten yards wide at its narrowest and not much more at its widest, and several times he led the group into water and had to adjust.

The lightning wasn't helping—just as he felt like his eyes were adjusting to the sudden gloom of the storm, a flash would leave streaks and flares inside his eyelids and he'd have to start all over again.

He turned to check on the others.

Valenti was five feet behind him with the M4, looking like something out of a Vietnam movie.

Domm was further back blowing streamers of rain away from his mouth, still recovering from the swim.

The sand below Turley's feet turned into grass and he moved to the left until he found the shoreline, then back-tracked to the grass and followed the ragged border.

Bush Key was much wider than Long Key—almost two hundred yards at its bulge—and he didn't want them wandering around in the storm. He figured, if he kept to the fringe between grass and sand, they'd hug the cove's shoreline but stay far enough away from the water and the damn powerboat, wherever it was.

They kept going and curving to the left and Turley tried to picture the islands and the water around them.

How far had they gone?

Were they near the anchorage yet?

He stared down at the grass and sand and moved faster.

When the southern blasts of wind started pushing his back instead of his left side, he knew they were curling to the north.

This, he thought, put them near the spot where Dunbar had dropped the yacht's anchor.

Turley peered through the downpour around him and shook his head.

The squall made it impossible to see anything out in the water, even a ninety-foot yacht.

He turned to tell the others where they were but Valenti's hand shot up in a halt gesture and his eyes bored into the cove.

He dropped to one knee and Turley followed him down.

A moment later Domm appeared over Valenti's shoulder and joined them in a tight triangle so they could hear each other.

Valenti said, "You hear that?"

Turley focused on his ears.

He heard rain and wind and thunder.

"Hear what?"

"Engine. Powerboat."

Now that he knew what to listen for, Turley heard it.

A low, constant rumble beneath everything else.

The pitch of it changed but the cadence remained the same and Turley's seaman brain recognized it as a large engine getting tossed around on sizable waves, muffled then exposed, muffled then exposed.

Then the sound faded and Turley wasn't sure if it was gone or the storm just got louder.

"I don't hear it anymore."

"Me either," Valenti said.

Turley pointed toward the water.

"The yacht's right out there. They're boarding it."

Valenti licked his lips and blinked rain out of his eyes.

"I'm not swimming out there again."

Turley knew it was the right call but didn't like it.

He covered his own concerns by saying, "They can't go anywhere anyway. Not until this shit lets up."

Domm's head bobbed in agreement. Raindrops exploded off his shaved scalp and hit Turley in the eyes like he was standing next to an umbrella.

Domm said, "So, what? We wait here?"

"Nah," Turley said. "We get in front of them. They have to sail past the dock and around the ruins to get out. We set up there, we can put it on them from the front and side. If the powerboat is in the lead, we let it go past and hit the yacht first. If the storm dies down and we can move on it before then, great."

Valenti and Domm both nodded.

Turley led the way again, glancing to his left in case he got a lucky glimpse of the yacht.

The grass and sand curled to the left again, taking them west, and he was looking out into the cove when Valenti grabbed the back of his belt and yanked.

Turley reeled backward and was about to come around with some venom but Valenti's finger pointed over his shoulder and Turley saw it.

Two shapes, about fifteen feet ahead.

The backs of two men crouched on the beach.

Turley's eyes widened in anticipation.

Dunbar and Kline?

He could picture them abandoning the yacht and swimming to shore and waiting for a chance to make a move, just like he and his crew were doing.

Or maybe they were just waiting for the sheikh's men to leave.

Then the one on the left turned to say something to the other and Turley saw the shape of the black mask and goggles pushed up on his head.

These *were* the sheikh's men.

What the hell were they doing on shore?

The one on the right yelled, "Bruder! Come out! We have a message from Mr. McIntyre!"

Turley frowned.

Who the hell was Bruder?

The man yelled, "We have your money!"

And Turley thought, *Ohhhh...*

He was thinking about what to do—sit back and let these guys go after Kline, or Bruder, or take them on and cut the powerboat crew by two—when a sound like thunder, but not thunder, crashed from somewhere ahead.

The two men crouched lower and spoke to each other, the words lost to Turley in the storm.

He glanced back and Valenti fired a finger gun with a questioning look on his face, and Turley nodded.

Gunshot, probably a shotgun.

Valenti put his mouth next to Turley's ear and whispered, "That was the Sweeper. Kline had it on the yacht."

That became a factor in Turley's decision on what to do next, then one of the men in front of him pressed a palm to the side of his head and said, "Say again, say again!"

A moment later both men lunged to their feet and ran forward and disappeared into the rain.

Turley waited a full minute, then told Valenti and Domm, "We're the cleanup crew. We take our time. Let 'em fight it out and burn ammo. Whoever's left, we finish them off then go for the yacht when the squall passes."

The other two nodded.

They all moved higher up on shore, into the grass and low scrub, and crept toward the fort.

***

Bruder heard the splashing footsteps coming from behind him and eased his head around.

A slope-shouldered person in a poncho trudged through the inner archway of the tunnel and came spluttering toward him.

The person was slightly backlit by the archway and Bruder could see them fumbling beneath the poncho.

He kept himself low and pressed against the wall, avoiding a similar silhouette, as the person whipped one side of the poncho up and came out with a massive handgun.

No, Bruder realized—it was a flashlight, the kind used for shining wildlife and, from the size of it, signaling aircraft.

The person slopped forward in soaked boots and was ten feet away when Bruder leaned the shotgun against the wall and stood and said, "Hey."

"Yah!"

The person, a man by the sound of his scream, lunged away and brought the flashlight arm up to protect his face.

"Easy," Bruder said.

"Oh jeez! Oh man!"

He was hunched over, still holding the flashlight toward Bruder but not thinking to click it on.

"Here, let me help," Bruder said and tried to take the flashlight away.

"Hey, no."

The man held on and pulled, surprisingly strong, and Bruder let it go.

The light clicked on, and the man at least had the sense to keep it pointed at the floor so he wouldn't blind anyone.

Still, Bruder's hard-earned night vision was ruined, and now he was spotlit for anyone coming through the fort's entrance.

There was nothing to be done about it, so he used the light to get a better look around.

The man's poncho was dark green and still hung up on his right shoulder. Bruder saw the boots and shorts and part of a tan shirt.

A park ranger.

Bruder checked the tunnel.

The opposite wall had an indentation just like the one he'd been crouched in, and further along toward the inner gate were narrower openings that looked like doorways.

The one behind the ranger had a sign on the floor with information and rules about the fort and park.

The ranger said, "Are you with the campers or boaters?"

"Campers," Bruder said.

"Is everybody okay out there? We heard some odd booms."

Bruder moved a bit to his left to make sure his shadow fell over the shotgun.

"Thunder. This storm is crazy."

"Well, let's get you all inside until it passes. Did any of you talk to those boaters who came in right before everything hit?"

"No," Bruder said. "Do you have a phone?"

"Cell phones don't work out here."

The ranger sounded proud of it.

"I mean any phone."

"Well, yes, but—"

Bruder clipped him beneath the ear and the man slumped and dropped the flashlight, which gave off a cracking sound and died when it bounced on the stone floor.

Bruder caught the ranger before he fell and dragged him toward the sign.

He clamped his eyes shut, willing the lingering fireworks from the flashlight to die, and moved by memory until he kicked the sign.

He left the ranger on the ground and opened his eyes again.

Still ruined.

He waved his hands around until he touched the sign, then moved it and reached into the arched doorway.

His fingertips touched brick right away—it was just a deeper indentation in the wall.

But it was deep enough.

He dragged the ranger into it and sat him up in the corner and pulled the poncho over him, then moved the sign back.

The man snored softly but Bruder couldn't hear it after one step backward.

He turned to retrieve the shotgun and saw a black shape leaning from outside the entrance, a head, trying to get a better look before coming in.

Bruder took a step toward the shotgun and froze when the person outside the archway kicked on a flashlight of their own, this one pure white and similar to the one on the M4.

He thought, *Valenti?*

Then another beam sliced through the rain from the opposite side of the entrance.

The first beam pushed through the waterfall as the man holding it came around the corner.

Bruder looked at the shotgun, too far away, then stepped backward through the inner curtain of rain and disappeared.

***

Bruder was still facing the tunnel and looked to his right at more light—yellow and softer compared to the harsh tactical beams—coming through the windows of a closed door.

Some kind of office, or the ranger station.

Bruder went the other way.

The wind in the courtyard was mostly blocked by the fort's two-story wall but the rain poured almost straight down and bounced off the bricks on his right. He was already soaked to the bone from the swim and storm, so running through this car wash didn't make it any worse.

He glanced up and the wall seemed to tilt inward toward him.

It had large, dark openings made vague and endless by the storm.

If someone wanted to jump down on him or shoot or drop something heavy, he'd never see it coming.

He ran past a tree offering paltry shelter and kept going, then the acoustics on his right changed.

The drum and sizzle of rain dropped and was replaced by something bigger, something hollow.

He turned that way and stepped through a wide arched opening into a deep room with a window offering gray light at the far end.

Out of the rain again, Bruder shook his head to get rid of some of the water and moved to the window, which was just a small rectangular loophole in the outer wall.

There wasn't much to see except more rain and wind but he identified the moat below and knew he was inside the fort's rampart, facing toward the anchorage.

The bridge across the moat was somewhere off to his right and he leaned forward, trying to spot it and the flashlight beams of the men coming after him, but it was a lost cause.

Those men were already in the tunnel, sweeping the nooks and corners.

They'd find the ranger.

When they moved on they'd probably split up, and who-ever came Bruder's way would poke the beam into this chamber and pin him like a rabbit on asphalt.

He thought about squeezing through the loophole and dropping to the moat but had no idea how the landing would go, and staying in the fort meant he didn't have to worry about the powerboat.

Just the men coming in to hunt him.

Bruder stepped back and looked down.

The floor was uneven and he knelt and touched it—rough and gritty.

He didn't know if it would show wet footprints in the flashlight beams but had to assume it would.

From his lower angle he saw a shape along the right wall, another arched opening, and went through that into another chamber, identical to the first.

He could picture it now: Soldiers manning cannons in each of these casements, yelling commands in the smoke while they poured overlapping fire through the loophole at ships in the anchorage and men struggling across the bridge and moat.

He appreciated the engineered brutality of it but still scowled, knowing he most likely would have been one of the men storming the walls.

This casement had an identical narrow opening on the far wall and he moved to it and stood beneath the archway, between the two rooms.

It was a good spot.

He could look back through the previous opening into the first casement and watch for trouble, and had a decent angle on the courtyard and anyone moving close to the inner wall.

Bruder kept himself still, except for the drips falling from his clothes, and thought about McIntyre.

The bastard had played him.

Put him in a bind from the beginning—do the job or else—and Bruder had fallen for it.

Now he'd completed the job, more or less, and McIntyre wanted him dead.

Bruder was angry at himself for playing the sucker, but he'd take it out on McIntyre.

Lightning hit something on the fort, a sizzling flash, and thunder simultaneously shook the ground.

More bolts flashed, striking who the hell knew what, but Bruder only cared about the constant while light coming from the courtyard.

The beam swept left and right, then flooded the first casement.

A voice echoed through the archways: "I got footprints."

Bruder's right hand went to his pocket.

Ignoring the pain from the holes in his side and shoulder, he slid the knife out and eased the four-inch blade open.

***

Bruder stepped backward into the next casement, watching through the two openings into the first one he'd entered.

The white beam sprang from the walls to the floor, probing every shadow, and grew narrower.

The man was moving toward the doorway.

Bruder used his free hand to squeeze his shirt as he moved to the left, toward the outer wall, and he stayed close to that while he passed the narrow loophole and made another left at the next corner.

He rushed along the wall and ignored the doorway into the next casement over, moving all the way to the courtyard entrance and cutting back to the wall where he'd stood in the archway.

He peered along the bricks and looked for the trail of water he'd tried to leave near that opening but the gloom was too heavy.

Then the white beam spilled through the opening and across the floor and he saw the damp spots and small puddles kicking off reflections.

Bruder stepped out into the rain and pressed his chest against the end of the brick wall separating the casements.

He checked to his right and saw another beam, a flicker through the rain.

The second man was still in the tunnel, probably in case Bruder doubled back and tried to slip out.

Bruder turned his head and scraped his right cheek against the brick, easing an eye around the corner.

The beam was pointed at a forty-five-degree angle down at his trail.

He slid to the right and checked the casement on that side of the wall.

A man was backlit by the flashlight's halo.

He was leaning into the opening with his back to Bruder, trying to slice the pie into the next room as he followed the trail.

Bruder took a deep breath.

He hated knife work.

It could be loud and messy and dangerous, and if it was required, it meant things had gone horribly wrong.

This, he felt, qualified.

He moved forward in a crouch and kept his eyes low, off the man's head and neck so he wouldn't trip any primal alarms, and lunged up when he was a yard away.

The knife went in beneath the man's right ear and Bruder clapped his left forearm around his face to keep him quiet and pull him further onto the blade.

He worked the knife back and forth a few times until the body stopped fighting and started twitching, then dragged it toward the corner at the outer wall.

Bruder turned and got his back in the corner so he could see anything coming and eased the body down and used the blade to cut through the sling looped over the man's shoulder so he could pull the gun free.

It was an MP5SD, a submachine gun he'd used before but wasn't intimate with.

He cleaned the knife on the man's shirt and put it away, then aimed the flashlight beam at the body and pulled the balaclava off, hoping it was Reed or Penza, meaning McIntyre may have made the trip.

He didn't recognize the slack face.

The man was tanned and looked to be in his forties, likely part of the sheikh's security detail or a hired heavy who didn't mind working on boats and pulling the trigger if he had to.

He had a radio bud hooked into his right ear and Bruder pulled it free, frowning when it came completely loose from the black wire trailing down toward the man's belt.

He looked at the bud in the flashlight's beam and saw where he'd severed the wire with his knife.

Bruder shook his head and tossed the trash away.

A radio without an earpiece was worse than useless—the volume he'd require to hear over the storm could give his position away.

He scanned the archways for any sign of the second shooter, saw nothing, then used the beam and his free hand to quickly check the rest of the body.

The man wore quick-dry clothing more suitable for a safari than a fishing trip. He wasn't wearing a tactical vest or any sort of body armor and didn't have any spare magazines on him.

This told Bruder two things—these men were here for an execution, not a gunfight; and if they were all outfitted the same, the man he'd shot with the Sweeper was dead or close enough to it to be out of the game.

Even with a vest on, that slug might have put him down for good.

He wondered why they were even bothering with masks if the plan was to kill everyone on the yacht, but they probably didn't know what they were getting into coming into the cove on U.S. soil—cameras, witnesses, rangers...

To make sure the MP5SD was ready Bruder removed the curved thirty-round magazine and stuck it under his arm, then pulled the charging handle back and ejected the 9mm round from the chamber into his palm.

He slid the round into the top of the magazine and used the flashlight, turning the mag this way and that in the beam, searching for any sign of how many rounds were left.

There was no indicator other than weight, and it felt heavy enough, so he replaced it in the weapon and sent the charging handle forward to get the round back in the chamber.

He used his thumb to check the fire selector switch—the dead man had it set on a three-round burst—and flicked it to single shot.

Thirty rounds used one at a time should be more than enough, and if it turned out he didn't have that many, he'd just fire until the gun went *click*.

Then he found the switch for the flashlight and turned it off so he could hunt.

CHAPTER TWENTY

Turley led his crew along the moat, all three men walking in a crouch and bracing for another glimpse or bark from the two men they were following.

Turley also kept an eye on the water.

He couldn't see anything out there. His eyes had to fight the wind pushing the wall of rain at him and the strobing lightning, and he constantly thought he heard the rumble of the powerboat but couldn't be sure.

He wanted some kind of confirmation that the yacht was still there, just for personal satisfaction, but at the same time knew it had to be; moving the vessel in this shit would mean you wanted to sink it, and nobody at the fort wanted that.

So he offered a silent promise to the yacht that he'd be back aboard her soon and moved along the moat until they hit the low brick sign for Fort Jefferson.

The sign was on the right side of the walkway into the fort, he recalled, and sure enough, a few steps later he kicked a piece of the wooden bridge.

He peered to the right where the fort would be and caught a glimpse of an archway outlined by white light coming from within.

He blinked and it was gone, making him think it was either lightning or the afterimage of a bolt, then Domm was next to him.

"I see flashlights."

He pointed to the right of the bridge and now Turley was sure he saw it too, a white light bouncing around inside a small rectangle.

That would be in one of the—what did they call them—casements.

Turley watched the light move.

He wanted a muzzle flash, some signal they'd found Kline, or Bruder, or whatever the hell his name was.

Then the light vanished and he was staring at rain again.

The predatory part of him wanted to move in while they had an idea of where those lights and the men holding them were, but he tempered it and turned to lead the others back to the sign—it was a good place to hunker down and wait.

Valenti hissed and pointed back toward the walkway, in the direction of the docks, and Turley saw the lump on the ground about fifteen feet away.

They watched it and everything else around them for a few minutes and nothing moved.

Turley fanned the others out to the sides and took a few cautious steps, then he darted in and pressed the gun against the lump and grabbed a handful of fabric.

The lump rocked and shifted from his pressure but had no movements of its own.

Turley reached out and tapped Valenti, then drew a line across his throat.

He did the same to Domm, who nodded and went back to scanning the rain.

The dead man wore a black balaclava, so it wasn't Kline, but Turley pulled the hood and goggles off to be sure.

He had to lean close to get a good enough look.

Fat drops bounced off the open eyes in a face he'd never seen before.

Turley checked the rest of the body, which had no weapons and nothing in the pockets. His chest was a crater of sticky blood and rain.

This, he figured, was the result of the shotgun blast they'd heard.

Turley pictured the powerboat and recalled six men in the cockpit.

So there were five left, maybe less.

He pulled Valenti and Domm over to the Fort Jefferson sign and crouched down on the back side of it, somewhat out of the wind, but there was no escaping the rain.

The three of them crouched down and Turley said, "We wait here. They're inside, which tells me Kline is in there."

Domm said, "Who's Bruder? Is that the name they yelled on the beach?"

"Yeah, I think that's Kline."

"So Bruder's his real name?"

"Who cares? He'll always be Kline to me, until he's dead. After that, he'll just be that asshole we killed at the fort."

He smiled in the gloom and caught flashes of teeth from his crew.

"Domm, you keep an eye on the beach. We'll watch the bridge. Anybody who comes or goes has to pass by us. They don't get any farther."

***

Bruder stood at the inner end of the first casement and leaned into the rain to look toward the tunnel.

The white flashlight beam was still there, like a miniature lighthouse, sweeping back and forth through a half-circle in the courtyard.

Bruder frowned at it.

It was something he would do if he wanted to draw

someone in.

For two full minutes he watched the rain falling through the beam, looking like static on a screen, and was about to move around the corner when a dark shape broke itself away from the wall between him and the flashlight.

It moved in a crouch toward Bruder and angled into the courtyard and disappeared into the storm.

Bruder dropped to a knee and raised the submachine gun but nothing appeared in front of him.

He retraced the fort map he was building in his head— he'd run past a tree when he first exited the tunnel.

So there was more than one man at the gate, and they were trying to funnel him in.

When that didn't work they'd either keep waiting him out, siege warfare, or execute a search.

Bruder didn't know how many there were.

He'd killed two already, leaving four, but at least one of them was probably with the boat. It seemed too risky to completely abandon their best option for getting back to Havana at a fast clip, with or without the storm.

He'd assume there were three men out here trying to kill him, with the third on the far side of the fort's only exit.

It was a good setup, especially with the radios.

If he attacked one side or corner of the triangle, the others would close in.

The only advantage he could get was height.

He peered at the bricks arched above his head, thinking about how the fort's defenders would have gotten to the second level.

Any stairs would be well protected by the structure and serve as chokepoints for attackers who managed to get inside and needed to clear the gunners out of the second-tier casements.

The corners.

That's where he'd put them.

Bruder followed his drying footprints in the dark, through the arched doorway into the next casement, and kept going through archways and rooms until he came to a narrower space with a solid brick wall on the far side.

He went left, out into the rain, and kept his right shoulder close to the wall so he wouldn't wander into the courtyard.

He angled around two corners and the wall on his right turned into a narrow doorless opening.

The room was nearly pitch black, the only light coming from the gray gloom outside the doorway, which he was blocking.

Bruder figured he was standing in the inner corner of the bastion he'd run past on the beach, when he'd considered jumping into the moat.

He stepped to the right and followed the wall and knocked his forehead against something hard and sharp.

Biting back a curse, he probed with his fingers and found a horizontal stone ledge in front of his face, then another above and below it.

He reached as high as he could and felt more of them, curving up.

All of the ledges fanned away from a central stone column on his left and terminated in the brick wall to his right.

The shapes didn't make sense until he realized they were the underside of stone steps, and he was standing beneath a spiral staircase.

He slid to the left and found the first step with the toe of his boot, then checked the next steps with his hands to make sure they were intact and sturdy. They were wider at the outer wall and narrowed to a point at the central column and weren't going to move unless the fort collapsed around them.

He leaned forward and put his left hand on the outer wall, then the step level with his face, checking the path ahead to make sure he didn't tumble out a window, and started up into the darkness.

The MP5SD was in his right hand pointed up and the shoulder nagged him as he eased onto the next step, then the next.

The wind pushed against his face as he climbed, rushing through an upper doorway and funneling down the stairway like a drain. It smelled of salt and dampness and fish.

When thunder boomed, which was about every two or three seconds, it echoed through whatever rooms were on the upper level and rolled at him on the wind.

He'd gone ten steps and thought he might be about halfway up the spiral when the wind and acoustics changed.

Bruder stopped moving and held his breath.

He could still hear the sounds echoing through the upper tier, but the wind no longer touched his face.

He waited, watching the blackness above and the dull gray outline of the doorway below for sign of light or movement.

After a few seconds the wind returned, but in addition to the salt and dampness and fish, it now carried hints of sunblock and body odor.

Bruder eased his weight down and before he moved his left hand off the step something small landed on the back of it.

He tipped the hand and felt around on the step until he found the small piece of stone, mostly smooth with one sharp edge, like it had just been chipped loose.

In the darkness, someone was coming down the stairs above him.

***

Bruder snaked back down the stairs and stayed near the center post so he wouldn't be silhouetted against the doorway.

He crouched beneath the steps and waited in the pool of blackness.

The man made no sound as he came down and Bruder began to think he'd moved on, then he caught another whiff of the sunblock.

So the third man wasn't waiting at a triangle point near the tunnel—he'd had the same thought as Bruder, taking the high ground, and must have gone in the opposite direction to another corner or found a ladder or climbed up the wall like a spider.

Maybe he'd found his dead friend, or when that man didn't respond to radio calls they figured he was dead and knew Bruder must be somewhere between the bastion and the tunnel if he wasn't running around like an idiot in the courtyard.

Either way, they'd close in on him.

Bruder moved the MP5SD to his left hand so he could wrap it around the central post without exposing his entire body.

The part of his brain that never stopped judging angles and leverage points wondered if the fort's designers planned it that way, forcing any attackers coming up the stairs to use their left hand to wield a weapon.

With a muzzleloader, it would be a pain in the ass.

The first sign of the man other than his odor was a black shape moving along the outer wall of the staircase.

Bruder also thought he heard a long, slow exhale, but it could have been the wind.

When he identified the outline of the man's right shoulder leading the way down the stairs, he kept the submachine gun tucked in close and tracked where center mass ought to be with the barrel.

As the man got closer to the doorway the gray light gave him more definition. He had his back against the wall and was sliding along it, trying to peer through the opening into the rain, where he thought the threat would be.

Bruder rose from the pit of black beneath the steps and jammed the suppressor under the man's ribs and pulled the trigger three times.

The man shuddered and tried to bring his gun around but Bruder pinned it to his chest with his right hand and held it there while he fired twice more, then stepped back and let the dead weight topple over.

He took the magazine from the man's gun and stuck it inside his belt, then tugged his balaclava off. It was too dark to get a good look at the face and it didn't matter if Bruder knew him or not—he just wanted the radio.

He plucked the earbud loose and found the radio on the belt, then drew the wire from under the man's shirt until the gear was free.

Crouched at the base of the stairs, Bruder stuck the earbud in and listened.

Silence, so far.

He dragged and rolled the body under the stairs and started back up, moving faster this time.

If the other two were still at the tunnel, he wanted to kill them before they realized this one was dead.

***

Bruder stepped into the first second-tier casement, likely retracing the steps of the man cooling at the bottom of the stairway, and saw the same layout of narrow arched openings leading along the fort's front rampart.

He paused, wondering if the storm was lifting because of how much detail he could see, then saw the outer wall of the casement had a large, ragged hole in the bricks rather than a loophole like the rooms below.

He went that way and peered around the edge of the hole.

The storm was just as bad, whipping rain through the opening into his face, and even with the random flashes of lightning he couldn't see across the churning moat.

A voice came through the earbud: "Thompson, check in."

The man had a gravelly British accent and, to Bruder,

sounded like the person who'd shot Fulton.

He'd be the boss.

Moving faster, Bruder stepped away from the outer wall and approached the narrow opening into the next casement from the left side, checking for silhouettes against the arched courtyard opening, then darted into the doorway and pushed off the archway's bricks with his right foot.

He stalked into the nearest corner with the outer wall, found no one crouched there, and curled away from the ragged hole to check the next corner before turning right.

"Thompson."

When Bruder came to the opening into the next casement, he went through the process again, and again, until he stepped into a much darker casement with three narrow vertical loopholes in the outer wall.

He eased closer to them and had to work the angles in order to see down, and in a strobe of lightning saw the bridge below.

He was above the tunnel.

Another voice, also British, said, "I don't see his torch."

"He won't turn it on unless the job's done," the boss said.

Bruder frowned, then remembered people raised in England said torch instead of flashlight.

He checked the far corner and slid along the wall, sweeping the next casement as he passed the opening, and dropped to one knee and hugged the bricks as he leaned forward to look down into the courtyard.

The white beam of light still poked out of the tunnel, panning around, trying to draw him in.

The rest of the courtyard was a gray pool of wind and rain. He could barely make out the tops of a few trees flailing in the storm.

The nearest one on the right, he thought, was where he'd seen the man waiting to ambush him.

Bruder had no idea if he was still there, but he did know

where the one with the flashlight was.

He eased onto his stomach and moved to the center of the ledge above the tunnel.

The boss said, "Thompson, check in. Just click if you can't talk, mate."

Bruder inched toward the edge.

The second voice said, "Hold on, hold on, I've got something."

Bruder froze.

He pressed his cheek into the floor, which was made of something rough and gritty and stank of the sea.

The second voice said, "Nah, disregard. It's a piece of trash getting blown about. Fucking storm."

Bruder exhaled.

Keeping his eyes and the gun on the tree for any more signs of alarm, he eased his upper body out over the ledge until he could reach over with his left hand and brace himself against the bricks just above the entrance to the tunnel.

His right shoulder and side flared from the exertion but he ignored them, and when he was confident he wasn't going to get spotted by the second man, wherever he was, Bruder looked down.

He saw the end of the gun with the flashlight, starkly outlined by the tactical beam, which told him where the man holding it would be.

Bruder took a deep breath and held it to brace his torso, then brought the gun down and lowered his upper body and fired twice at the spot behind the flashlight.

The beam shook and jumped to the left, then fell back and clattered to the tunnel floor.

"I'm hit, I'm hit," the boss said.

He sounded calm, very matter-of-fact about it, and Bruder was impressed.

The second voice said, "What? Where is he?"

"Ahh. Dunno. Ah, shit."

Bruder pulled himself up and slid away from the opening but stayed close enough to watch the ground between the tree and the inner wall for movement.

The second voice said, "Coming to you."

A moment later the boss said, "No, wait!"

But he was too late.

Bruder tracked the man coming in from the right, still near the same tree, and when he stepped into the beam from the flashlight Bruder shot him twice in the chest and once through the top of his head.

The man stumbled and collapsed just outside the tunnel mouth.

The flashlight offered enough of a halo to see how far the drop was, ten feet at the most, and the grass on both sides of the entrance.

Bruder moved to his left and sat on the ledge, then trapped the submachine gun between his knees. He turned onto his belly and pushed himself over the ledge until he hung by his hands, his right side a burning with pain, then dropped to the grass and got the gun up and ready again.

The boss grunted and panted in the tunnel.

Bruder pressed his back against the bricks near the entrance and re-checked his math.

One man at the end of the bridge, with the shotgun.

One man in the casement, with the knife.

One man in the stairway, with the gun.

Two more at the tunnel.

That was five.

He called out, "Is one of you still with the boat?"

"Fuck you," the boss said.

It sounded like he spoke through gritted teeth.

The tactical flashlight hadn't moved, so the gun attached to it was still on the ground, but Bruder assumed the man had a backup piece.

And since the other light was already burning, he didn't

see the harm in adding another.

He switched the light on and stuck the gun around the corner, slicing the white beam into the tunnel and waving it around.

"Ah!"

The grunt was followed by two shots, unsuppressed and wild, and Bruder killed the light and dropped and leaned around the corner low, firing as soon as he saw the shape on the ground.

He kept firing and followed the bullets until he stood over the boss, who still had a grimace of defiance on his face even though was dead.

The body was sprawled next to the floor sign offering details and rules for the fort, and when Bruder heard a muffled groan he remembered the park ranger.

He pulled the sign away from the wall and found him there, bound with his own bootlaces and gagged with his belt. His eyes bugged above the belt, staring up at Bruder while he shook his head and tried to speak.

So the men from the powerboat weren't stupid—they knew better than to murder a U.S. government employee and had trussed him up instead.

Bruder didn't know how many times he'd fired.

To be safe he swapped in the magazine taken from the man in the stairway, took the one from the boss's gun, and stuck the two loose mags in his belt.

The ranger was making more noise now, trying to wriggle deeper into the nook in the tunnel wall.

Bruder told him, "Take a rest. Somebody'll find you."

He didn't like standing in the tunnel with the light around him, so he killed the boss's flashlight and returned the space to darkness with gray light and curtains of rain at both ends.

He blinked, letting his eyes get used to it again, then headed for the exit and the bridge.

CHAPTER TWENTY-ONE

Turley wasn't sure if the faint light coming from the tunnel was caused by the rain getting whipped around, or some kind of lightning trick, or what, but he was looking that way when the light suddenly flared and framed the arched entrance perfectly, and he jumped when two shots barked from inside the fort.

"Here we go," Valenti said, and Turley sensed him turning to put his back against the sign so he could aim the M4 at the bridge.

"No, let's move," Turley said, and went around the corner of the sign, putting the brick base and wooden panel between him and the fort.

Domm was already on the beach side, watching the cove and looking miserable in the downpour, waiting for something or someone to tell him which direction to move when the time came.

Valenti went around the other end of the sign and stayed at that corner.

Turley stared at the white light coming from the tunnel, willing someone to appear, then it disappeared. Now the bridge just led into a veil of grayness with occasional flashes of lightning showing the fort's massive rampart, which looked like it extended forever, the Great Wall of Florida.

Turley tried to ignore the rain pounding against his back and head—much worse on this side of the sign—and watched the bridge over the sights of his gun.

**

Bruder stepped out of the fort onto the bridge and searched for any sign of trouble.

It was useless.

The wind knocked him around and sent needles into his eyes. The worst part was the rain drumming on his right trapezius, refusing to let him ignore the wound there.

The only consolation was that, other than the bullet holes, anyone out here looking for him was dealing with the same situation.

Still, he didn't like the bottleneck created by the bridge.

They'd tried to use the fort's only access point as a trap, and if the last man was out here somewhere, he might get the same idea and use the bridge.

Bruder crouched along the right edge of the wood and looked down into the moat. It was still impossible to tell how deep it was, but he thought he saw shapes—maybe rocks—not too far below the pocked surface.

Off to his left, a concrete block stuck out from beneath the walkway like a narrow step.

Below the block was a support column made of brick.

He went that way and set the MP5SD on the bridge, then rolled onto his stomach again like he'd done on the fort's second tier and held the block and put his boots against the column to lower himself into the moat.

With his arms still bent he stretched a leg down, feeling for purchase, but found nothing.

Deciding it was still better to swim than walk the plank,

he grabbed the submachine gun off the bridge with his right hand and let his left arm extend all the way until he let go.

His boots hit the moat floor when the water was at his armpits, and even though he was already soaked and the water was warmer than the air he had to fight his body's urge to gasp from the sudden submersion.

He kept the gun above water and waded under the bridge.

Rain slapped across the surface of the moat and hammered the wood above him.

There was another column ahead and he wrapped around it on the right side. He wanted to keep the bridge between himself and the yacht, in case the sixth man had put himself on the flybridge and happened to get a lucky view of the head bobbing across the moat.

He went around two more columns, feeling his way across the uneven floor and staying under the bridge and out of the rain as much as he could.

Then there were no more columns, just the outer brick wall of the moat about ten yards in front of him. When he got there the ledge was low enough to grab.

He tossed the gun over the bricks and used the ledge and the bridge to pull himself up in the corner.

When he got his left elbow onto the wood and his right onto the bricks, he started to lever his right leg up, then glanced across the bridge.

About thirty feet away he could make out the squat, blocky shape of the brick and wood sign he'd almost shot with the Street Sweeper on his way in.

It was hard to tell in the storm but he thought, maybe, a man was crouched at the corner aiming a pistol toward the fort.

Bruder eased his hand toward the MP5SD, retrieved it, and sank back into the moat.

***

Turley stared at what he could see of the bridge until his eyes started forming shapes out of the swirling rain.

He squeezed his eyes shut and rubbed his forearm across his face, then refocused on the bridge.

Nothing had happened since the two gunshots and the white light going out, and the lack of new activity was getting to him.

His eyes and mind were trying to create something to break the tension, the anticipation, and when he heard a rumble that sounded like the powerboat engines he dismissed it, accusing his brain of turning thunder into something else, then Domm said, "That's the boat."

Turley cranked around and listened hard.

"You're right. What the hell are they doing now?"

The rumble was nestled within the racket from the storm, like an undercurrent beneath some serious chop, and the acoustics were made even more confusing by bouncing off the wooden sign next to his head.

"They're moving around out there," Domm said. "Going for the yacht?"

"Ah, shit," Turley said.

They had three options for cruising away from the Dry Tortugas after they killed Kline—the yacht, the powerboat, and Dunbar's *Hawk*—and the yacht was the only one with the potential to bring them two million bucks.

Turley put on an irritated face, but he was secretly relieved to get a break from their half-assed stakeout of the bridge.

He told Domm, "Here, take my spot. I'll go check it out."

He jogged in a half-crouch straight into the wind and rain, slopping through sandy puddles until he found the brick path.

From his previous visits to Garden Key he knew there were two boardwalks running off the bricks, one on his left leading to the dock for the ferry from Key West, and one on his right, leading to an open boathouse.

He went right, seeking the shelter of the boathouse.

He took care not to slip on the wooden planks as he passed a small group of trees growing between the board-walks, their leaves slapping around in the wind and rain, and nearly sighed with relief when he entered the boathouse, which was like a small barn with large, doorless openings facing the water and the fort.

He made quick work of checking the corners and tested a door leading into some kind of office or storage room, found it locked, and left it alone.

It felt amazing to get out of the rain, and Turley shook water from his arms and head as he crossed the boathouse and peeked around the left side of the cove-side opening.

He could still hear the powerboat grumbling somewhere out in the water. The sound of it rose and fell with the wind and seemed to be coming from somewhere off to his left.

Looking out at the cove, he knew the yacht had been anchored at about his nine o'clock, and it and the powerboat would have to cruise past this spot to get out into the Gulf.

He didn't see a damn thing but didn't know if it was be-cause the yacht wasn't there or the storm was keeping him from seeing it.

He shook his head and blew rain away from his face.

Even in this mess, the yacht would be hard to miss.

The powerboat, though, was like an oversized surfboard. It could skim by undetected if it was more than twenty yards away from the dock.

Turley listened and looked and it didn't make a difference.

"Goddamit," he said.

He didn't want to go back to his crew and tell them he had no information—hell, he didn't want to go back to the sign at all.

Two men were enough for that duty, and it made sense to stay put until he learned something new.

And yeah, being protected from the storm had something

to do with it, he admitted to himself.

But he was the head honcho, and that came with perks.

He settled in next to the opening and was looking for a life jacket or something soft to sit on when a dark shape slid toward the dock from the left.

Turley stopped moving and saw the lone man standing at the helm of the powerboat, his head craned up and moving side to side as he scanned the dock.

He idled along a good ten or fifteen feet away from the pilings, so he wasn't coming in to tie off, and any closer would put him in danger of getting slammed by the wind and waves into the dock.

So he was searching for someone—maybe the two guys who'd come onto shore on Bush Key—but it looked like the rest of the crew had left the boat as well, which explained the lights and shots inside the fort.

Alarmed, Turley looked back through the boathouse toward the boardwalk.

If the men from the boat had taken care of Kline and were coming out to get picked up, they'd find him waiting here.

But Domm and Valenti would handle anybody who left the fort...

So this guy on the boat was just making a pass.

Turley licked his lips and tasted salt and rain.

***

Bruder moved along the outer moat wall away from the bridge and the man with the gun.

The moat floor rose and fell, putting the water as shallow as his stomach and as deep as his neck, and he kept a hand on the bricks to move faster without losing his balance.

When the bridge and the Fort Jefferson sign beyond it were lost in the storm, he pulled himself over the outer wall and crawled on his stomach across short grass until he was under a picnic table set near the moat.

A low rumbling—possibly the powerboat engines but he couldn't be sure—rolled toward him from the water.

He waited under the table for a full minute to see if anything happened.

When no one shouted or ran at him or fired a gun, he crawled out from under the table and ran in a crouch, taking a wide loop across a muddy path and into more grass, heading for the vague shape of some trees where the docks ought to be.

He came to a wooden railing and dropped to one knee.

A soaked boardwalk was on the other side of the railing, and if he had his bearings correct, the dock was to the right, the fort to his left, past a small copse of trees.

Bruder eased over the railing and glanced toward the water.

The dark shape of a boathouse was there, with a large opening in the middle framed by gray light spilling through from the anchorage.

He went over the far railing and crept into the trees, which had leaves shaped like ping pong paddles. They provided a canopy of darkness and shelter and he wiped the rain away from his eyes and looked around.

Another boardwalk was to his right, also leading toward the dock, and he was irritated about having to worry about two of them.

The low rumbling was louder now, definitely the power-boat, and Bruder spent a brief moment wondering if the pilot would leave the engine running while he went ashore to set up an ambush near the sign.

He shook his head at boats and boaters, at water in general, and peered toward the fort.

The sign and the man next to it ought to be straight ahead.

And if he hadn't moved, his back would be to Bruder.

An aggressive gust of wind whipped the branches around and Bruder used the disturbance to crawl out from under the tree on his stomach, snaking through more grass toward where the sign should be.

After five yards he picked out the top corners of brick and wood against the backdrop of rain.

He slowed, moving one arm and leg at a time with the MP5SD cradled across his forearms.

His right side burned with each movement, stretching and flexing, and his shoulder felt like someone was steadily rapping it with a hot nail, but he shoved the pain away and kept his head up, searching.

The grass turned to wet sand, then wet bricks, and he knew he was getting close.

Halfway across the brick path the man took shape on the left side of the sign, still crouched, and still staring toward the fort.

Bruder stopped and brought the submachine gun around and up, leaving it at an angle so the long magazine wouldn't scrape the bricks.

His finger was on the trigger when another shape moved at the right end of the sign.

Bruder frowned.

There had been six men on the powerboat, and he'd already killed five and pegged the man on the left as the sixth.

Then that man's head turned to the right, saying something to the man at the other end, and Bruder saw the shape of a bald head and pug jaw.

Domm.

Bruder looked back over both shoulders, oblivious to the pain streaking through his right side.

If Domm was here, the man on the right was either Turley or Valenti.

Where was the third?

Still out on their Whaler, dead or injured, or trying to get it operable again?

Or sneaking around?

Bruder put his eyes front again and thought about Turley and his crew.

They'd come to shore, past the yacht, to set an ambush outside the fort.

So they weren't here just to retake the boat.

They were here to kill him.

He moved the fire selector switch to the center setting, a three-round burst, and shot Domm in the back.

The man on the right turned at the sound of the bullets slapping into Domm's body—the suppressed gun was too quiet to be heard above the storm—and Bruder saw the outline of the M4.

Valenti.

He fired again and Valenti reeled away from the sign, dropping the M4. The shape of him fell to the ground and Bruder rose and advanced, concerned about backup pistols, but when he got to Valenti the man was face-up in the rain with both hands clutched to his chest.

He blinked up at Bruder, who said, "Where's Turley?"

Valenti opened his mouth and blood fell out.

Bruder went back to single-shot and fired once, then went around the sign and found Domm crawling toward the bridge.

He fired again and used his boot to send Domm's body over the brick wall and into the moat, then hauled Valenti's body to the edge and rolled him in.

If Turley came back this way before Bruder found him, let him wonder what happened to his crew.

He tucked Domm's Glock into his belt and tossed the M4 into the moat after Valenti, preferring the quiet submachine gun over the racket of the assault rifle.

Then he went back to the Fort Jefferson sign and knelt at the same corner Domm had used, but on the fort side, somewhat out of the rain, to think about what to do next.

He could still hear the powerboat somewhere out in

the anchorage, telling him the sixth man was out there somewhere.

But where the hell was Turley?

***

When the powerboat was almost straight out from Turley's position he darted out of the boathouse toward the edge of the dock.

The man at the helm saw him and lifted a hand in welcome, and when Turley raised the pistol the man yelled and reached toward the console.

Turley fired three times and hit the pilot at least once.

The man fell away from the wheel and dropped between the two front seats.

Turley stalked along the edge of the dock, keeping pace with the idling boat as the wind and waves pushed it closer to him.

He was almost out of boards when the wounded man pulled himself onto the captain's chair and looked up.

Turley took careful aim and shot him in the face, then watched the boat bump its way into the much smaller docks west of the boathouse, the ones reserved for small, private watercraft.

The engines continued to rumble but Turley didn't think the boat was moving fast enough to cause any real damage, just scratches and dents, and now he knew where the powerboat was if they needed it to get off Garden Key.

Pleased with himself and the news he carried, he walked through the boathouse and headed down the boardwalk.

The rain and wind against his back didn't seem as bad now, so either he was feeling invincible or the storm was petering out.

Maybe both, he thought, smirking against the downpour.

***

Bruder waited, moving his head and eyes slowly to watch every direction while his mood fouled by the second.

He was thinking about how he was going to retrieve the gold and get the hell off the island, assuming he managed to survive long enough to get back onto a working boat.

But which one?

There were only three left as far as he knew.

If Dunbar's had gotten beached, he'd have to find it and haul the gold out himself, then get aboard the yacht or the powerboat, wherever it was.

If Dunbar's *Hawk* had drifted away with the gold...he didn't want to think about it.

Regardless, he didn't know how to drive any of the damn things.

It probably wasn't difficult—just work the throttle and wheel to go where you wanted—but he didn't know anything about reefs or shoals or depth charts or how to read the cockpit screens he'd seen aboard the yacht and Dunbar's boat.

The powerboat, he figured, would try to kill him right away out of pure disdain.

The ranger had said something about campers...

Maybe, after he got the gold, he could blend in with them and slip aboard the next ferry, or bribe his way onto a personal craft.

He didn't see it going well.

Maybe they'd turn part of the fort back into a prison just for him so the tourists could see what happened when you caused trouble.

But that was all for later.

He needed to deal with the problems in front of him first, and those were Turley and the last man from the powerboat crew.

Bruder was thinking about retracing his steps along the beach and following the sand to where he figured the *Hawk* and Fulton's body would be if they blew ashore, because at least then he'd know where the gold was, when three quick shots came from the water.

He ducked behind the sign but the shots hadn't come with the distinct sound that meant the barrel was pointed his way, so he slipped around the sign and moved in a crouch back to the trees between the two boardwalks.

He ducked under the branches and knelt next to a trunk, watching through the leaves.

The powerboat's engines were very loud now, echoing through the boathouse ahead on Bruder's right side, then another shot barked in the storm.

Bruder heard sounds he couldn't identify—faint thumps and creaks—and when a shape came out of the boathouse and walked toward him Bruder kept still except for the barrel of the MP5SD, which tracked the movement.

When he saw the wet ponytail drooping off the back of the head he led it by a few inches and fired.

He did recognize the next sounds—a body thumping onto the boardwalk and a gun clattering away from a loose hand.

Bruder stepped out from under the tree and checked Turley's body, which was smirking around a bullet hole high on his right cheek.

Bruder left him there and walked through the boathouse and followed the sound of the powerboat's engines, then saw it nosed up onto a smaller boat tied off to a short dock.

He realized he wasn't getting battered as much by the wind and rain and looked up, and to the south he could see a faint line of lighter gray, possibly the back end of the squall line.

Then he went to find the gold.

CHAPTER TWENTY-TWO

Bruder walked along the beach in the storm—which was starting to feel less like the end of the world and more like a mere hurricane—and stopped when he came to a spot that looked like where he'd come ashore.

Any sign of his passing had been erased as soon as it was created, so he looked left at the grass and low scrub, which looked like all the other grass and low scrub, then right, toward the cove, and could barely make out the shape of the anchored yacht.

So there it was, if he wanted to try to drive the damn thing.

He slogged further along the beach.

The thunder and lightning were still going strong but had carried north, and he'd stopped ducking his head into his shoulders and making the right one complain with each flash and boom.

Bruder followed the gentle curves of the shore, replaying the scene when the men on the powerboat had cruised up to the *Hawk* and executed Fulton.

He looked back at the spot where the yacht would be, though he couldn't see it anymore, and figured Dunbar's boat ought to be within a small arc from where he stood.

He made sure Domm's Glock was secure and waded in and did his best to keep the MP5SD above the water, but after a few waves rolled over him and he came out the other side coughing and spitting he let the submachine gun sink and used both arms to keep from drowning.

The dull aches along his right half were joined by a sharp stinging as the salt water found the wounds again, and he gritted his teeth and wondered how much of a fool he was going to be before he gave up.

He never got to find out.

Dunbar's boat appeared off to his right, toward the yacht, pushed and pulled by the storm and current.

Bruder swam that way and managed to pull himself aboard in the narrow space between the engines and stern rail, then rolled over onto the deck and lay there for a minute, next to Fulton's body, catching his breath and waiting for the black spots around the edges of his vision to fade away.

They were almost gone when he heard a thump and a curse from somewhere on the boat.

He reached for Domm's Glock, which was still wedged in his belt, and grabbed the .45 out of Fulton's chest rig as he willed himself to his feet and pointed the guns over the cabin's rear bench toward the cockpit.

No one was there, until a head rose out of the hatch centered in the console.

The man wore a diving mask and scuba breathing gear, which wasn't in his mouth but blocked it from Bruder's view.

A loose snorkel flopped on one side of his head as he lugged two sacks of the gold up from the cabin.

His eyes grew inside the mask when he saw Bruder standing with the two guns.

He set the gold down on the deck, the bars thudding and clinking together, and held his palms out toward Bruder as he reached up and pulled the breathing apparatus down and the mask up.

Dunbar's face broke into a huge grin.

"Holy shit, man. You made it."

"So did you," Bruder said, still holding the guns up.

"Yeah, I ducked into the yacht's engine room and grabbed this gear. I've been bobbing around in the water trying not to get slammed into a reef or chummed up by that fucking powerboat trolling around. I heard shots—was that you?"

"Turley. He shot the powerboat driver."

"*Turley?*" Dunbar looked vaguely to his right, processing it. "What about the others? Domm and Valenti."

"Dead," Bruder said.

Dunbar nodded. "And the rest of the powerboat crew?"

"Same. What was your plan here?"

Dunbar glanced at the gold and realized how it all looked.

"Oh, shit. Well. My plan was to cruise on over to the yacht, tie this girl off the stern, and motor on out of the anchorage and head for Mexico with the gold. I don't know if the tow would work in this chop, but figured—»

He saw the look on Bruder's face and said, "Hey, now that you're here, it's the same deal as before, man. I'm not looking to cross you up."

"That's good."

Bruder believed him, so far, and didn't want to kill him unless he absolutely had to—Dunbar solved the problem of getting away from the Dry Tortugas.

Bruder let the guns fall to his sides.

"We're not messing with the yacht anymore, though."

"We're not?"

"No. We're getting the hell out of here before the storm clears and people start finding bodies."

Dunbar gave a longing look in the direction of the yacht, then shrugged.

"Damn thing has a bunch of bullet holes in it, anyway. But we do need to swing by her and siphon some fuel."

"Let's go," Bruder said.

***

Dunbar had a set of gear that looked custom-made for doing the job, and when they dropped anchor near the yacht's stern he swam over to the diving platform with a long hose in one hand.

He disappeared into the engine room, then came out a minute later and gave Bruder a thumb's-up.

Bruder hit the switch as directed and a pump began to chug, filling a fuel bladder almost identical to the one on Turley's Whaler.

He sat and watched the bladder grow and kick out wrinkles.

The squall had passed and left a steady, cold rain in its wake, and Bruder dared to start thinking about his next hot shower.

Then he thought about Julie, the woman at the impound marina who'd maybe asked him to come to the next auction as a first date.

He pushed the notion away—he could never show his face around there again after what had happened with the yacht, and what was about to happen when people found it and the surrounding carnage.

When the bladder was full he killed the pump and waved to Dunbar, then called out, "Hey!"

Dunbar stopped in the engine room hatch and turned.

Bruder said, "While you're over there, do something for me."

***

Dunbar took the *Cooper's Hawk* around the ancient dock pilings and turned north, chasing the squall for a while before cutting toward Key West.

Bruder looked off the starboard side and could see the black smoke above Garden Key getting scattered in the dying winds of the storm.

Dunbar stayed well north of the usual lane to the Dry Tortugas, avoiding any authorities rushing out in response to the inevitable call from a park ranger, telling a story that would make him a legend in the community.

When they were hours away from everything and no other boats were in sight, they pulled anything useful or identifiable off Fulton's body and sent him down to join Hendrick.

One of the items in his pockets was a cell phone, and Bruder turned it on.

When enough bars showed up he called the number he had for McIntyre.

Penza answered.

"Who is this?"

Bruder didn't say anything at first.

Then: "Put him on."

It was Penza's turn to be silent, for other reasons, then he said, "Where are you?"

"You won't know until it's too late. Put him on."

After a moment McIntyre came on, sounding tough.

"What the hell is going on out there?"

"I sank your yacht."

"Say that again."

"I set it on fire," Bruder said, "and if it hasn't sunk yet they'll tow it out into the Gulf and let it drop."

The line hissed, then McIntyre said, "That was a mistake."

"No. It's the latest casualty on my way to you."

"Be careful, my friend. I still have everything we discussed before you agreed to take this job on. Need I remind you? Lola. And once we have her, a slow progression through everyone you've ever worked with."

"They can handle themselves," Bruder said. "How about

you?"

He killed the call, then dialed the number he had for Lola.

When the answering machine picked up with no outgoing message, he spoke a single phrase that would let her know she was burned.

Then he hung up and did the same for Kershaw.

For Gator, he called a diner in Louisville and winced when his least-favorite waitress said, "Diner."

"I need to leave a message for Pablo."

"Who?"

"Pablo."

"Oh, right."

"Ready?"

"No, I'm waiting for the planets to align. Snap it up, pokey."

Bruder shook his head.

"Tell him the oranges are late."

"That's it?"

"Yeah."

"Bye then."

Bruder tossed the phone overboard and sat back on the bench and closed his eyes, letting the rhythm of the engines and water lull him.

Now the three other surviving people who had anything to do with the job in New York had fair warning.

They could do with it whatever they wanted.

Bruder figured, like him, they would rather hunt than hide.

A LOOK AT: TOOTH & NAIL

AUTHOR JEREMY BROWN BRINGS YOU A COLLECTION OF
FIRST-IN-SERIES THRILLERS FULL OF BLOOD-SPLASH-
ING COMBAT...

The tiny Alpine village of Lontan is the perfect moun-
taintop retreat for assassins who need a place to relax,
recover and hide. Villagers welcome the quiet, low-profile
professionals and their cash-heavy wallets. Daniel Rorque,
chief of the one-man communal police corps in Lontan,
doesn't mind the lethal visitors spending time and money
in his jurisdiction as long as they leave their business at the
base of the mountain.

Go from Lontan, to the Texas/Mexico border and all
the way to eve of the Second Peloponnesian War. Here is
where Akoniti of Sparta is recruited into the krypteia, a secret
society of assassins, spies, and covert operators who do
whatever is necessary to ensure the survival of Sparta and
her people.

"The snake smiles but shows no teeth."

AVAILABLE NOW ON KINDLE

ABOUT THE AUTHOR

Jeremy Brown is a novelist working in many genres, including crime thrillers, murder mysteries, and military thrillers. He has worked as a narrative designer and lead writer for a massively popular video game and enjoys kettlebells, stockpiling firewood, and using coffee as a delivery system for cream. He lives in Michigan with his wife, sons, and various animals.